Amphibian

a novel by
Carla Gunn

Coach House Books | Toronto

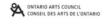

Published with the generous assistance of the Canada Council for the Arts and the Ontario Arts Council. Coach House Books also acknowledges the support of the Government of Ontario through the Ontario Book Publishing Tax Credit and the Government of Canada through the Book Publishing Industry Development Program.

LIBRARY AND ARCHIVES CANADA CATALOGUING IN PUBLICATION

Gunn, Carla
    Amphibian / Carla Gunn.

ISBN 978-1-55245-214-1

    I. Title.

PS8613.U57A65 2009   C813'.6   C2009-901300-2

For my sons
and other amazing animals

This morning Bird and I got in trouble. We were pretending to be spies. Our job was to decipher our enemies' cryptic messages. In our Grade 4 classroom, Prime Enemy Number One is Mrs. Wardman. We were sure she had some undercover allies, but we weren't sure who they were. So, to figure it all out, we were keeping track of Mrs. Wardman's commands. At the point our covert operation was blown wide open, this was our list:

1. Kelsie, hold your tongue. (Beside this, Bird had drawn a picture of a tongue in a hand. It kind of weirded me out.)
2. Ryan, don't play with your thing. (What Mrs. Wardman said to Ryan, who was spinning his X-Men eraser.)
3. Gordon, it's time for your medication.

All I can figure is that the list must have slid off my desk while I was watching a spider by the window. I was thinking about how I sure hoped nobody mean spotted him. If Lyle caught him, he'd rip his legs off one by one. Then, just as I was thinking about how my grandmother always says, 'If you wish to live and thrive, let a spider run alive,' my eyes were pulled away from the spider and made to focus on something quite a bit bigger but not so interesting: Mrs. Wardman. She was standing over me. My brain blinked, and then I understood what that meant.

She said, 'Phin! Are you even listening to me? Why are you staring off into space?' Just as I opened my mouth to say something that wasn't the truth, I saw her see the list. As she reached down to pick it up, it was like she was moving in slow motion, like when I flip a flipbook's pages reeaaallllly slowly. When she stood back up, she looked at me and raised her eyebrows, and then she looked at Bird. She didn't say a word, but I knew we were in trouble.

It didn't take long for Mrs. Wardman to get her revenge. She moved Bird to the front of the room and left me at the back. Now all Bird's stuff is in Kaitlyn's desk and all of Kaitlyn's stuff is in Bird's desk. Kaitlyn didn't like the picture of Dr. Evil on the inside of Bird's desk, so she erased it. To top it all off, last week Kaitlyn was out sick with lice and I'm not so sure she's completely cured.

In my pencil case I have a humongous blue eraser with the words *Big Mistake* on it. That's what this day was. If I had an eraser of life, I'd start at the top of the morning and work my way down. I have a feeling, though, that whoever drew this day pressed the pencil really hard and even if I rubbed and rubbed and rubbed, little horrible bits of it would still be left behind.

When I got home, my mother was on the telephone, likely interviewing someone for a story. She's a journalist. She works at an office building in the mornings but mostly at home in the afternoons. Sometimes when she gets off the phone or home from an interview, she's really sad. She won't tell me why, she'll just say, 'Hard story, Phin.' That's the code for don't talk to her until after she comes out of her bedroom.

I lay down on her office sofa and looked up at the ceiling. I counted the face patterns I saw in all the little blobs of paint. Seven. And one looked just like a mouse.

When she got off the phone, my mom said, 'Why the long face, Phinnie?' So I told her about how Bird got moved to the front of the room and I got left at the back with Kaitlyn and Gordon who aren't even my best friends.

'Oh, that's disappointing, sweetheart,' said my mother, 'but maybe it's good to sit beside someone new for a change.'

'But I don't want to sit beside Kaitlyn – I want to sit beside Bird. That's one of the only things that makes school fun.'

'I know you don't like it, Phin, but you can put up with it. And look at it this way – adversity builds character.'

'What the heck does that mean?'

'Well, when I was your age, Granddad used to tell me a story about a man who found a cocoon and thought he'd help the butterfly out by cutting it open. Problem was, the butterfly wasn't ready to emerge and so it ended up with shrivelled wings and was never able to fly. What Granddad meant was that it's good to struggle – it builds muscles.'

'Well, that might be true, but I'm getting too much of a workout.'

'That which doesn't kill you makes you stronger.'

'Or weak or crippled,' I told her. 'And that which *does* kill you makes you dead.'

'Oh, but just think of all the character you're building.'

'I have enough already.'

My mom laughed, 'Yes, well, you're certainly quite the character.'

I rolled my eyes at her and went to my room and got out my Reull drawings and stories. On the planet of Reull there are lots of different kinds of cats. I drew one called the Electric Cat, which you wouldn't want to come across. I wrote about how if you mistake him for a domestic cat and take him into your house, he will shut down the power and you'll get the shock of your life. His body reacts to things like TVs and electric mixers and sends a high voltage through them that ruins their motors. You cannot keep an Electric Cat as a companion animal.

My companion animal is Fiddledee. She's a really furry black and white cat with blue eyes. I went to look for her in my closet where she sometimes sleeps on top of my stuffed animals, but she wasn't there. So then I turned on the TV to the Green Channel. The Green Channel has shows about animals and nature and how humans are ruining the environment. The life on earth is in deep trouble. Deep, deep trouble. In fact, 25 percent of all mammal species are on the Red List of Threatened Species.

Partly because of this, my New Year's resolution is to save at least one animal from going extinct. I have a cat-whisker collection in a matchbox. I also have feathers from different types of birds and some squirrel fur. This way I will at least have their DNA.

On the Green Channel I watched a show about sadness in animals. When an elephant in Africa dies, sometimes more than a hundred elephants will come from all over and trumpet around the dead elephant with their trunks up in the air. Then they cover his body with branches. When a baby elephant dies, often his mother won't leave the graveside. Mother elephants love their babies. Once, after a man in Africa used his tractor to haul a baby elephant out of a mudhole, the baby's mother rushed up to him and wiped the mud off his clothes with her trunk.

Last year when I was eight, I had to say goodbye to Granddad MacKeamish at a human funeral. Just a few months before that, I said goodbye to my father too. But he's not dead. It just feels like it sometimes.

Today after school, I didn't stick around the playground like I sometimes do. Bird had gone home with his mother, and besides, I saw Lyle over on the monkey bars and just didn't feel strong enough to risk being picked on. My mother says Lyle is the spawn of similarly small-minded cretins and that I should just stay away from him. She says I'll meet lots of small-minded, life-suck-ing cretins all through my life. Why does she torture me like that? The Lyles in my life are going to grow bigger and bigger and that's supposed to help me feel better?

Sometimes I have really, really bad thoughts about Lyle – the being-picked-apart-by-vultures-and-bursting-into-flames kind. And one day I said *póg mo thóin* to him. It means *kiss my something*. It's Gaelic and I learned it from my grandfather. Lyle just looked at me confused. He doesn't speak Gaelic. In fact, he's not very good with languages, period. In French class, he asked Mrs. Wardman what *je ne sais pas* means and she said, *I don't know*. He got really mad and gave her the finger behind her back.

The reason I didn't feel like I had enough strength left over to risk Lyle is because I was still thinking about how Mrs. Wardman was irritated with me again today. It happened in math class when we had to do logic questions. First we read this sentence: 'Paula gave out 47 treats for St. Patrick's Day.' And then this one:

'Paula received 50 treats for St. Patrick's Day.' Then we had to read ten statements and write T for true or F for false or M for maybe. For the question 'Everyone who received a treat from Paula gave her one as well,' I answered M for maybe, but Mrs. Wardman marked it wrong and put a T for true.

I just couldn't figure out why Mrs. Wardman had done that so I went up to her desk to ask her about it. She said that since Paula got more treats than she gave out, she must have gotten a treat from everyone she gave one to.

I said, 'But how can we know that for sure?'

She said, 'Phin, it's logic. Go back to your seat and think more about it.'

So I did. I thought really hard about it, but it didn't seem like logic to me. How could anybody be absolutely sure that Paula got a treat from everybody who gave her one?

I went back up to Mrs. Wardman and told her I thought really hard about it, but it still didn't seem like logic to me.

Mrs. Wardman sighed and said, 'It *is* logic, Phin. Here, I'll show you the answer in the teachers' book.' She showed me and, sure enough, it said exactly what she said.

I went back to my seat and thought some more, but still it didn't seem like logic to me. So just to be sure I had it right in my head, I drew one hundred stick kids and put a big circle around forty-seven of them to show who Paula could have given treats to. Then I put a big circle around a different fifty stick kids to show who Paula could have gotten treats from. I took my drawing up to Mrs. Wardman's desk and showed it to her.

That's when she sighed - again - and rolled her eyes. She said, 'Phineas, there are fifty kids in Paula's class, not one hundred. Now that's enough of that - please go back and get out your social-studies notebook like everyone else. Mrs. L'Oiseau will be here in a minute.'

I could tell she was mad with me, so I went back to my seat. Her being angry made me angry, and it sure made that logic sheet *cac*, which is Gaelic for something most people do about once a day.

It did make me feel better to see Mrs. L'Oiseau, though. She's Bird's mother and she works as a Thumbody who travels around to all the schools in the city. She came into our classroom wearing a funny hat and dressed up like a big thumb – although she looked more like a big peanut to me.

She gave us each a sheet of paper and then got us to press our thumbs on an inkpad to make prints. It made me think of how it would feel to be a prisoner, except our prison was the school. I put eyes and whiskers on my thumbprint and made it into a cat. Bird put teeth on his, and it looked like I don't know what. Then we cut out our prints and put them into round pieces of plastic and made them into pins, which we put on our shirts.

Bird's mother told us that we're all special, and that we should all feel good about ourselves because we all have our own thumbprints and no two thumbprints are the same. I didn't know how that made us special, but I didn't say anything. No two worms have exactly the same skin pattern, and nobody thinks they're special. On the Green Channel I learned that humans have 50 percent of their DNA the same as worms. And we're 50 percent like bananas too.

After the Thumbody thing, school was over. It was kind of embarrassing seeing Bird and his mother walking to their car together, with her still dressed like a big thumb. I figured I may as well be embarrassed for Bird since he wasn't embarrassed for himself. I think I even blushed for him. I do a better job at that anyway because his skin is dark and you can't see his blushes very well.

When I got home, my mother was working in her office but she wasn't on the phone. I was still upset about the logic problem so I told her about it. My mom agreed with me. She said Mrs. Wardman was making an assumption that wasn't really in the problem; she assumed there were only fifty kids.

I said, 'But doesn't *assume* make an ass of u and me?' I learned that from Bird who learned it from his cousin. He also learned from his cousin that you can guess the size of somebody's penis – only he didn't use that word – by looking at the distance between the tip of that person's pointer finger and the tip of the thumb when he makes the letter L with his hand. But he's wrong because I checked it out.

My mother told me that *ass of u and me* wasn't a very nice expression, and that I shouldn't use it.

I said, 'Why is it so bad? It's more of an insult to donkeys than to humans.' But I was just pretending that I didn't know the other meaning for that word. I still felt angry at Mrs. Wardman. I imagined her face on an ass – on a donkey ass, not on a human one.

My mother said that sometimes people – even teachers – make mistakes. She says that sometimes it's not a good idea to point out to people that they're wrong. She said that sometimes it's better to just let it go and be right inside your own head instead of worrying what's inside the other person's head. I have to think more about it. Don't people want to know when they're wrong? Why does being wrong make people happy?

I told my mother that if I was wrong about something and somebody told me the right answer, then that would make me happy. She said she would always do her best to tell me when I'm wrong. I think she already does that, and that made me happy.

Then I went up to my room to draw and try to forget about whether or not Paula got treats from all the kids she gave treats to. Who gives out treats on St. Patrick's Day anyway?

I drew the Oster, which was a species hunted by Gorachs – who think they're the most intelligent beings in the universe – for their five-nostrilled noses, which the Gorachs used to hold things upright, like pens and pencils and things like that. Gorachs also liked to use them for sprinkler nozzles. They did this by drying them out for weeks and weeks and then using glue from the stomachs of the Tussleturtles (kind of like earth turtles but with bulging stomachs that slowed them down even more and made the Tussleturtles really, really wise because they were never in a hurry) to coat them so that they would be waterproof.

The Oster is now extinct. The other creatures of Reull are very, to-infinity sad about this. They know that with the extinction of the Oster, one more string of the web of life has been torn away forever.

Then I drew the web of life that was holding Reull in place in the universe. Lots of the web strings were in place but lots of them were broken. There can only be a few more destroyed before the whole planet falls into space.

Today we had to take Fiddledee to the vet. She has red in her poop, and Mom says that can't be good. The vet's name is Dr. Karnes. She is really big and has lots of sticking-up hair that looks a little like a lion's mane and makes her face look bigger than it really is.

Dr. Karnes listened to Fiddledee's heart, checked her body for lumps and weighed her on a scale like the one at the grocery store. Then she took her temperature. When my mother takes my temperature, she has an instrument that she sticks in my ear. Then she presses a button and the instrument beeps, and then she takes it out to read what it says.

Fiddledee wasn't so lucky. Dr. Karnes had to put the thermometer in another place, and I can tell you it wasn't her mouth. I held her while the vet did that because Fiddledee likes me best, and the vet said I would help reassure her that she would be all right.

I looked into Fiddledee's eyes, and she looked just like the cats on those birthday cards with the bulging eyes that are supposed to show that they're surprised by how old you are. I think I know now how the photographer gets their eyes to bulge like that.

Finally, it was all over and I let Fiddledee go. She climbed right back into her cat carrier, which was kind of funny because it took Mom and me a long time to get her in there in the first place.

Dr. Karnes said she doesn't know for sure if there's anything wrong with Fiddledee. She said we have to keep an eye on her and bring her back in another month to see if she's lost any weight. We're also supposed to watch her litter box for more red poop and to bring a fresh piece in for a test if it looks red. I hope there's nothing wrong with Fiddledee.

When we left the animal clinic, we ran into a man my mother knows. He had a dog who got bitten by another dog and had to get stitches. My mother introduced me to the man, whose name is Brent. I said hi, but I decided I'd rather talk to his dog, so I did.

On the Green Channel, I learned that a human can check to see if he's top dog by taking one of his dog's toys or chewies and putting it in his own mouth and walking around with it proudly. I think it might be a better idea to only pretend it's in your mouth. If the dog growls or chases the human, the human is not top dog. If the dog doesn't do anything or just tries to play, the human is top dog.

Another test is to wet your dog's food with your own spit and offer it to your dog. If the dog eats it, he's submissive, but if he growls or won't eat it, he's dominant. To wet your dog's food, you can just spit on it and not really put it in your mouth.

I patted Kooch on his head and his back and on the top of his muzzle and he looked happy. Submissive dogs look like they're smiling. If you want a dominant dog to start being more submissive, you can hold his mouth into a smile once in a while, and that will start to make him feel more submissive.

That works for humans too. If a person holds his face in a smile, he doesn't feel angry or dominant. I saw that on Discovery Channel.

Some biologists think a smile makes a human feel less dominant because the smile evolved thousands of years ago from the fear face. If you were afraid of your enemy, you would smile to show that you weren't a threat. I think humans are sometimes big liars, though. Some of them smile to pretend not to be a threat and then have you for lunch. For instance, sometimes Lyle smiles at you as if he's your friend – then next thing you know he's got you in a headlock or he's kicking you in the shins. The smile's only to get you to let your guard down. My mom says that's pretty much how it works at her office too.

Brent had on a light green shirt with a dark green and purple tie. He looked a lot like a leprechaun, partly because of all the green, but partly because he was really short – much shorter than my mother, who is really tall for a woman. My mother is a little bit taller than my father, but she's a lot taller than the man named Brent.

I got the feeling Brent is one of those grown-ups who doesn't really like kids but pretends to. I like people who don't like kids and don't even pretend to like them – like Mr. Byers, who owns the big apple tree that Bird and I play on. At least with Mr. Byers you know to stay away from him because he might grab you by the ear and march you over to the principal's office like he did to Justin who fell out of the tree and into his backyard one day.

But with people like the man named Brent, their voices say, 'I like you' and 'Aren't you a cute little kid,' but that's not what their faces say. He reminded me of the alligator snapper turtle, which has a bright pink tongue that looks like a worm that lures fish right into his mouth. Or like one of those shiny cards that if you tilt it one way you see one thing but if you tilt it the other way, you see something different.

Afterwards, I asked my mother if she actually liked that man. She said she likes his company.

I said, 'Is that man going to be your boyfriend?'

She paused for a moment – too long of a moment, if you ask me. Then she said, 'Phin, I enjoy Brent's company. We have a lot in common. Listen, Phin, if I ever were to have a boyfriend, it would never come as a surprise, okay?'

I said, 'Good, because bad surprises upset my homeostatis.' I learned that word in *Discover* magazine, but I had never had a chance to use it until then. When a person's homeostatis is upset, he feels uncomfortable and is motivated to do something about it. For example, if you are cold, you will shiver and get a sweater. I didn't want to think about what I would be motivated to do if Mom made that man her boyfirend.

Besides, my mother and he would make a funny-looking pair. They would be different than most mammals since the male is usually bigger than the female. There are some mammals where the female is bigger, but only a bit bigger. That would be like the spotted hyena. The female spotted hyena has to be bigger than the male in order to stop him from eating her pups.

Of the species where the female is a lot bigger than the male, many of them are spiders. For example, the average female golden orb spider is twenty centimetres long, but the male is only five to six millimetres long. Some of the golden female orbs are a thousand times bigger than the male. The male is so tiny that he can live on the female's web and steal her food without her even noticing him. He mates with her usually while she's eating and is distracted. But if she notices him, she will try to eat him too. I can always hope that happens to Brent.

My father looks better with my mother, but they got separated when I was eight. I live with my mom because my father travels a lot. He's a foreign correspondent. Right now he's in Helsinki. It is six hours later in Helsinki than it is here. That means my dad is living in the future.

L ast night I drew land formations and natural disasters on Reull. Spikequakes are natural disasters where spikes come up out of the ground. Virex is a virus when everything you touch starts to get bigger and bigger and when it's ten feet big, it explodes and your skin turns purple, then blue, then red, then green. Firex is when you get hotter and hotter but don't catch on fire, you simply melt into a pool of fluids.

I showed them to my mother and she said, 'Wow, Phin, that's very imaginative. Do any nice things happen on Reull?'

I said, 'Sure, there's Mover Island, a piece of land that moves from place to place. The people who live there could go to sleep near a country like Canada and wake up next to a country like Australia or Greenland. The problem is, they're hardly ever dressed for the weather and sometimes freeze or boil to death in their beds.' That got me thinking about Lyle, who I would like to put on Mover Island.

At lunchtime I was swinging and playing a game in my imagination – until Lyle came along. In the game, I was swinging over a big gully. The object of the game was to swing high enough so that my feet looked like they were touching a certain cloud in the sky. If they couldn't touch that cloud, I would be sucked into a gully of brain suckers. I had fun doing that until Lyle came over and did an under-duck and pushed me out of my swing. I landed in brain-sucker gully and was really mad. So I yelled some Gaelic words at him and then called him a name he'd understand. If Lyle was in a pit of brain suckers, and he was the only food they had in months, those brain suckers would starve to death. I really wished right then that I was a stinkpot turtle that releases a foul scent when its predator attacks. But the only thing that stank right then was Lyle.

Lyle ran to Mrs. Wardman. I watched him as he talked to her, and I knew he was snitching. Mrs.Wardman listened to him, and then she looked over at me and made a motion with her hand for me to come over. As I walked over to her, I had seventeen thoughts go through my brain. Then I had a thought about there being seventeen thoughts, and that made it eighteen.

Mrs.Wardman said, 'Lyle says you called him a rude name. I don't know what it was and I'm not even going to ask you, because saying it once is enough. I don't want you to call names again, is that clear, Phin?'

I nodded my head, but I was really, really mad. I hadn't told on Lyle for pushing me, so why did he tell on me for calling him a name? He does it all the time, and not behind my back like some of the other kids. Lyle's the biggest front-stabber there is. I said 'Whatever' to Mrs. Wardman, but I said it really low so that she could hear me only in her unconscious.

I wished really hard that red fire ants would swarm Lyle. Their sting hurts as much as wasp stings. The problem is there aren't many red fire ants around here. They're usually where it's warmer. Then I started thinking that maybe with global warming, they would begin a giant march north and eventually end up here.

This made me think about climate change and how the earth is heating up. Scientists say that if it heats up by more than two degrees, we'll all be in big trouble, and it's heating up even faster than anyone thought. Thinking this made me feel shivery inside. When I told Bird I was feeling worried, he tried to distract me by getting me to pretend the teachers could shoot laser rays out of their eyes and we should dodge them. But I just didn't feel like it.

I tried putting a stick between my teeth to make my mouth into a smile, but it didn't work. Bird said I looked like a jack o' lantern, and then he put a stick between his teeth too. When he did that, I saw something black crawling toward his mouth.

I said, 'Umm, Bird, I think you should take that stick out of your mouth.'

He said, 'Why?' but it sounded more like *Eiiii*.

Then I said, 'Because there's something about to crawl into your mouth, and it's something that people might eat in Cambodia but we don't eat them here.' Actually, 80 percent of the world's people eat insects of some kind, which means they can't be all that bad for you, but just as I was about to mention that to Bird, he saw the beetle too. He flung the stick really far, and it hit a Grade 5 kid on the back. That kid turned around and pushed the kid behind him, who must have been confused. Bird started dancing around and shivering. He was still shivering and saying, 'Gross, gross, gross,' when the bell rang. That made me smile a little bit for real.

We mostly did boring stuff the rest of the day, so to keep myself from falling asleep, I made up a game to play each time Mrs. Wardman told us to take a Duo-Tang out of our desk. The game was if I reached in with my eyes closed and pulled out the right one on the very first try, I got fifteen points. If I got it on the second try, I got ten points. Third try was worth five points and fourth try got a big fat zero. The goal was to get at least fifty points by the end of the day. I only got to forty-five.

The only good part of the afternoon was silent reading, when I got to read a book about dolphins. I learned that a dolphin mother sometimes has a dolphin midwife with her when she gives birth. The midwife pushes the baby up to the surface as soon as he's born so that he can get a breath of air. I also learned that if you plug a dolphin's blowhole, that feels to a dolphin like how covering your mouth and nose at the same time would to you. I wondered what that would feel like. I tried holding my breath to see what it felt like, but I didn't really think that would be the same.

After school, my mother showed up to take me home but I told her that I wanted to walk home today.

She said, 'But, Phinnie, I'm already here.'

I said, 'But I really want to walk home.'

My mother sighed and said, 'Fine then, walk home.'

It was a good thing I did because on the way, I saw a plastic shopping bag on the side of the road. I picked it up and put it in my backpack because it could blow out to the ocean and a sea turtle or an albatross could choke on it. Albatross babies are fed things like plastic lids and Lego blocks by their mothers, who find them floating in the ocean and mistake them for food. Every year thousands of babies die because plastic gets caught in their throats and esophaguses, which makes them choke or starve to death. I wondered why the person who littered the plastic bag didn't think of that.

When I got home, my mother wasn't there. In a few minutes she showed up and told me that she had had a little talk with my teacher. This is never good news. I sucked in my breath and held it as long as I could. I remembered the rule of threes when I did this. The general rule is that you can live three minutes without oxygen, three days without water and three weeks without food. I was careful not to hold my breath for longer than the count of fifteen, because I wasn't sure that rule was completely accurate.

My mother still hadn't said anything else, so then I took another big breath and did the same thing over. She said, 'Phin, what are you doing?' I didn't say anything right away because I was still trying to let out the air I had breathed in and didn't want to break the pattern of it. She crossed her arms.

When all the air was out, I said I was just breathing, waiting for her to get to the point. She said she was getting there but was waiting for my full attention. I said I could never give her my complete full attention because some of it had to be used for things like breathing and blinking my eyes. She said most people could do those things without paying attention. I said not me because I had to keep part of my mind on those things in case they got out of control.

My mother said, 'I heard you used a few select words today, Phin. What was that all about?'

'Lyle pushed me. Twice.'

'Well, I hadn't heard about that part. Did you tell Mrs. Wardman?'

'No.'

'Well, you should have. Lyle needs to learn a lesson. You'd actually be doing him a favour by telling on him.'

'I don't want to do him any favours.'

'You know what I mean, Phin. You'd be doing everyone a favour,' said my mother.

Then I told her that Lyle had pushed me before today too. She got really quiet, and I could tell she was mad. She said that she would talk to the teacher about it and that I should stay away from that kid like she told me to before. I said I was trying to, but the problem is Lyle has legs too. And also a few times Mrs. Wardman made me do group work with Lyle – even though I told her my mother said I should stay away from that kid.

Then came the part I was hoping wouldn't come. 'What did you call Lyle?' asked my mother.

'Lady,' I told her.

'You called him *lady*?'

'Yes.'

'Since when is *lady* a bad word?'

'Since fourth grade.'

'Oh,' she said. 'Well, how about next time you insult Lyle you call him *man* instead?'

I just rolled my eyes at her. Sometimes she just doesn't get it, but I was glad to get off that subject.

Then I said, 'Mom, if I lie down on the couch, could you sneak up on me and cover my nose and mouth at the same time?'

'Why?' asked my mom in a surprised voice with a surprised face.

'Please. Just do it, please.'

'That's kind of a creepy request, Phin. I need to have a good reason for doing something like that.'

'What's creepy about it?'

'Well, Phin, it sounds a little like a smothering and, you know, I rather like you. Besides, I don't want to spend the rest of my days in the penitentiary. I've written stories about some of those inmates, you know, and I don't think they'd be very nice to me.'

'Yeah sure, Mom, sure.'

'Seriously, why do you want me to do that?'

'Because I read in a book today that if you plug a dolphin's blowhole, that feels to him like having your nose and mouth covered at the same time would to you. I want to know how that feels exactly.'

My mother said, 'Oh, okay.' So I lay down on the couch and closed my eyes. A few minutes later, she covered my nose and my mouth with her hand – but only for a couple of seconds. She wouldn't do it for any longer than that, but I think I know a little bit better what that feels like to a dolphin. Not good.

At lunch today, Bird and I went to the edge of the playground by the apple tree. The tree has a branch that sits straight out and it's almost like sitting on a bench except that it is a lot higher off the ground and it bounces up and down a bit when we move around on it.

Bird and I were careful not to jump down on the side of the tree facing Mr. Byers' house. At the beginning of the year we were told in school assembly that we could play only on the school-facing side of the apple tree. Mrs. Wardman even went out to show us where we could go and where we could not.

Bird said, 'Can we step here, Mrs. Wardman?'

And she said, 'Yes.'

Then he said, 'How about here, can we step here, Mrs. Wardman?'

And she said, 'No.'

He said, 'But what about right here, Mrs. Wardman, can we step right here?'

And she said, 'You can, but you may not, Richard, and your allowable questions are up.'

Richard is Bird's real name. Everyone calls him Bird because his last name is L'Oiseau, which is bird in French. Bird likes his nickname better. It irritates him that Mrs. Wardman won't call him by that, so he makes sure not to call her by the name she prefers either – just not to her face.

Bird stopped asking questions. But when Mrs. Wardman wasn't looking, he stepped over to the side she told him he couldn't step on, and then he jumped back before she looked around. But nothing happened to him when he was where she told him he shouldn't be.

I don't want to go anywhere near Mr. Byers anyway. He makes the hairs on the back of my neck stand up.

One day I got Silly Putty stuck in the hairs on the back of my neck. I'm not sure how I did it – I think I forgot to put it away before I went to bed, and I lay down on top of it. When I got up the next morning, it was stuck to me.

I went to my mother and she said, 'Geez, Phin, you're turning green.' She tried rubbing it off with soap and water but it wouldn't come off. Then she tried baby oil, and she pulled some off but the problem was she pulled off the hairs on the back of my neck too.

I yelled because it hurt, and then I said, 'Great, Mom, now how am I going to know when I'm scared of someone?'

She said, 'Phin, sometimes you exhaust me.' She says that a lot. But then she smiles.

When we were on the tree branch I told Bird that I thought I hated Lyle who pushed me yesterday and then told on me for calling him *lady*. Then I told Bird I would like to call Lyle an F-er to his face instead of behind his back.

The F word is one of the very first words I think of when I'm really mad. For example, in third grade we had to write down words that described our French partner, and the only word I could think of was the F word because I really didn't like him. Maybe it was a good thing that I didn't know what that word was in French – especially after he bit me. When that happened, I yelled the F word, but just inside my head.

This morning I woke up to an awful sound – it was like a wolf trying to howl after swallowing one of those birthday-party noisemakers. And it was standing over me.

I was a little worried about what I might see – maybe a pack of wolves having a birthday party and the cake just happened to be me – but I took a chance and opened my eyes. My mother was standing there and that awful noise was coming from her. She was smiling so I figured she wasn't choking on something, so I asked her what the heck she was doing.

'I'm yodelling, Phin,' she said.

'But you're not on a mountain,' I said. 'You're standing over me making that awful sound. I thought you were a wolf with something caught in its throat. If you were a wolf, you'd have to be the alpha because if you were a submissive, the others would attack you for making a sound like that.'

Since my mother seemed to be interested in awful sounds, I told her that a science show I watched was about how researchers asked people across lots of countries to rate how horrible different sounds are. The top five were:

5. a metal drawer being opened
4. scraping wood

3. scraping metal
2. Styrofoam being rubbed together
1. scraping slate with a garden tool, which makes the fingernail-on-a-chalkboard sound

I told Mom that I figured her yodelling would be pretty close to the top of the list if the scientists had used it in their study.

'Ha ha,' she said. 'I actually think I'm pretty good. Anyway, I've been asked to give you a message. Your father is in Switzerland covering a story about how the permafrost is melting in the Alps and he emailed me and asked me to say hello to you and to give you a big lick from him.' Then she reached for me and pretended to lick me and it felt like I was being mauled by a crazy wolf mother. I told her to stop before she gave me the creeps.

As I ate my breakfast, I wondered how close Switzerland is to where I live, so I went up to my room and got out my distance globe. It's a globe where you touch one part of it with an electronic pen and then touch another part of it with the pen and then the globe tells you how far apart those two places are.

My father bought it for me on my last birthday so that I could always know how far away he was from me. I think he thought it might make me feel better to be able to see exactly where on the earth he was, but it doesn't. Now not only can I see how far away he is but I can hear the exact number of kilometres. That's like not only knowing that you're about to get a needle but also knowing how far it's going to go into your muscle. The robot-sounding voice said 5,403 kilometres.

I wondered which animals will start dying if the permafrost melts, so while my mother was having a shower, I got on to her computer and did a Google search. My mother told me to figure out the most important words when doing a search and type them in. So I typed in *animals* and *melting* and *permafrost* and it came up with 217,000 hits. One said that melting permafrost in Siberia is releasing carbon that's been trapped there since the Pleistocene era. As it bubbles to the surface, it releases methane gas into the atmosphere, and since methane is twenty times more potent than carbon dioxide, this means global warming will happen even faster than the scientists originally thought.

The article said that this news is not good for human and animal life. This made me worried and scared. My insides, even my heart, felt like they were getting skinnier and skinnier.

I turned off the computer when I heard my mother coming downstairs. She saw me sitting in her office and asked me what I was up to. I told her I was reading about the melting of the permafrost.

She said, 'Phin, right now you should be getting on your snow pants and boots because there's nothing melting here today – it's minus 21 degrees.'

'But,' I said, 'doesn't it worry you that the permafrost is melting? The *perma*frost?'

'Yes, Phin, sometimes it does, but I don't have time to think about it right now. Now, come on, we have to get going – quick as a bunny!'

She handed me my jacket and snow pants, and I put them on, but what my mom said didn't make any logical sense. If a starving grizzly bear walked up to a person having a picnic, would it be good for her to say she doesn't have time to be scared because she hasn't finished her sandwich?

When I walked into my classroom this morning, I noticed right away that there were two things out of the ordinary. The first was that Mrs. Wardman's desk was moved over too far to the right at the front of the classroom. I sit in the back row, which has seven desks. The middle row has eight desks and the front row normally has seven. But today it had eight. I counted twice to be sure. Eight.

The other out-of-the-ordinary thing was that there was a lump on the show-and-tell table with a white sheet over it. It looked about the shape of the big box where I keep my Reull drawings.

When everybody sat in their seats, the extra desk was taken up by a kid I had noticed in the hallway hanging up her jacket. I don't usually pay much attention to girls, but I noticed this one because I had never seen her before. Also because she's a big girl.

Mrs. Wardman went over and stood beside her desk and said, 'Children, this is Mitty. She's new to our class. Please say hello.' And then we all said, 'Hello, Mitty.' I felt sorry for and happy about Mitty at the same time. I felt sorry for her because she had a weird name and was also big, which meant that Lyle was bound to give her a hard time. I could already think of a few bad things that rhyme with Mitty, and I knew that even 'waste of flesh' Lyle, with brain cells for nothing but thinking up really mean things, was bound to think of them sooner or later. Mitty was definitely in for it.

But I felt a bit happy too because having Mitty in the class might take some of the pressure off me and a few of the other kids since Lyle would have someone else to pick on. I felt a little guilty about feeling happy about that – but not guilty enough to stop thinking it. Maybe that's what people mean when they say misery loves company. Maybe when misery is spread out it's not so hard to take. Maybe it's like when we have reading groups and there are five in each group instead of three, which means you don't have to answer Mrs. Wardman's questions as often.

After we said hello to Mitty, we sang 'O Canada.' Then Mrs. Wardman announced that we were going to gain another new friend in our classroom – a class pet. She said we had to use our logic skills to guess what was under the sheet. I was a little worried when she said that because of the last time we did a logic exercise. She gave us ten minutes to write down what we thought was under there.

I thought nine thoughts:

1. There are only a few animals that are domesticated and would make good companion animals.
2. One is the cat.
3. We can see things eight times smaller than cats can.
4. Another animal that makes a good companion is a dog.

5. It can't be a cat or dog because they would be making noises.
6. A horse could be an animal companion.
7. The show-and-tell table couldn't hold a horse.
8. Some people think pigs make good domesticated companion animals.
9. We shouldn't eat our companions.

But I only wrote one: It is not a cat, a dog, a horse or a pig. I didn't have a guess as to what was under the sheet because I had ruled out all suitable companion animals.

Mrs. Wardman told us to pass in what we had written down. Then she said, 'Okay, are you ready for the big surprise?' All the kids yelled *yes* and Gordon nearly fell out of his chair because he jumped out of it and then plopped back into it really quickly, which made it tip. Mrs. Wardman told him to be careful because he could fall backwards and split his head wide open.

Then Mrs. Wardman pulled off the sheet slowly and said, 'It's a ... frog! Who guessed a frog?' she asked. Nobody raised a hand. Then she said, 'Welcome your new class pet, everyone!'

I raised my hand and Mrs. Wardman said, 'Yes, Phin?' I asked her what kind of frog it was. It looked like a White's tree frog to me but I wasn't absolutely sure. It was smaller than my hand and a greenish turquoise colour, which is what they look like, but White's tree frogs are nocturnal and I doubted that Mrs. Wardman would get a pet that would sleep all day and be awake all night when we weren't even here.

'It's a White's tree frog,' said Mrs. Wardman.

Mrs. Wardman told us that frogs make excellent pets because they are quiet and don't need a lot of care. I wondered how that makes a pet excellent. Wouldn't a rock be a good pet then too? I only thought this – I didn't say it because Mrs. Wardman would think I was being sarcastic. I wasn't being sarcastic, I was being serious. But I didn't say it anyway.

Next Mrs. Wardman told us that we all got to vote on a name for our class frog. I knew that since this was a White's tree frog, it was male and not female because he had a greyish throat and females have white throats. Each of us wrote one name on a piece of paper and put it into the voting jar. I wrote *Cuddles*. I meant to be sarcastic that time, but I didn't have to put my name on it so I knew I wouldn't get in trouble for it.

Then Mrs. Wardman went to the jar and asked us what the chances were that our entry would be chosen. Gordon shouted out, 'One in twenty-three,' and Mrs. Wardman said, 'Yes, Gordon, you are right, good thinking.'

But both she and Gordon were wrong because I heard Katherine and Amy talking in the row in front of me and I knew that they had both voted for *Kermit*. That would mean that they had a two-in-twenty-three chance of having their name chosen and the rest of us would have a one-in-twenty-three chance but only if there were no others of us who chose the same name as someone else.

Mrs. Wardman put her hand into the jar and pulled out a piece of paper. 'The name of our class pet toad is ... Cuddles!' she said. She smiled and some of the kids clapped and cheered. Mrs. Wardman asked whose name was Cuddles, which I didn't think she'd ask. I raised my hand slowly and she said, 'Nice name, Phin, congratulations.' Then we opened our readers to page 123.

Nobody seemed to think that was weird – a frog that was quiet, slept all day, didn't need much attention and that you couldn't cuddle called Cuddles. Sometimes sarcasm just doesn't work.

Today at school a kid got in trouble – big trouble. Her name is Jody and she got caught telling other kids that eating breath mints will make them jump higher. The teacher said this is pretending to take drugs and that there's a zero tolerance policy for drugs. After Jody got her misbehaviour, she started crying so hard that her mother had to come get her.

I felt bad for Jody, which made it hard to concentrate on my spelling exercises. The word activities were all about animals. One of the questions was 'Lions live in the j _ _ _ _ _.'

I raised my hand and Mrs. Wardman came over. I asked her if this was a trick question since there's no J word for savannah. She said, 'Phin, the answer is jungle. Just write *jungle* down.' Then she walked back to her desk.

I thought about not telling her that lions don't live in the jungle because I could tell she was irritated with me. I knew this mainly because when she told me to write *jungle*, her eyelids fluttered and she took a deep breath.

I thought about it for a few seconds. I remembered what my mother had told me about how maybe I shouldn't point out to Mrs. Wardman that she's wrong when she's wrong. But then I decided that she should know the right answer. She was the teacher and it wouldn't be good if she was teaching everybody the wrong thing for years and years and years. So I raised my hand again.

'What is it, Phin?' said Mrs. Wardman. She said this from her desk, which made what I had to say a little bit tricky. I didn't want to say it out loud in front of everybody but now that I had raised my hand and she had answered, I had to say something.

'The answer to question seven can't be jungle,' I said, 'because lions don't live in the jungle. They live on the grasslands and savannah.'

Then all of a sudden other words popped into my head, but they didn't stay in my head. It was almost like they dropped down out of my brain and into the back of my throat and I had no choice but to spit them out – it was either that or choke. But after they came out, I immediately wanted to grab them from the air, shove them back into my mouth and swallow. But it was too late. The words 'and frogs shouldn't live in cages, they should live in wetlands' were out into the air making their way to Mrs. Wardman's ears and all I could do was hope for the best.

Mrs. Wardman didn't say anything for a few seconds. She just looked straight at me and then she said in a really low voice with her mouth hardly moving, 'Phin, then just leave that one out, for pity's sake.' She didn't say a thing about what I said about frogs.

So I left the jungle answer out. I should have known it was going to be a stupid exercise. On the first page there was a picture of a polar bear and a penguin sitting on the same ice floe. On the same ice floe! They live on opposite ends of the world, for pity's sake. Whatever that means.

I couldn't get to sleep last night at all. I tried to. I tried counting sheep. I got to 1,011, but then the sheep started bumping into the fence they were jumping over. I think that was because I was getting a bit tired and couldn't make them jump high enough after about 1,000. When they hit the fence, they would fall down. That didn't make me feel sleepy.

Then I tried to think nice thoughts. I thought of the animals on Reull. I thought of Whirly Eye who has one big eye but also little eyes at the tips of his tentacles so that when he whirls around he can see in all directions. He is never surprised by what may be around a corner because all he does is put out one of his tentacles to look for danger. Whirly Eyes have predators but they're hardly ever caught, not even at night, because the eyes take turns sleeping – half of them sleep during the daytime and half during the night.

That made me think of dolphins here on earth. The left and right sides of a dolphin's brain take turns sleeping so that one part can watch for danger. Whales and seals and manatees do this too but no other mammals do.

There are thirty-five different species in the family *Delphinidae* and five of them are critically endangered, endangered or vulnerable on the Red List of Threatened Species. Most of the others could be in big trouble too but scientists don't have enough information about them to know for sure.

Lots of different species of birds can sleep one half a brain at a time. The eye that is controlled by the part of the brain that is awake stays open and the other one droops closed. If birds sleep together, the brains of the birds at the ends of the rows sleep one part at a time but both sides of the brains of the birds in the centre sleep because they feel safe.

This thought made me think of feeling safe and then I wondered if Cuddles was feeling safe. I started to worry that he was lonely there in the aquarium cage without any of his species around to listen to. Last summer, my mom and I went to a marsh-mallow roast in the amphibian park where there are three different types of frogs. As it was getting dark, they made a lot of noise. But for Cuddles in his lonely cage in the quiet school there would be nothing for him to see or hear at the very time he's most awake. That made me worried and sad, so I got up to find my mother.

I found her working in her study. She didn't even look up from her computer because she knew it was me behind her. When I was little she told me not to make faces at her, that she had an eye on the back of her head and could see me. I believed her because anableps are fish that have two eyes to see the world above the water and two eyes to see below.

Before I even said a word, my mother sighed. 'What is it, Phin? Why are you up when I put you to bed over an hour ago? How are you going to do well in school tomorrow if you're tired? Don't you know I have a lot of work to do after I put you to bed? Don't you understand that?'

She said it in her sandpaper voice and she didn't even have her 'I'm a ticking time bomb' sign around her neck. She sometimes uses that sign to signal to me that I'd better not give her a hard time. I hate it when she asks me a lot of questions in a row because then I have to remember them in order so that I can answer them in order. It's hard to remember after about three or four and it's even harder to answer them all really quickly because most often she doesn't give me time.

I complained to her about this once and she said that some questions are rhetorical, which means that they're asked for a purpose other than to get answers to them. She said for example that asking 'Why me?' when something bad happens is an expression of emotion more than a question that you want answered.

But when I say 'Why me?' I usually really am looking for an answer. But mostly I never get one so maybe that makes it rhetorical too.

The problem with rhetorical questions is that I usually don't know which ones are real and which are not. So the answers to my mother's questions were:

1. I am worried about Cuddles.
2. I can't sleep.
3. I'll be fine, school is easy.
4. Yes.
5. Yes.

But all I ended up saying was, 'I can't sleep because I'm worried about Cuddles' – which I guess answers two of her questions at once.

She said, 'Phin, for the love of God, Cuddles will be fine. He's safe in his aquarium.'

I said, 'The being-in-the-aquarium part is the part that worries me. And I think he might be in pain because of it.'

She said, 'Phin, he's a frog! A frog! He doesn't even know where he is.'

I said, 'How do you know that? How does anyone know that?'

She said, 'Phin, you have to stop anthropomorphizing. Do you know what that means?'

'Yes,' I said. 'But why is that wrong? Why the heck do you think animals don't have pain and feel scared? They do, you know. The Green Channel has lots of shows about that.'

'Phin, please – it's late. Just go back to your bed and try to think nice thoughts.'

I said, 'I'm all out. And I can't sleep. I know this is one of those nights that I won't be able to sleep – not even a little bit.' Then I had a sudden thought and ran to Fiddledee's litter box and checked for red poop because I hadn't checked it for two days. I lifted some of it with the scoop and looked really carefully. It looked mostly black, which was a relief.

My mom said, 'For the love of God, Phin, get up those stairs to bed.' I ran up fast in front of her because she didn't look happy and I thought maybe her brain cells might go all wonky and she might pounce on me or something. But then she sighed and said, 'Let's go to bed and get some sleep.' She let me climb into her bed, which is very big, a king's bed.

I said, 'I love you, Mom.'

She said, 'I love you too, Phin. Now go to sleep.'

I didn't say anything else after that because I wanted her to not be mad at me and I wanted her to be happy and I thought maybe this was as good as I was going to get tonight. I snuggled close to her and she put her arm around me and kissed the back of my neck.

But do you know what I think? I think that some people can't stand to think that animals feel a lot like human beings. I think it's hard enough for people like my mom to write and hear about what's happening to other human beings around the world – let alone other animals too. Knowing that so many more of the earth's animals feel sadness and pain is just way too much hurt for their minds to let them see.

My mother woke me up this morning saying, 'Good morning, sleeping beauty.' She kissed my cheek and I opened my eyes. She had a pad and a pencil and said, 'What can I get you this morning, sir?'

I said, 'How about toast and peanut butter?' I must have been still sleepy because then I remembered I'd decided not to eat peanut butter. Last night I checked the ingredients on the jar and it contains palm oil. I told my mother to forget the toast and peanut butter because of the palm oil.

She said, 'But you're not allergic to palm oil.'

I said, 'Don't you even care about the orangutans?'

'What do you mean?' asked my mother.

I told her that the peanut butter we have is made with palm oil and that palm oil comes from palm-tree plantations that have been built where the orangutans used to live. Now those orang-utans are endangered because so much of their habitat has been destroyed.

'But, Phin,' she said, 'we already have the peanut butter and so we're not going to help the monkeys by not eating it.'

'They're not monkeys,' I said, 'they're primates. And it's the principle of the matter.'

My mother sighed and said, 'Okay, Phin, if you don't want peanut butter, what do you want?' But then she remembered she was pretending to be a waitress and her voice got nice again. She said, 'I'm sorry, sir, we're out of orangutan-free peanut butter this morning, is there something else that you might like?'

I said, 'Mom, the peanut butter doesn't have orangutans in it – it's made with palm oil that comes from plantations that are being built on orangutan territory and making them go extinct!'

My mother slammed closed her notepad and said that her sanity was going extinct. She said, 'I'll get you some orangutan-free Shreddies. They'll be on the table waiting for you.' Then she left the room.

My mother doesn't understand and I don't know why. Actually, I think I do know why: I think it's because she's too busy. She's always hurrying around. I'm not too busy so I know there are almost 400 species in the order Primate and one third of them are vulnerable or endangered or critically endangered on the Red List of Threatened Species. All of the orangutans are endangered or critically endangered. In fact, all the individual remaining primates in the twenty-five most-endangered species could fit in one single football field.

I know something else too. I know Cuddles is in trouble. And I know I have to do something about it.

Today at school, I carefully checked Cuddles for any signs of sickness. Frogs can get fungus diseases that make them dry out and lose weight. I'm really worried about him in there but I don't think he's losing any weight. In fact, to me he looks like he's getting heavier, but that might be because he's sitting on a white sheet today whereas a few days ago he was sitting on a black one.

I learned that trick about black and white from my mother. Once she was trying on pants at the mall and one pair was white and she asked me if she looked bigger or smaller in the white pants. She definitely looked bigger in the white ones, and so I told her that I thought she looked the best in those. My mother always trusts my opinions on fashion because she says I'm only nine and practically incapable of telling white lies.

Later I asked her why it was that she looked bigger in the white pants and she said, 'What do you mean I look bigger? I thought you said I looked best in the white ones.'

'You do look best in the white ones.'

'But do I look bigger in them?'

'Yes.'

'That doesn't make any sense.'

'You look better when you look bigger.'

'Phin,' she said, 'women don't want to look bigger, they want to look thin.'

My mother told me that people in our culture think thinner women look younger and better-looking and that she was trying to buy an outfit to make her look young and pretty.

I told my mother that in the animal kingdom, animals are always trying to look bigger because the bigger they are, the less likely they are to be attacked by predators. For example, the bull-frog blows itself up to look bigger and fiercer, and so does the puffer.

My mother sighed and said, 'Well, that's good – at least I won't be eaten today.'

Mrs. Wardman had to change Cuddles' sheet because he pooped on it. Frog poop is kinda brownish and you can see the things they eat in it. I could see some cricket parts in Cuddles' poop. We're supposed to take turns feeding him crickets and my turn is who knows when since we're going by last name and mine starts with W. Well, actually, I do know when. I'm kid number twenty-two and we're only at kid number nine.

The other kids seem excited about dropping crickets into Cuddles' aquarium, but I'm not. All I can think is poor Cuddles, a tree frog from Australia snatched out of his tree, packed into a crate and sent on a plane to a pet store, who ends up in an aquarium in a classroom in a foreign country with only a single tree branch to climb on with a bunch of ugly faces staring in at him through a glass wall. This isn't the least bit exciting – it's really, super, to-infinity *sad*. Cuddles should be in his natural environment living his natural life with other White's tree frogs in Australia.

I just couldn't stop thinking about that and even when I got home from school all the cells in my body felt like they were buzzing. To calm myself down, I went to Pete's Pond in Africa. Well, not really, just virtually. I typed in the address on the internet where you can see and hear the the animals around the pond at that very minute. Since it was night in Africa, I couldn't see much, but I could hear noises. I closed my eyes and pretended I was right there with them.

When I woke up this morning, I had a feeling that something really bad was going to happen. It made my chest feel empty and my stomach ache, almost like my heart was dangling by a string into my belly. Usually I don't feel like that except for when I wake up in the middle of the night, but then I feel good again in the morning.

I felt yucky and couldn't eat much breakfast and when my mom dropped me off in front of the school, I told her that I still didn't feel right. I told her I had a bad feeling that I couldn't get rid of. She said, 'Phin, I feel like that some days too but my feelings don't make bad things happen. Your thoughts can't do that either, Phin. You're not magic.'

I asked her how she knew that for sure and she said, 'If my thoughts could make things happen, then there would be some people at my office with giant ears and no mouths. So far that hasn't happened.'

'The luna moth has no mouth. It can only mate and lay eggs and then it dies because it can't eat,' I told her.

My mother said, 'Phin, you never cease to amaze me.' Then she told me to jump out of the car because she was going to be late for work. I didn't want to get out, but I did.

I spotted Bird over by the teeter-totters. He was hanging around two kids from Grade 2. The kid with the white hair was showing Bird the T-shirt he had on under his jacket. It had a picture of a chart like the one at the eye doctor's office where the letters start out really big and then get smaller and smaller. It said 'Iseedumbpeoplelookingatmyshirt.' That made Bird laugh when he figured it out.

Bird and the white-haired kid and the other kid and I played freeze tag while we were waiting for the bell to ring. I kept having to be It because I couldn't run very fast. My head and my chest felt heavy and I figured the part of my brain that normally controls my legs was likely being used up by thinking about something bad happening.

I got tired of being It, so I went up onto the top of the slide and made a list in my head of some of the bad things that could happen today:

1. Mrs. Wardman might have been abducted by aliens who implanted an alien's consciousness in her body.
2. My mother could get necrotizing fasciitis in the paper cut she got on her finger when she pulled a notice out of my backpack.
3. Today a species that all other species depend on could become extinct. That would mean the end of the living earth.
4. I could get spontaneous human combustion.

Even though my logic told me that these things likely wouldn't happen, my imagination fooled me into thinking they might. This made me even more worried and my chest started to get really tight and hurt. It turned dark purple and the only way to get it to stop hurting was to think of it as being light purple and then to think of it as being mostly whitish. Sometimes when I concentrate hard, I can think my chest white with only a few purple spots, but I couldn't do it. Besides, I didn't want my chest to go white because then I wouldn't be prepared for the bad thing that was about to happen. Purple is a good colour for quick reflexes.

During first and second periods, my mind tried to play tricks on me. It tried to make me think that maybe my mother was right and I was wrong and nothing bad would happen today. My mind went: 'Something bad is going to happen' (times 82), and then it would say, 'Nothing bad is going to happen' (times 3). Then it went, 'Something bad is going to happen' (times 54), and then it said, 'Don't be crazy, nothing bad is going to happen' (times 23). It kept going on like that until the 'something bad' thoughts were the same in number as the 'nothing bad' thoughts, and then, finally, the 'nothing bad' thoughts were more than the 'something bad' ones, and I felt nearly back to normal. My chest stopped hurting and went whitish.

My mind almost had me fooled. Almost, but not quite – which is a good thing because it was about then that my mother's theory was proved wrong. I used to keep track of all the times my mother was wrong but as I get older, she has started to be wrong a lot. Today she was wrong again. Just like my feeling told me, something bad – very, very bad – happened: Cuddles started making really weird and really loud noises. I knew this was a distress call.

Mrs. Wardman went over and looked in his aquarium. Kaitlyn asked if we could look too and she said yes. We all got up and stood around the aquarium and that's when Cuddles jumped into the glass wall and fell backwards. Then he got up and did it three more times. On the fourth time, he stayed still and didn't make any more croaking noises.

I was really worried that he had zoochosis, which is what animals can get when they're taken out of their natural environment and put in teeny cages. It's kind of like psychosis – which is what humans get when they're driven crazy like in solitary confinement in prisons. All you have to do is visit just about any zoo and you'll see zoochosis. It's when big cats pace back and forth, back and forth, bears and elephants sway from side to side, and the giraffes twist their necks over and over again. I think it must be extra hard to be in a zoo if you're a giraffe – such a long neck and nothing to look forward to.

I asked Mrs. Wardman if she thought Cuddles was sick or something, and she said, 'No, he's fine.'

I'm not at all sure about that. My guess is that Mrs. Wardman is wrong even more than my mother is.

I looked carefully at Cuddles in his aquarium and I wondered if maybe the water at the bottom had too much chlorine in it. Or maybe he needed more than the fake tree branch to climb on. Or maybe he doesn't like the feeling of the big rock under his sticky-pad feet when he climbs up on it to get out of the water. Or maybe he doesn't like the dead crickets and mealy bugs that Mrs. Wardman buys for him at the pet store – most frogs will only eat insects that are moving. Or maybe the pine chips at the bottom of the tank are not the right kind for him? Do they even have pine trees in Australia? There are so many things that could be wrong for Cuddles because that glass aquarium is not his natural habitat.

I was still so worried about Cuddles that just before bed I called Grammie to see if she knew what might be wrong with him. She used to work as a biologist and knows more about animals and plants than anyone else I know.

The phone rang and rang and rang. I was about to hang up when finally she answered. She sounded like she had been sleeping even though it was only 8:30. I think she sleeps a lot these days. Even when she's awake she looks a little like she's sleeping.

'Oh, Phin, it's you, sweetheart,' she said. She sounded happy it was me but her voice was quieter than it used to be.

Since I hadn't talked with her in a few weeks, I told Grammie all about how there's a White's tree frog trapped in a glass aquarium in my Grade 4 class.

'Oh, that's a shame,' she said.

'You think so? Nobody else seems to think so.'

'Well, there are different opinions about that, honey, but if it makes you feel any better, I think White's tree frogs belong in trees.'

It did make me feel better. But my grandmother said she didn't know what could be wrong with Cuddles. I'm going to keep a close eye on him.

A few days ago, I emailed my dad a story about the very last Ozie couple on Reull. I worked really hard on it because I really wanted him to like it. Because he's a journalist, I think he'll be proud of me if I can show him that I can write really good stories.

I got nervous when I was just about to press the Send button. I read over the story again. It looked to me like I'd gotten all the grammar and spelling right, and that it had a beginning, middle and an end, just like they teach you in Language Arts. But to be sure, I asked my mom to read it first. She said it was incredible and that I'm a fabulous writer. But Mom would say that even if all I wrote was my name.

Here is my story:

On Reull there was a small animal called an Ozie that looked like a dog but that was no larger than a rat. The Ozie absorbed carbon dioxide through its skin and cleaned the air just like plants do. Its digestive system made the carbon dioxide into Ozone, which it farted out all the time. The Ozone farts floated up into the sky and healed the atmosphere of Reull.

The problem is, there were only two Ozies left – one male and one female.

One day, the last two Ozies went out for a walk and were captured by a Gorach scientist who was hiding in the jungle. The scientist put the Ozies in a cage where they cried and cried. He thought about how he could make hundreds of Ozies in his lab to heal Reull's atmosphere. He got more and more excited as he thought about how the other Gorachs would love him now that he'd found a solution to all of their problems.

But then later that night, the scientist looked at the Ozies, wondering what they would taste like. They looked a bit like a creature he had tasted before – the Coonit. The Coonit was one of the most favourite foods of the Gorachs. The richest Gorachs got to eat Coonit every day and the poorer Gorachs were very jealous of this.

The scientist tried really hard not to think of cooking the Ozie. But each time he heard one of them fart, the more he drooled and drooled. Each fart was like the smell of a Coonit to him.

Finally, he couldn't stand it anymore. He grabbed the screaming and farting male Ozie and killed it and cooked it up to eat. It tasted even better than he had imagined – even better than a Coonit. He was so excited about its taste that he ate it all in about three seconds.

The scientist still had the taste of the Ozie in his mouth when he killed the female Ozie without even thinking. After she was cooked and eaten, the scientist screamed in horror. He had just discovered the Ozie, which could have been the solution to many Gorach problems, but then, because of his appetite, he ate the very last one.

Then I drew a picture of the last Ozie couple ever. I drew what they were thinking in a thought bubble. They were thinking, 'Help, help,' and even though all the other animals in the web of life on Reull heard their thought, nobody could do anything about it. They all cried, which made the Ozies cry all the harder, and that Ozie couple died knowing only fear and sadness.

After I sent my story, I checked the email every chance I got. It took my dad forty-one hours to write back. This is what he wrote:

Dear Phin,

I am impressed! That is a wonderful story and an excellent example of a satire. I really enjoyed reading it and hope that you'll continue to write and to send me your work.

I hope you and Mom are doing well. Right now I'm in France covering the labour riots. I hope to get a chance to call you within the next few days. Say hi to your mom for me. Love, Dad xoxo

I went to find my mother. She was sitting at the kitchen table reading the paper. When I started to talk, she raised her finger to say just a minute. I sat down and counted the tiles from one end of the kitchen to the other. Still twenty-seven. Then she said, 'Sorry, Phin, just wanted to finish reading that story I wrote.'

'Don't you already know what comes next?'

Mom laughed and said, 'Well, sometimes the editor changes things around.'

'Mom, Dad says hi.'

'Thanks, Phin. How is your dad?'

'I think fine. He liked my Ozie story.'

'It's an incredible story.'

'What's a satire?' I asked my mom.

'Well, it's when someone writes something that ridicules people or things happening in society. Why?'

'Because Dad says my story is a satire. But how could I have written a satire if I didn't even know what *satire* meant?'

'Well, Phin, we don't have to have a word for something before we understand what it is.'

I thought about that for a moment. 'I guess that makes sense.'

'Remember irony? Satire is a bit like irony,' said my mom.

My mom explained irony to me when she wrote a story about a man who ran into the very tree that he took the protective foam off to use for his sled. Mom said that is an example of irony of fate.

'How about another muffin? Thank goodness for the word *muffin* or else we'd be eating a lot of cake,' joked my mother.

I sat down and ate a raisin bran muffin. As I chewed, I thought about how I haven't seen my father for nineteen days. Last time he was home, it was only for four days. I stayed with him in his apartment. There's only one bedroom in it so I slept in his bed and he slept on the pull-out couch. We did lots of things together like play chess and go to the theatre and carve Ivory soap into little animals. But now he's gone again, and I don't even know when he'll be home next.

Sometimes I wonder why my mother and father got separated. I remember when it happened, though. It was just a few days after they had a big fight, which was just after Dad got home from South America. On that day we were all in their bedroom and my mother was helping Dad unpack, and I was somersaulting across their big bed. I had just learned how to do a backwards somersault, and I was feeling happy because of it, and because Dad was home.

I remember that Mom and Dad were talking and Mom was putting away Dad's clothes, and then she stopped talking. And then my dad stopped talking too, and I stopped somersaulting because it was really quiet all of a sudden. I sat up and looked at them. My mother was holding a piece of paper, and they both looked really weird. Then Dad asked me to go downstairs to watch TV for a while.

I don't know what they said when they had the big fight, but I could hear that their voices were louder than normal, and I could hear what sounded like my mother crying. When she came downstairs later, her eyes were red and her hands were shaking. She sat down beside me and didn't say anything, she just hugged me and I could feel her whole, entire body shaking, and I was really worried, but I didn't say anything either.

Then, after a while, my father came downstairs carrying the suitcases he had just brought home. He came into the room and my mother got up and left, and my father sat down and told me that he was going to stay with my uncle Roger for a few days and that he would give me a call later to say goodnight.

A few days later, when my mother and I were out getting groceries, my father came and got his things, like all of his books from the study and his desk that used to be his father's and the big picture of a sandpiper that he got in the Magdalene Islands. Then later my mother sat me down and told me that she and Dad were separating. She said that it was because some people just can't live very well together. That didn't make much sense to me. I asked why they can't get along, and she said they have personalities that are too different from each other.

The thing is, my mother and father seem to have pretty much the same personalities. And they both like the same sorts of things. And they also have almost the same kinds of jobs. And they also both have me. So why couldn't they just fight and then make up like other animals?

In the animal kingdom, when there is a fight among animals that depend on co-operation to live, they make up. For example, when two chimpanzees fight, sometimes one of the others butts in to help the chimp who is losing. When everything quiets down, sometimes the chimp who won the fight goes over to the other chimp and reaches out a hand to him and hugs him and kisses him and grooms him. This is called *reconciliation* by primatologists.

Once a teenaged female chimp called Amber went too close to another chimp's baby and the mother got upset and hit her. But when the mother calmed down, she went over to Amber and kissed her on the nose and let her get close to her baby again.

I don't understand why my mother and father couldn't live together after their fight. Fighting is just a part of life. All the animals do it but those in the same social group – like my mom and my dad – mostly make up afterwards.

After my parents separated, my father started working even more as a foreign correspondent. Now he is hardly ever, ever home. Among primates, the only ones who just get up and leave the social group are the kids who are grown up. They go off to find another group so that they can mate. Parent primates don't just pick up and leave. If there was anyone who was supposed to be doing the leaving around here, it should be me, when I'm older – not my dad.

Tonight before bed I couldn't stop thinking about Cuddles. I thought about him when I was watching the Green Channel, I thought of him as I was eating my bedtime snack, I thought about him when I was brushing my teeth. I just couldn't get him out of my mind. It was like he was in there hopping through my brain pathways and each time he made a turn, he split into two and went down two more roads and those roads split into two and so did he and so on and so on and so on until there were thousands of Cuddleses hopping all through my brain until it overflowed and frogs started coming out my ears.

I told my mother this and she got a weird look on her face.

Her lips twitched a little bit and then she said, 'Phin, why can't you stop thinking about that frog? It's a frog, Phin. A frog! Would you like me to look up some information on the web to show you how little frogs know and experience compared to us? Maybe it would help you to stop worrying about him.'

I shook my head no. I already knew all about frogs. *That* was my problem.

My mother said, 'You know, Phin, like I said before, you can't think of a frog as though it's a person. They're just not as intelligent.'

I asked my mother if aliens came down to the planet earth and they were one million times smarter than humans, would it be all right to capture all the humans with nets and put them in solitary cages and feed them once in a while and watch them bang their heads against the glass until the day they died?

My mother opened her mouth to say something and then closed it again. Then she opened it again and closed it. She told me to jump in my bed and then she went downstairs to get me her relaxation CDs. They didn't work. In fact, they made me feel more scared and worried. One CD was of thunder and lightning storms and all I could think of was being struck by lightning. The next one was of the ocean and it made me think of drowning. The next was called *Rainforest*. That was the worst of all. If you went to a rainforest these days likely all you'd hear would be the sounds of power saws and big trucks and animals running and howling and crying because their homes are falling down all around and on top of them. That's supposed to relax me? What I really want is for my mom to let me have a computer in my room so that I can listen to what's happening at Pete's Pond.

I got up out of bed and walked down the stairs really quietly. I peeked into my mother's office and when she heard me I ducked and then ran in behind the couch so that she wouldn't hit me with her mad rays.

She said, 'Phin, what are you doing? Why aren't you in bed? You know I have two hours of work to do after you go to bed, you know that! Why are you doing this again? You're making me crazy! I have a deadline to meet and I don't have the time to lie down with you, I just don't, Phin, I don't!'

I said, 'I know, but I can't sleep and the CDs aren't helping a bit.' She sighed a really loud sigh and slammed her book shut and walked me back up the stairs. I ran up them fast because I couldn't see her behind me. She's scary when she's mad.

Sometimes I look at my mother and say *Mom Mom Mom* over and over again and the more I say it and look at her, the more she doesn't seem like my mother anymore. She seems stranger and stranger to me the more I stare at her and think the word *Mom*. It's almost like she becomes an alien or something and if I do this for too long, I get scared and then I have to look at something else. When I look back to her again, she's back to normal.

When my mother was mad at me, she wasn't at all normal. But then she lay down with me and she went back to normal. Especially after she fell asleep.

I listened to her snore and thought about Cuddles some more. I am starting to think of a plan for getting him free. I am going to talk to Bird about it.

My mother told me that after school tomorrow she's taking me to a psychologist. His name is Dr. Barrett and she says he helps kids with their problems, like worrying about things. My mother's eyebrows were kind of scrunched up and her lips got a little thinner when she told me this. I told her she looked like the worried one, not me, and that maybe she's the one who needs to go to a psychologist. She said maybe so, and that she'll talk to him about her problems too. I wonder if she means me.

I saw on the Green Channel that psychologists sometimes imprison animals in cages and do experiments on them. A lot of scientists who work for big companies also keep animals in cages and test soaps and shampoos and things like that on them. They put rabbits, mice, guinea pigs, hamsters and ferrets in restraining devices so they can't move and then put chemicals on their skin and in their eyes. Sometimes they don't even give them painkillers because they want to know how much it hurts. Sometimes animals break their necks or backs trying to escape the pain.

Those scientists say animal testing is absolutely necessary. This doesn't make any logical sense to me because other companies make the same sorts of things without any animal testing at all. So how can it be absolutely necessary?

My mother said that Dr. Barrett works only with humans, not animals. She means not-human animals. But I'm not so sure about this whole psychologist thing.

I saw Dr. Barrett today. After he explained to me who he is – somebody who can help me feel less worried – he asked me if I wanted to talk about anything in particular. When I didn't say anything, he did mostly all the talking.

He said, 'You know what a thought is, eh, Phin?'

I said I did. In fact, since I had sat down on the chair that was too high for me, I had four thoughts:

1. Dr. Barrett smelled like parmesan cheese.
2. I hate parmesan cheese.

3. It smells just like throw-up because they have the same
   molecular structure.
4. The U.S. military has tried to find a smell for stink
   bombs that everyone would find horrible but they
   can't find one – not even toilet smells.

'You also know what a fact is, right, Phin?'

I said I did. He asked me for a fact and I told him that a pistol
shrimp has a small claw and a large claw, and when it snaps the
large one shut, the two halves squeeze water out at such a speed
that it's the loudest sound made on earth by any animal. It can
even deafen sonar operators in submarines. Dr. Barrett said,
'That's very interesting, Phin. That fact is in your head with lots
of other thoughts, right?'

I nodded my head.

'Well, here's another thought for you, Phin: right now I'm
having a thought about a purple people-eating monster. Is this
thought like your pistol-shrimp thought? Is this thought a fact too?'

I shook my head, but I felt like there might be a trap ahead.

'Because thoughts and facts aren't necessarily the same, right,
Phin?'

I nodded my head.

'Do you know, Phin, that thoughts make emotions?'

'Yes,' I said.

'The trick, Phin, is to know that lots of the thoughts that make
unhappy emotions like sadness and worry are not really facts at
all – they're just imaginary thoughts. For example, if I was thinking of a big purple people-eating monster and I had the thought
that he was following me all around my office, I would be scared.
Would you be scared, Phin, if you thought that?'

I said I would.

'What I do when I have a thought like that is say to myself "a
thought is not always fact" and then I put it in a bubble in my
imagination and send it away,' said Dr. Barrett. 'How about you
do that with the thoughts that make you worried, Phin? What
thought has been worrying you lately?'

'Well,' I said, 'I'm worried about our classroom pet who is a White's tree frog who shouldn't be stuck in a cage here in Canada. And I've also been thinking a lot about animals going extinct and the earth dying.'

'Do these thoughts make you really worried and not able to sleep?' asked Dr. Barrett.

'Yes.'

'Remember, a thought is not always a fact. A fact is something like two times three equals six and how pistol shrimp make loud noises. A thought, on the other hand, can be something that's just imaginary and can lead to bad emotions like the ones you've been feeling lately. How about we put those thoughts in a bubble and send them away? How about – '

'But they're not just thoughts. It's a fact that Cuddles shouldn't be in a cage. He should be in his natural environment. And it's also a fact that the animal species of the earth are dying. A quarter of mammals are already endangered. Just check the International Union for the Conservation of Nature's Red List of Threatened Species if you don't believe me,' I said.

Dr. Barrett stopped talking for a moment. Then he said he wanted to teach me something that would help calm me down. He said it would also help me get to sleep at night. He told me that for each breath I took in and let out I should concentrate on a word that pushed other thoughts out of my mind.

I said, 'What word?'

He said, 'How about the word *calm*?' I could breathe in deeply and then when I breathe out, I could say the word *calm* to myself.

I told him I couldn't use the word *calm* because it might make me think of the word *comet* and then that would make me think of one hurtling toward me from outer space.

I told him that comets aren't as dangerous as asteroids because they have bigger orbits, which don't bring them as close to earth as often. 'But that doesn't make them not dangerous,' I said. I told him that the chances of an asteroid or comet hitting the earth in the next hundred years is one in 5,000, which is quite a big chance – about the same as dying in a plane crash if you fly twice a year. And that's likely a bigger chance than a gunman going into our school and shooting at us, which is something my teacher made us prepare for.

He said, 'Okay, then let's try to think of a word that doesn't really mean anything.'

That wouldn't be a word then, I didn't say.

He asked me what my word could be and I said I don't know. He said, 'Just give it a shot and try out a sound.'

I thought for a minute and said, 'How about *turu?*' I don't know what made me think of that unword.

He said, 'That's a good word. Try it in your head, say *turu turu turu.*'

So I said *turu turu turu*, but at the second *turu* I thought about how that word sounded familiar. I think *turu* is a culture in Africa or Asia or something that I watched on Discovery Channel. That got me thinking about the book I read on Asia last week, the book about the tsunami. Then I wasn't at all relaxed.

I told Dr. Barrett I couldn't use that unword because it made me anxious. He asked why and I told him. He said, 'Okay, let's pick another word.' I thought and thought and finally came up with *buba*. 'Good word,' he said. 'Say *buba, buba, buba* in your head and nothing else.'

So I tried it. This time I got to the third *buba* and then I thought of something that wasn't relaxing. I tried not to think of that not-relaxing thing by saying *buba* again, but it didn't work. I said *buba buba buba buba* fast and then faster and faster. It felt like there was a rock band of aliens chanting *buba* in my head. And they weren't pretty aliens – in fact, they were really scary, each with ten tentacles coming out of its head and ten mouths that each said *buba*. The more I said *buba*, the more real the aliens became. And how much scarier can a scary thing be than right inside the most important part of your whole body? The only thing I can think of that can live without a brain is a cockroach – and that's only for about nine days.

I moved around in my chair and Dr. Barrett asked what was the matter. I told him that *buba* reminds me of *bubo,* which is a type of infection of the bubonic plague.

Dr. Barrett said, 'Okay, how about the word *piece?*'

I told Dr. Barrett the word *piece* would remind me of pieces of things, like bits of animals.

'No, I mean *peace* as in *peace and love,*' said Dr. Barrett. 'But okay, that's enough for today. We'll try it again next time.'

When I got home from school today, my mother said, 'Come here quick, Phin, I want to show you something cool.' I started to take off my jacket, but she said, 'No, you might want to leave that on, Phin, it's really, really cool.' I just rolled my eyes at her and she said, 'Don't roll your eyes at me like some muley old cow.'

I sat down beside my mother and she showed me a letter Grammie sent with a picture that my uncle John took of her skating on the river. The river looked like a big plate of glass. She said in the letter that she could see right down to the bottom of the river because the ice was so clear. She said that she skated about two miles down the river and back and that the river hadn't been that perfect for skating in fifteen years because mostly it's covered with snow in the winter, but not this year.

I told my mother that's because of global warming. Farm animals' farts and burps make up 17 percent of the methane gas in the atmosphere.

'Phin, doesn't your brain ever get tired? Doesn't it sometimes scream, "Please stop! Stop! You're killing me in here?"'

'No.'

'How about we go see Grammie on the weekend and skate on the river?'

'Yes!' I like visiting my grandmother – but I reminded my mother that I can't skate very well. Actually, when I do it it's not called skating, it's called falling. Last time we went to the rink I fell so many times my butt felt like a whacked piñata.

She said, 'Butt – pardon the pun – practice makes perfect.'

I said, 'That's not always true about practice makes perfect. Bird and I have been trying to lick our elbows for two weeks now but we haven't been able to do it. But Bird gets closer to licking his than I do to licking mine because he has a longer tongue than I do. In fact, his tongue kind of gives me the creeps because it looks like a Gila monster's except that it doesn't have a fork in it.'

I don't think anything is possible if you set your mind to it like they say on *PBS Kids*. I think the only way Bird and I could lick an elbow is if he licked mine and I licked his. But that would be gross and I'm not going to mention it to him in case he tries to do it.

My mother said, 'Well, some things are impossible, you're right, but skating is not one of them.'

Today was a *cac* day at school. My mother picked me up and I let her drive me home because I didn't even have the energy to walk. It was like Lyle just sucked it all out of me. He's like a Dementor in the Harry Potter books except he doesn't even have to put his lips on me to suck out my soul. In Harry Potter, Dementors have no eyes and there's a large hole where the mouth should be and they grow in the darkest, evilest places and bring a cold fog wherever they go. Maybe the woman who wrote that book has met Lyle.

I described to my mom how Lyle walked by my desk and knocked over my pencil case on purpose. My pencils and markers and eraser and lunch money went all over the place. Lyle just looked back at me and laughed. Kaitlyn helped me pick them all back up but I thought maybe her licey hair would touch my hair when we were both down on the floor crawling around and that worried me.

I told my mother that I would really like to tell Lyle that I hate him. She nodded and said that she understood why I felt like that but that it likely wouldn't solve anything. I told her maybe not, but it would make me feel better.

Then I told her that I would like to use the F word with Lyle.

She said, 'What F word?'

'You know, the F word.'

'What? *Fart?*'

'No, the really bad F word.'

'What? *Frig?*'

'No, the one that rhymes with *duck*.'

'Oh, that one.'

After a few seconds she said, 'Well, how would you use it with Lyle if you could?'

'I don't know – how about "Leave me alone, Lyle, you fucker"?'

She laughed and said, 'Yeah, or maybe "Fuck off, Lyle."'

'Either one would work for me,' I said. 'I think it would make me feel better.'

'Well, then, go ahead and say it out loud to me. Tell me how you feel about Lyle,' said Mom.

'Really?'

'Sure, when I'm mad at someone, I like to express it to my friends and not have them tell me what I should or shouldn't say or feel, so I guess why should it be any different for you?'

'Okay,' I said. 'Lyle is a fuckface fucker and I hate him.'

'Yes, I agree,' said Mom. 'Lyle acts like a fucker. Did that make you feel any better?'

'Yes.'

'Good, but you likely shouldn't say that word anyplace else. A lot of people are really offended by it.'

I told her okay, I wouldn't say it.

Then I asked her what *fuck* meant exactly, and she said, 'It's just a rude word.'

'But what does it mean?'

'You know about reproduction, right, Phin?'

'Yes, I know about that.' That was the second time this week she'd asked me that.

I have a book called *The Lifecycle of Nature*. It says that animals reproduce when the male puts a seed in the female, which already has a seed, and then the two seeds grow together into a baby.

My mom said, 'When a male is putting his seed into the female, mostly this is called sex or copulating but some person made up a rude word for it years ago and called it *fucking*.'

But why would someone make up a rude word for something that makes more life and makes everything grow? How can that be bad? Why isn't there a swear word for eating since that makes things grow too? Why isn't there a swear word for breathing because that's something animals have to do to survive too? Humans are weird.

After supper, my mother put on the Celtic Chieftains, which is music with fiddles and the guitars. We call it our joyful music. My mom just started putting it on again. For a long time I think she was too sad.

Sometimes Mom plays the fiddle along with it. Sometimes she misses some notes and it's all messed up but messed up in a funnier way. Sometimes she doesn't play along but instead grabs me by the arms and swings me in a circle until I feel like I am dancing on the ceiling. Sometimes I feel like I am going to throw up but since I am on the ceiling I would be throwing down instead.

When we dance, Mom laughs and laughs. I get worried when her head is back and her face is in a big laugh but no sound is coming out of her mouth, not even the sound of a breath, so I poke her in the stomach and make her breathe in loudly and still she laughs. When my father lived with us, he would dance too. Sometimes he would even put me up on his shoulders and bounce me around. That used to worry my mom and she'd yell, 'Will, put him down! You're going to shake his head off his shoulders!'

This evening, though, I didn't really want to listen to the music or dance because there was a show coming on the Green Channel that I wanted to watch. It was all about tigers. Tigers and joyful music just don't go well together because in India there are fewer than 1,500 tigers left and the scientists and conservationists who are telling the truth about how the tigers are being killed are being threatened by the people who want to make factories and mines. That's not the least bit funny.

There are thirty-six animals in the family *Felidae* and twenty-three of them are near threatened, vulnerable, endangered or critically endangered. The Iberian lynx is the closest to extinction and if it's completely killed off it will be the very first wildcat species to go extinct in 2,000 years.

I saw Dr. Barrett again. He told me he wanted to show me a new exercise to make me feel calmer and I said okay.

Dr. Barrett said, 'Okay, sit back, close your eyes and take deep breaths.'

I breathed in, and then I breathed out.

'Do any of your muscles feel tense, Phin?'

'Yes.'

'Which ones?'

'My hands and arms and legs and shoulders and neck and chest mostly.'

'Okay, let's start with your hands and arms. Just open your hands and let your arms hang loosely like you would if you were to lie down in your bed.'

I spread out my fingers and let my arms flop against the arms of his chair.

'That is very good, Phin. Just relax. Relax,' said Dr. Barrett in a slow, quiet voice that made me think of practicing a lockdown at school.

After a few seconds he said, 'Now, do you have a favourite place – a place that makes you feel calm and relaxed and happy? It can be a real place you've been before or it can be one you imagine. Do you have such a place, Phin?'

'Yes, Pete's Pond.'

'Great. Wonderful. Now go to Pete's Pond in your imagination. Let me know when you're thinking of this favourite place by raising a finger on your right hand.'

I raised my finger after a few seconds. I thought about how I saw a honey badger on the Pete's Pond webcam a few days ago. Although it's a small animal about the size of a skunk, a honey badger is listed as the fiercest animal in the world in one of the books of records.

Dr. Barrett said, 'This is a calm, safe place where all your worries disappear. Look around at this place and look at all the sights ... How does it feel to be here?'

I said, 'It makes me feel happy.' In fact, the day I saw the honey badger was really exciting because they're hardly ever seen in the wild. They're vulnerable on the Red List of Threatened Species.

'That's good. You are safe and feel very peaceful and calm. Notice what you hear or don't hear in your special place. Look all around,' said Dr. Barrett very slowly. Then, after he paused for a minute, he said, 'Notice what you smell ... Now, notice what you feel. Say to yourself, "I am relaxed. All of my worries are gone. I am very calm and peaceful."'

I said those words to myself and they did actually make me feel calmer. Dr. Barrett said that I should go to this place inside my mind whenever I want. He told me to repeat, 'I am very calm and relaxed here ... This is my favourite place to be,' to myself. He asked me if I thought this would help with my worry. I said sometimes. He said he'd settle for that and told me to practice over the next week.

I went to Bird's house this afternoon and we played Ping-Pong down in his basement for a long while. Bird is good at Ping-Pong. I suck. Almost every time I hit the ball it flew up into the air and hit the ceiling. Then it would bounce down and hit the floor and roll away under the couch or toys or stuff and we'd have to search for it. I think we spent more time searching for the ball than playing. Once Bird's dog, Ranger, grabbed it and Bird had to reach inside her mouth and pull it out. Some of Ranger's drool got inside the ball and then for a while each time we hit it, drool flew out of it and all over the table.

Bird says Ranger is actually a big pain in the butt and a lot of work because he and his brother have to take her for walks and pick up her poop. Sometimes when Bird is walking on the street and a car comes, Ranger pushes him and knocks him over onto the sidewalk. I don't think I would mind that so much and sure wish I had a companion dog. But Mom says Fiddledee is enough for now and that Fiddledee likely wouldn't like sharing my attention with someone. When I grow up, though, I'm going to have lots of companion animals – at least six or seven.

A female dog like Ranger is called a bitch. Once Bird said *bitch* because he thought it was a bad word. When I told him what a bitch really is, he was a little mad at me because I took all the fun out of saying that word. But then he started calling people who made him mad a female dog. He'd say things like, 'Get out of here, you female dog.' He asked me if the male dog was called *bastard*. He was hoping it was because then he could say, 'Get out of here, you male dog,' and that would be funny too. But I told him that *dog* actually means a male dog and that the species is hound.

While Bird and I were looking for the Ping-Pong ball, we could hear Bird's mother and father having a fight upstairs. At least it sounded like a fight to me. I couldn't tell what they were saying but it was as loud as the fight my parents had just before my dad moved to his own apartment.

I mentioned it to Bird. I said, 'Um, Bird, your parents sound like they're having a fight.'

'Yeah,' said Bird.

'Doesn't it worry you?'

Bird just looked at me like I was crazy and shrugged. 'Nah, it's probably about my brother. My mother yells at him and my dad says she should just leave him alone because he's going through "The Change," like growing hair all over his body and stuff. I think he's turning into a werewolf.'

I didn't say anything else because I don't want to worry Bird. But I sure hope he doesn't become one of 'those kids.' Then he would be like me. One day he could have a whole family and the next day half of one. One day he could have a father who was home 80 percent of the year who took him to swimming lessons and played chess with him and ate supper with him and read books with him and talked with him about lots of stuff, and then the next day he could have a father who's only around 20 percent of the year and who he mostly only talks to on the phone or on email. And it could happen in the blink of an eye, just like that.

I think it's a good thing I didn't tell Bird that. There's no point worrying him about it, I guess, because it's not like he'll be able to stop it from happening or anything. So I'll just be worried for both of us.

Today I saw Dr. Barrett again – twice in one week. He asked me if there was anything I wanted to talk about and when I said no, he said, 'Today, Phin, we are going to talk more about facts.'

Oh great, here we go again, I thought but didn't say.

'Do you know what *propaganda* means, Phin?'

'Yes.'

'Well, that's good. So do you know that some people on the Green Channel may say things so that you and the other viewers get upset about the environment? That way they can get money for their projects or put more pressure on the government to support their projects. Do they do that – ask viewers for money?'

I nodded my head.

'Well, the people on the Green Channel get more money from viewers if they can get them upset about animals.'

That makes sense. Why would you bother doing something if you weren't the least bit concerned about it? It's easier to do nothing.

Dr. Barrett asked me to tell him about one upsetting show I saw on the Green Channel. I picked a show about factory farms. That's where mostly all the meat in grocery stores comes from. On factory farms cows and pigs and other animals are raised in tiny stalls. Their whole lives are spent standing, sitting or lying down.

They don't develop muscles in their legs because they never get any exercise. They get sores on their bodies because of the constant rubbing against their stalls. They spend their whole lives there. Their whole entire lives.

Dr. Barrett said, 'Hmmm. I bet they showed lots of pictures of animals penned in that way and it made you feel really sad, right?'

I said, 'Yes.'

Then Dr. Barrett said, 'Well, Phin, I think the story is a little more complicated than that. Factory farming is how many people around the world make enough money to feed and clothe themselves and their families. Was any of that discussed on the show you watched?'

'Not as much.'

'If you got the other part of the story – the part that I just told you – would you still think they should stop factory farming?'

I nodded my head.

'But, Phin, what about the men and women and children who depend on farming in order to survive?' said Dr. Barrett.

'My grandmother says organic farmers can make money. She said that by letting their animals move around in the fields, the animals are healthier and don't need all those antibiotics and stuff to keep them alive. So that means the meat that comes from them is healthier for people. And even though they end up eaten, at least the animals are treated humanely.'

I stopped for a second to think about the word *humane*. It comes from the word *human,* which sometimes makes it kind of ironic – like calling death a cure for a sickness.

'Well, Phin, I don't want to disagree with your grandmother, but I think it may be even more complicated than that. I think the factory farmers are doing it that way for a reason. It may be the only way they can produce as much food as we need and make a good profit at the same time.'

I didn't believe him. I think they do it that way just because they can. 'The Green Channel says it doesn't have to be like that either,' I told Dr. Barrett.

'Well, I would still argue that it's much more complicated than what you're watching on the Green Channel. Companies need to be able to make a profit to keep people in jobs so that they can support themselves and their families.'

'My grandmother says that less than .2 percent of the world's people own more than 25 percent of the world's wealth. So I figure mostly people can afford to make their stuff in a way that doesn't totally destroy the animals and the environment,' I said.

'Well, Phin, that would be nice for sure, but accumulating wealth is how our free-market economy is structured, and we can't really change it.'

'Why do people tell kids that we're all equal and to treat everybody equally if that's not the way the real world is?' I asked Dr. Barrett.

When Mrs. Wardman talks about being considerate, the only kids who really listen to her are the considerate kids. The kids like Lyle don't pay any attention. So what ends up happening is that the nice kids become even nicer so that the not-so-nice, greedy kids can get away with taking more and more from them with less and less of a fight. Sharing might work if we were all capuchin monkeys or bonobos but some humans are more like chimps. Alpha chimps do things like give food only to those other chimps who are most likely to give them something back. And a wannabe alpha chimp grooms the real alpha chimp just so he can mate with a female without the alpha interrupting.

Dr. Barrett changed the subject. He said, 'Phin, how about we learn some more relaxation exercises?'

So that's what we did – we relaxed ... again.

This is what I wonder: I wonder if Dr. Barrett is working for the alpha humans. And I think *he's* the one with the propaganda.

This evening my mother put on her new white pants and her favourite grey shirt made out of a silkworm's life project. She said she was going out to interview someone about the homelessness problem in our city and that Rena, my babysitter, was coming over to stay with me.

I don't like the word *babysitter* because I'm not a baby. I like the word *caregiver* better. The thing with Rena, though, is that she's not even much of a caregiver. When mother meerkats go out to hunt, the mob's subordinate and teenage meerkats look after all the babies. Those teenagers chase and play with the pups and let them climb all over them. It's not that I want to climb over Rena or anything, but playing a game of cards or chess or something might be nice. All Rena ever does is talk on the phone.

On her way out, my mom wrapped a blue scarf around her neck and put on some hand lotion that smells like jasmine. She even dabbed a little bit on her neck. As she was zipping up her leather boots, I noticed that her face looked smoother, her eyes looked bigger than usual and that she had big red guppy lips. Then I realized that she had makeup on. She hardly ever wears makeup.

'Mom, where are you going?' I asked.

'I told you, Phin – to interview an activist who works with the homeless,' said my mom.

'Is that it?' I asked.

'Yes,' said my mother, 'but I may stop for some dinner afterwards. Why do you ask?'

'No reason,' I said.

While Mom was gone, I worked on my Reull stories and watched the Green Channel. I helped myself to lots of chips since nobody was around to see how many I had. Rena didn't get off the phone even when Fiddledee knocked a dish off the counter and it smashed onto the floor. She didn't hang up until she heard a car come in the driveway.

I ran to the front door and looked out the side window. What I saw almost made me choke on my chip. It wasn't my mother's car in the drive. She was getting out of a shiny red car instead.

I opened the door and stood on the doorstep. My mom was talking with a man inside the car. It was Brent!

I put my hands on my hips. Still they talked and talked and talked, like they didn't even see me.

I walked down the the driveway in my sock feet even though it was super cold out. I stared at the car. They didn't even turn to look in my direction.

I walked over to my mother's side of the car and put my face up to the glass of her window. That's when Brent saw me and he jerked his head back as though someone had slapped him. My mom's head swivelled in my direction. She looked like she did once when I caught her eating my Halloween candies. Then she gave a little wave.

She stepped out of the car. Brent leaned across the seat and said, 'Hi, Phin. How are you doing?'

'Fine,' I said, turning and walking back to the house.

I gave my mother the silent treatment. I pretended not to listen to her when she explained that she had had a few glasses of wine and didn't want to drive home in her own car after dinner. I didn't even let her read to me before bed.

My dad called this evening to talk to my mom. I couldn't hear all of what she was saying because the dishwasher was running, which made it really hard to eavesdrop. I could tell, though, that they were arguing about something. I was hoping it wasn't about me.

I didn't ask my mom what she and Dad were fighting about because I didn't want to make her say something about Dad that I didn't want to hear. She's only said a few things bad about him, but I wondered if there were a lot more bad things inside her. I don't want to hear any of them, especially since I'm part Dad. Because of that and because I can tell it makes her upset, I don't like to bring up the Dad topic with my mom.

Sometimes I send Dad an email that says, 'Dad, you're the best dad in the world. Love, Phin' – even when it's not even Father's Day. Sometimes I also draw pictures of our family and put me in the middle. My mother didn't like my first one like that after my parents got separated. When she saw it, she sat me down and told me again that she and Dad were separated and blah blah blah – another reason not to bring up the Dad topic. Once she told me that their not getting along had nothing to do with me and that I shouldn't blame myself. That didn't make me feel better at all. I wished it was my fault because then maybe I could fix it. After that talk I added horns to my picture of Mom. But then I felt guilty and erased them. Now when I draw pictures of all three of us, I just don't show them to her.

I hope that when Dad sees the letters and pictures I mail him maybe he'll think of me – and maybe even remember that he misses me and then come home to stay. But so far it's not working.

Today something shocked me. When I first heard it, my body got cold and my teeth chattered. It was something I would never have expected – never in a million years. It was a thing worse than the sound of Lyle's voice, a thing worse than getting sick with lice, a thing worse than having your eyelids held open for a week with toothpicks: MY MOTHER TOLD ME THAT I CAN'T WATCH THE GREEN CHANNEL ANYMORE!

After the shock, I got really really really, really, to-infinity mad, which made my body hotter than normal. Now I'm so mad I'm practically burning up and my brain is buzzing like a whole hive full of bees. And my arms are shaking so much that the only thing that could steady them is to grab hold of something – like Dr. Barrett's neck. I just know this is all that friggin' psychologist's fault because after he talked to me, he talked to my mother and then she told me this HORRIBLE, TERRIBLE, SHOCKING news. That's no coincidence.

I yelled at my mother that this was not fair. I screamed that she was ruining my life and that I won't be ready for my job when I grow up if she doesn't let me watch the Green Channel! I asked her how she would like it if she wasn't allowed to get ready for her job.

She said, 'Phin, this is for your own good. There is too much on the Green Channel that is making you worried.'

I yelled, 'The Green Channel isn't what's making me worried! The extinction of animals is making me worried! Everybody should be worried! Why aren't you worried?'

She said, 'Phin, I am not going to change my mind on this. I'm your parent and I've decided this is what's best for you. I am not going to talk about it like this. If you'd like to talk about it calmly and listen to my reasons, then we can do that.'

I screamed, 'I want a different parent! This is not best for me! I need a better parent who makes better decisions!'

She walked away and went to the bathroom. I screamed at her through the bathroom door. Then I went to my bedroom and slammed the door. I cried for a long time. Then my mother came to my door.

She said, 'Phin, how about we play cards?'

I screamed, 'No!'

She said, 'How about we draw?'

I screamed, 'No!'

She said, 'How about we go out for an ice cream?'

I screamed, 'No!'

She said, 'How about we look up things on the computer that you want to know?'

I screamed, 'No, leave me alone!'

I would not talk to her about things she wanted to talk about just like she wouldn't talk to me about what I wanted to talk about.

Later my mother told me that she was speaking with Dr. Barrett on the phone and that he'd like to speak with me too for a few minutes. I screamed at my mother that I didn't want to talk to the friggin' psychologist, but she whispered in an angry voice with her teeth clenched together that if I didn't speak to him civilly, I would lose something worse than the Green Channel.

'What? What?' I screamed. She wouldn't tell me, she just kept staring at me, looking like the picture of the Maori warrior that my grandfather had hanging in his den. So I picked up the phone. Dr. Barrett asked me if there was anything I wanted to talk about and I said no – he's the one who wanted to talk to me, not the other way around. And besides, it was talking to him that got me into this friggin' trouble to begin with.

Dr. Barrett said he understood how frustrated I must feel, but that he and my mother are going to work really hard to help me feel better. He told me that one thing I can do when I'm frustrated is called deep breathing. He told me to breathe in through my nose to the count of seven and then hold it to the count of four and then breathe out through my mouth to the count of seven. Because my mom was watching I tried it, but it made me feel like I was going to pass out. I guess that's one way to stop being frustrated – just pass out and fall on the floor.

Dr. Barrett said that likely the reason I am getting angry easily is because I'm not getting enough sleep. That's not true but I let him think it because I figured that would get me off the phone quicker. The real reason I'm angry is that I'm worried. Nobody is listening to me, not even my own mother! Aren't mothers supposed to listen to their kids? Aren't they supposed to understand them? When she doesn't listen to me, it makes me even more worried than I already am about Cuddles and other animals and climate change and stuff. So I guess you could say my mother is the reason I'm not getting enough sleep. And it's also Dr. Barrett's fault because he's making my mother not listen to me even more than she already doesn't.

When I went to bed, I told my mother that I hadn't changed my mind about this – it was definitely not right that I can't watch the Green Channel. I told her that not being able to watch the Green Channel will just make me more worried. I will be more worried because the bad things I can imagine are worse than the bad things that may really be happening – much, much, to-infinity worse.

I didn't sleep a wink.

Tonight after supper I was really super upset and really wanted to talk to someone who wasn't my mother. The first person I thought of was my grandmother, but when I called her number, there was no answer. Maybe that was okay because I wouldn't want to wake her up again. Sometimes even when I talk to her face to face, it's like there's no answer. She has this blank look like someone has pressed the Pause button or something. Since Granddad's been gone, she's like a goose widow who hangs her head and droops her body after her mate dies. Can you die even before you're dead? I want Grammie to be like she used to be.

My mother wanted to talk to me, but I didn't want to. She kept coming into the living room and sitting next to me and taking my hand. But I wouldn't talk to her. I just kept rubbing Fiddledee and thinking about how unfair it was that I couldn't watch the Green Channel. After a while I got up and turned on the TV and watched a different channel, but I was not happy about it.

MythBusters was on. They were testing the myth that you could kill yourself with your own farts. Jamie and Adam and Tory counted the number of farts they had on a normal day, and then they ate only certain foods all day long. Adam ate only beans, Jamie ate meat and Tory drank pop. Adam's farts went up the most. He farted twice as much – which shows that 'Beans, beans, good for your heart, the more you eat, the more you fart' is true. Then they put Adam in a tub that had a tube over it to hold in all his farts, but he didn't die so they busted that myth. But they did find that there are three deadly gases in farts: methane, carbon dioxide and argon. But it wasn't enough to kill him. The death-by-fart myth was busted.

How come it's all right to watch a TV show about myths, but it's not all right to watch shows about truths?

After *MythBusters* I watched a show on the Travel Channel called *The World's Ten Most Dangerous Animals*. The animals from ten to two were:

10. Bears – kill about 6 people each year
9. Sharks – kill about 8 people a year

8. Hyenas – kill about 50 people a year
7. Jellyfish – kill about 55 people a year
6. Big cats like leopards, lions and tigers – kill about 80 people a year
5. Elephants – kill about 130 people a year
4. Scorpions – kill about 500 people a year
3. Crocodiles – kill about 2,000 people a year
2. Bees and wasps – kill about 10,000 people a year

I was sure I knew what number one was going to be. I watched about fifteen commercials waiting for the final animal. I was absolutely sure I knew what they were going to say, but I had nothing better to watch. But when finally they got to the big moment, it wasn't at all what I thought it was going to be. The man on the Travel Channel said, 'The world's most dangerous animal is ... ' There was a pause and then a drum roll and then he shouted, 'The snake!'

I almost fell out of my chair. The snake? What kind of dumb show was this anyway? The snake kills only 100,000 people each year. What I was sure was the world's most dangerous animal didn't even make the list!

Just to make sure I was right and the Travel Channel was wrong, I went to my mother's computer and typed in *murders*. On Wikipedia it said there were about 500,000 people murdered in the year 2000. That makes humans five times more dangerous than the snake! If you count the murdering of other animals too – which should count because the Travel Channel included inter-species killings – the human kills billions each year. Do you know how big a billion is? It would take a person sixty-seven years to count to a billion if he counted two numbers every second. The human is the most dangerous animal in the world! Stupid, bleeping, crappy channel.

This just made me even angrier. I wasn't getting good information anymore. If I kept watching channels like that, I was going to get stupider and stupider, and then how was I going to know everything I need to know to save animals from extinction? To make it even worse, on one of the channels I was allowed to watch, there was an advertisement about a program that will be on the Green Channel tomorrow. It'll be all about symbiotic relationships in the animal kingdom. But I can't watch it. The only thing that made me feel a teensy bit better is that I already know a lot about symbiotic relationships.

A symbiotic relationship is when one animal gets something from another animal and that animal gets something back from it. An example of that is the oxpecker and the ox. There are two species of oxpeckers, the red-billed and the yellow-billed. They live in the African savannah and have strong feet to hold on to the backs of mammals like oxen. They eat the ticks and parasites on animal skins. So in return for the oxpecker's meal, the ox gets rid of the insects that make him itchy and sore.

I once saw on the Green Channel that all over the earth, animals and birds and insects are all in what is called a dynamic symbiotic relationship with all the other animals and birds and insects. This means that if one is taken out of the food chain, many other animals could suffer or die out.

But if humans went extinct, all of the other species on the earth would stay alive and mostly get healthier and increase in number. That's because humans are at the top of the food chain and there is no mammal species on earth that needs humans to survive, except maybe the little dogs that humans have bred to need them. Besides them, the only living things that need humans are the parasites that live only on them, like the crab louse and certain types of viruses, like human chicken pox and tuberculosis. This makes the human relationship with the other species mostly a parasitic one.

What I think is weird is what humans are doing: killing off their hosts. That doesn't make any kind of sense for a parasite.

When I thought of all this, I had to tell my mother. I knew it was a risk but I really needed to share it with someone. Those facts were like a flood in my mind swirling around really fast and I knew that if I told someone about them, that would relieve the pressure. There would still be a flood, but a calmer one.

When I first started telling her, she listened and made jokes about how it would be neat if everyone had their very own oxpecker. But then she started to get a really weird look on her face and by the time I got to the part about humans being parasites, the really weird look turned into her really worried look. And I knew I was in big trouble.

She said, 'This, Phineas William Walsh, is why you are not watching the Green Channel.'

I said, 'What do you mean? What did I say that was bad?'

And she said, 'Phineas, the ideas you see on the Green Channel really worry me. Do you know that some environmentalists actually hope humans go extinct – that we're all wiped out by a virus or a meteor?'

I said, 'No, I haven't heard that on the Green Channel.'

And she said in a quite loud voice, 'Well, there are such people! They call themselves the Voluntary Human Extinction Movement. I interviewed them once and they're crazy, Phin!' Then my mother got really quiet and said in a very low voice, 'Phin, human life is very important.'

I said, 'But I didn't say it wasn't! All I said is the facts! How come nobody wants to know the facts?'

She said, 'Phin, I know that you're leading up to asking me if you can watch the Green Channel and the answer is no. No, final answer. And you *know* why – I have explained it to you and tomorrow Dr. Barrett will again explain it to you, and your little monologue just now makes me even surer of that decision. You may watch the Discovery Channel or the Learning Channel or PBS or CBC or YTV or Spike TV or Playboy or whatever else – I don't care what! But not the Green Channel. Do you understand?'

That's when I started screaming. I screamed that she was not being fair. I screamed that she was being stupid – more stupid than an acanthonus armatus, which is the vertebrate with the smallest brain weight compared to spinal-cord weight. The acanthonus armatus didn't have to evolve to be very smart because it lives at the bottom of the ocean and is not very active and doesn't have many predators.

My mother didn't like being called an acanthonus armatus, and she likely didn't even know what it was, which proved my point! She gave me her dragon-lady look and told me to go find something to do. She turned to the counter and tried to ignore me by opening a can of cat food for Fiddledee.

But I didn't go away. I stood behind her and screamed that she was not being a good mother. By the look on her face right then, if she were a crocodile carrying me in her mouth to the water, she would have swallowed me.

My mother held the can of cat food in one hand and took some peanuts to eat with the other hand. My mother often puts stuff in her mouth to eat when she is upset. The more upset she is, the more she eats. And she was eating a lot of peanuts really fast.

I followed her to Fiddledee's dish and screamed at her to listen to me. And she said, 'Phin, I will not talk about this.' Her voice and face were very mad. Then I yelled some more about how nobody wants the facts, everybody just wants the lies, and I followed her back to the kitchen counter.

My mother must have been really upset because then she did something that all of a sudden made me stop yelling and start laughing, and I really didn't want to do that, but I couldn't help it: she meant to put more peanuts in her mouth, but she put the cat-food spoon in by mistake!

She ran to the sink and started spitting and gagging, and I laughed harder and harder. I had tears running down my face. She kept saying, 'Phin, this is not funny,' but she was laughing a little bit too.

Then I told her that she shouldn't worry too much because even though cat food is made out of animal parts like intestines, bones and ligaments, Fiddledee hasn't died yet, so she would likely be okay from eating just that little bit on the spoon. She was bigger than Fiddledee, after all, and so it would take a lot of cat food to poison her.

Then I didn't feel mad anymore. I don't think you can be mad and laugh at the same time. I really don't think that is possible.

I told my mother that she wasn't as stupid as acanthonus armatus and she said, 'Why not? I ate cat food, didn't I?' And that made me laugh some more.

I asked my mother if it tasted good and she just made a face at me. I said, 'Well, Mom, you never know. There's only one thing that all cultures of the world won't eat and that's human poop. Everything else is eaten by someone somewhere.'

When my mom went to do some work in her study, I went upstairs and wrote about Reull and drew some pictures of them. I drew the Jingleworm, who is red and white and has a part on the end of its body that jingles like a bell wherever it goes. The Jingleworm's predator is the Three-clawed Wren and it jingles so much that the Wren doesn't have any problem finding it to eat.

But then the Jingleworm started to hide in the coat of the Green-tailed Squirrel, which didn't mind because the loud jingling noise of the Jingleworm scared away its predator, the Electric Cat. The Electric Cat's ears are very sensitive to the jingling noise. To it the Jingleworm sounds like somebody scraping their nails on a chalkboard sounds to us. So the Jingleworm and the Green-tailed Squirrel have a symbiotic relationship.

The problem again is the Gorachs. They are starting to collect Jingleworm tails for jingly bracelets, which they give to their Gorach children. The Gorachs are the parasites, so many of the animals are working on making more symbiotic relationships. The Gorachs are in for a surprise.

That night I slept with my mother and she didn't even complain. I think the cat food may have done something to her brain.

Today my mother made me see Dr. Barrett again. It was my fourth time in his office with the too-high chair. I'm really tired of sitting in that chair. I don't know why, but it's hard to think when your feet don't touch the floor. It's weird to have them dangling and it makes a fast escape almost impossible – which might explain why he has those chairs.

After Dr. Barrett asked me if there was anything I wanted to talk about (which is always how he starts off), and I said no (which is always my answer), he got out a little thing that looks kind of like a mouse for a computer. He told me it was called a galvanic skin response unit. It had a place for me to put two fingers and it was supposed to show how stressed I felt by measuring how sweaty the skin of my hand was. Dr. Barrett then hooked it up to his computer and clicked on a picture of a flying saucer floating in the sky. He told me that I could make the flying saucer go lower and eventually land by calming my mind and my body. He told me to concentrate on something that made me feel calm to see if I could do it.

With my fingers in Dr. Barrett's stress unit, I thought of sitting in a tree beside Pete's Pond. I imagined elephants doing a greeting ceremony. When they haven't seen each other in a while, they rush together loudly and flap their enormous ears and spin in circles while rumbling, roaring and trumpeting. This is how elephants show joy.

As I imagined this, the flying saucer got lower and lower. Dr. Barrett said quietly, 'Excellent, Phin. You're doing it. See how calm and relaxed your body is?'

I nodded my head. I was starting to imagine baboons drinking and playing in the water and I wanted Dr. Barrett to be quiet so I could keep the image.

Dr Barrett said, 'You've almost landed the spaceship. You are calm and relaxed. Very good.'

After a few more minutes, Dr. Barrett said, 'Excellent, Phin! You did that really quickly. Now, what I'd like you to pay attention to is how relaxed your body and breathing are. And whenever you're upset, try to get back to this bodily state again, okay?'

'That may be difficult.'

'Why?'

'Because of what makes me upset.'

'Which is worrying about animals, right? Well, when you worry about animals, just think of what you were thinking this afternoon and bring back that feeling of calmness ... '

'That likely won't help,' I said. 'Because I was thinking about Pete's Pond in Africa. I want to do work like Pete does, but you won't let me learn the things I need to know.'

Dr. Barrett didn't say anything for a minute and then he said, 'Phin, I know this seems confusing for you right now, but next week when you come in we'll talk more about why your mother and I think that not watching the Green Channel is for the best right now. Can you trust me on this and we'll talk about it more next week?'

I didn't say anything.

Then after a few moments, Dr. Barrett said, 'We'll talk more about this next week, okay, Phin? I'm really proud of how quickly you caught on to the relaxation exercise. That kind of exercise can really help make you feel better. And that's what your mom and I really want for you – to feel better. I'm going to lend you the little device we used here today to practice making your body feel calmer. Can you practice that for me every day until I see you next?'

He wants me to not worry at the very time I should be most worried – when I don't know what the crap's going on in the world.

Today at school Bird got in big trouble. He put his tongue in the cheek of his mouth and tried to say, 'Get the puck off the ice' – only it didn't sound like *puck*. He said it about six times louder than loud. Mrs. Wardman heard him. He had to explain for a long, long time what he was trying to say.

I could tell that Mrs. Wardman didn't believe what Bird was saying. Her eyebrows were low and her lips were closed together and her nostrils were bigger than usual. She looked like the gorilla I saw on the Green Channel who was trying to scare away a lion except she didn't hoot and beat her chest. But she did give Bird one of those misbehaviour forms that his parents have to sign and send back in. Last time Bird got one of those was for saying the names Hugh Jass and Oliver Closov and Mike Hawk. She didn't believe him when he tried to explain those ones either.

Before this year I got a misbehaviour only twice. The first time was when I said *whatever* to a teacher when she told me that I'd have to stay in at recess because I forgot to get my agenda signed to show that I did my homework even though she knew I did all my homework. I thought I had said it quietly enough, but I was wrong and had to go see Mr. Legacie.

I actually like Principal Legacie. When he's on lunch-hour duty he often asks me if I have any interesting animal facts to share. I can tell that he's really interested because he asks questions about what I've said instead of just nodding his head and smiling like a lot of people do – including my mother sometimes. One day I told him all about barnacles, which stay attached in the same place for their whole lives. I wasn't sure if I should tell him about how they make babies since they don't move around, but I figured I would take a chance with Principal Legacie because I've never seen him look shocked or even surprised – I figure that's because of all the weird stuff he sees every day. So I told him that I read in a book that male barnacles have penises that are four times as long as their bodies and these come out of the shell and search around for a female nearby. Principal Legacie laughed, but then one kid started taking off his pants and he had to go stop him so we didn't get to talk about it more.

But all that happened before this year. I have a feeling this will be the year of the misbehaviour for me, just like every year is for Bird. That's because of what Bird and I are planning for Cuddles.

At lunch, Bird and I went back to the big apple tree by Mr. Byers' house and climbed up really high. Usually Bird tests out Mrs. Wardman's idea that something bad will happen to him if he goes past the place she told him he could go. So far he's gotten about three math books away from the tree and nothing has happened to him yet.

When he got past where he was supposed to be and then jumped back, he covered up his footprints by brushing a fir tree branch over the snow and then he threw the branch away. He said that if the Crime Scene Investigation Unit came to the school to see who had been going past the line, they wouldn't be able to tell because all they'd see were the tree branch marks. The tree branch wouldn't have any fingerprints on it because he was wearing wool mittens. They might find traces of wool on the branch but that wouldn't help them much since many of the other kids have wool mitts too.

I told Bird that there might be eyewitnesses who saw me and him by the tree and that could lead to us being interviewed as suspects. But Bird said they wouldn't be able to hold us if they didn't have any evidence so he thinks we're out of the woods, but really we were in the woods.

I told Bird that they might be able to match up the wool they find on the tree branch with the wool on his mittens because no two pairs of mittens would be exactly the same. Bird said that if the CSIs show up at the school, he'll hide the mitts somewhere and put on his spare pair.

I said, 'But where would you hide them on such short notice?' And he said he would just put them in some other kid's pocket. I told him to put them in Lyle's. But then I told Bird that flakes of his skin would be in the mittens and that the skin would be his DNA and not Lyle's. He said, 'Oh.' I think Bird has decided to take his chances.

Today Bird didn't try getting more than three books away from the line because he wasn't himself. He was worrying about taking his misbehaviour form home to his parents. His father said that the next time he got one, he would be in big, big trouble. Bird said that usually means that he won't get to play his Game Boy for a whole week and sometimes that means no TV too. But usually it just means no Game Boy because when there's a no-TV rule, Bird follows his mother around the house talking until his mother tells him he can watch TV. She said to Bird's father that when Bird does something bad, she shouldn't be punished too.

I told Bird that I can't watch my favourite programs and I didn't even get a misbehaviour form. I just worry too much about animals going extinct and the earth being ruined.

He said, 'You got punished just for worrying about stuff?'

And I said, 'Yes.'

He said, 'That's too weird!'

And I said, 'Tell that to my mother.'

Bird and I have been talking a lot about Cuddles. When we first met him in that aquarium, Bird thought it was pretty cool to have a pet frog. But then I asked him how he'd feel if he were stuck in an aquarium with a bunch of ugly faces staring in at him. I told him about how pets aren't really pets if they don't want to be with you and how sad Cuddles must be to be here on the other side of the world from where his species is. I told him how frogs are disappearing off the face of the earth and how we need to free Cuddles and put him back in his natural environment in Australia. Now Bird agrees.

We have been trying to think up a plan. We don't have all the details worked out yet but it goes something like this: at the end of a school day, I pretend to zipper my jacket right by Cuddles' aquarium while Bird goes up to Mrs. Wardman and asks questions to distract her. Then I reach in, grab him and put him in my pocket and take him home. What to do next is the difficult part – what do we do with Cuddles after we rescue him? One idea is to give him to my dad to take with him to Australia. But the problem is, my dad is in Scotland right now. When he comes home next, I don't know where he's going – and neither does he because he can't predict what bad thing will happen and where. He's prepared for just about any bad thing, though, because he has taken hostile-environment courses. Come to think of it, kids like me should take those courses too.

So then we thought about mailing Cuddles back to Australia, but who would we get to let him out of his box when he got there? And would it take too long? I read that some desert frogs can live months and sometimes years without food and water, but I can't find that information on White's tree frogs. Another worry is that he would be bounced around too much in the package. I saw on TV that shaking a baby too much can burst blood vessels in its brain and give it shaken baby syndrome. Is there shaken frog syndrome?

We got a chance to answer some of these questions after lunch today when we had a technology class. We got to use the computers and Bird is my computer buddy. We were supposed to be looking up information on hurricanes for our science project, but when Mr. Sears wasn't looking, I typed in *frog rescue* on the internet. I found a site called the Frog and Tadpole Rescue Group, which is a group of people in Australia who save frogs. Sometimes frogs are mistakenly packed in food crates and building-supply boxes and shipped to other parts of Australia. If you find a frog in your bananas or fruit salad, you call the frog team and they rescue him.

I was almost finished reading the first page when Bird whispered, 'Hurry! Get off the frog site – here comes Mr. Sears!'

So I wrote down the phone number really quickly and then Bird clicked the backwards arrow twice so that we were back on the hurricane page.

Mr. Sears stopped at our computer and said, 'How are you boys doing?'

And Bird said, 'Those hurricanes can be really big, eh, Mr. Sears?'

And Mr. Sears said, 'What else have you learned so far?'

And Bird said, 'They're very windy.'

Mr. Sears said, 'Boys, I suggest you read some more.' Then he walked on to the next computer buddies.

Bird said, 'Phew, that was a close one!'

And I said, 'Hurricanes are windy? Geez, Bird, of course they're windy – they're hurricanes!' But then I told Bird thanks because he had saved us from getting a misbehaviour, or at least a growling.

I put the frog-rescue phone number in my shirt pocket. I am going to call them. I am hoping they will have some ideas about how to save Cuddles.

My mother and I drove to my Grammie's first thing this morning. My grandmother lives in the country an hour away from my house. There's a real forest in her backyard and she lives only five minutes away from a river and only fifteen minutes away from the ocean. She lives in a perfect place – except that she's not very far away from an oil refinery that blasts pollution into the air twenty-four hours a day every day. This is something that Grammie is upset about. Because she used to work as a biologist, she gets on the news a lot to talk about it. Lung cancer killed my grandfather and he didn't even smoke.

On the way to Grammie's, I counted all the graveyards I could see. Last time I counted twenty-eight, and I told my mother I wanted to break that record. I asked if she could please slow down when we went through the villages.

'Phin, do you really think there have been more graveyards added since the last time we visited Grammie?'

'No, but I may have missed some last time.'

'Oh, okay, keep your eyes open, you don't want to miss those dead people.'

I watched really closely and then when I was up to a count of eighteen, I spotted one in behind a church that looked like an ordinary house that I don't think I saw last time. I was starting to feel like I might break my old record.

'Mom, I just saw one I didn't see before!'

'That's wonderful, Phin. How many dead people do you think are in there?'

'There look to be about fifty gravestones. But sometimes there is just one gravestone for more than one person. So there's no way of knowing for sure – unless we dig up the whole graveyard.'

'The answer is all of them. They're all dead, silly!' And then she laughed. That was a good joke.

My mom laughs a lot. I like watching animals laugh on TV. When chimps play and chase each other, they pant laugh and their faces look a lot like human faces laughing. When a gorilla tickles another gorilla, the one who's being tickled makes a laughing face.

Dogs make that face too. And rats chirp when they play and it sounds like giggling. When the scientists on the show tickled the rats, they chirped happily and wanted to be tickled some more. But other scientists still think that only humans can laugh. I think that's because the animals they're keeping in their cages for experiments are not laughing – not one little bit.

By the time I got to Grammie's, I had spotted thirty graveyards, which broke my record.

When we got to Grammie's, she grabbed me and hugged me. She smells like the lavender she grows in the summer because she makes oils and lotions and bath balls from it. Last summer I helped her cut off all the lavender and hang it upside down in her garden shed. Then a few weeks after that I helped her make the bath balls. We broke up the lavender flowers into smaller pieces and then we mixed up sea salt in a blender and added baking soda, cornstarch and eggs and then the lavender. Then we made the mixture into balls and baked them in the oven. When you put a lavender ball in the bathtub, it dissolves and little bits of lavender float around. It smells really good, like my grandmother did when she hugged me.

We all went into Grammie's kitchen and talked and had some tea and biscuits. Mostly my mom doesn't let me drink tea, but when we're at Grammie's she does. I chose lemon ginger tea and put lots of honey in it to make it sweet.

When Mom went to my grandfather's den to make some important calls, Grammie asked to see what I'd been doing on Reull. I ran out to the car and got my box and showed her. She loved my story of the Ozie and the Oster. We talked about how plants, like the Ozie, actually help clean the earth.

Grammie knows a lot about plants because that's what she used to study when she worked as a biologist. She says the work she did then is the reason she's now an organic gardener. She found out things like that dogs whose owners use pesticides are more likely to die of bladder cancer. So to get rid of bugs like aphids, she just sprays them off with the garden hose on full blast instead of using poisons. She said that once they're on the ground, they often can't crawl back up.

I looked up aphids in my bug books and learned that aphids can be of the winged kind or the unwinged kind. The kind that are in the garden are usually unwinged, but if a plant gets too crowded, all of a sudden winged aphids start to be born and they fly off to other plants.

I mentioned that to my grandmother and it was something she didn't know about aphids – and she knows a lot about bugs and plants. I felt happy to tell her something she didn't know. She said, 'Well, soon humans had better start producing the winged variety too.' She was making a joke, but I think it was only a half-joke.

Just before supper, my uncle John got home from work. When he saw me, he said, 'Hey, little man, long time, no see.' He messed up my hair and said that I'd grown a foot. He says that every time he sees me because when I was three I looked down to see if I had actually grown another foot. He still talks about that, which is kind of irritating.

Uncle John works at a factory that makes potato chips. Sometimes the equipment doesn't work right and makes weird-looking chips. He brought home one that is shaped like the Loch Ness monster and another one that looks like a bus. He has another that he says looks like something I'll see when I get older, but he won't tell me what. He framed those three chips and hung them on his bedroom wall.

My mother says Uncle John needs to get a life.

At supper we had yellow beans, and I hate yellow beans. We also had carrots, and I hate carrots. My mother said to have three bites of each.

I said, 'Should I eat my carrots with my eyes open or with them closed?'

And she said, 'Why do you ask?'

'Because you say carrots are good for your eyes and I'm wondering if that's only when you keep them closed since they look so disgusting.'

'Phin, I don't care if you eat them with your eyes opened or closed, standing on your feet or standing on your head, just eat them.'

So I ate three bites of them but I made sure to pick the smallest pieces. They lunged down my throat like they were alive, which made me almost barf. I washed them down with organic milk, which is all Grammie buys because she's upset about commercial farmers using hormones in their feed for cows. And she doesn't like it when farmers use artificial insemination. That's when the farmer instead of the bull makes the cow pregnant.

After supper I sat at the dining room table and made some Reull animals. I drew the Digging Robin, which has a red or blue head. He crawls, has two small claws for digging and spikes to make tunnels. He also has a very sharp beak and a stabber on the end of his tail to break up rock as he digs. The problem for the Digging Robin is that his habitat has started to be taken over more and more by the Gorachs. The Gorachs are 90 percent liquid and 10 percent solids and when they move around they drip poison wherever they go. The Gorachs have been covering everything up with their cities, and they say that they are the supreme rulers of all of Reull. The Digging Robins have fewer and fewer places to dig and to live and they are worried. But there's a plan, and they're almost ready to put it into action.

I slept on Granddad's side of the bed last night. Even though I really wanted to sleep with Grammie, it made me miss him right in the pit of my stomach.

'Do you still smell Granddad on his pillow?' I asked Grammie as I was going to bed.

'Yes, but it's fading,' said Grammie.

'Do you still miss him a lot?' I asked.

'Every day,' said my grandmother. Then she sat in her rocking chair and brushed her long white hair, staring out her window at her garden, still all covered in snow.

I wanted to say more about Granddad but from the look on my grandmother's face, there are some things that are just too sad to say all at once. There needs to be spaces between – spaces to absorb some of the sadness, like a sponge.

I changed the subject. I told Grammie about my super-humungous problem of Mom not letting me watch the Green Channel. She asked me why I thought Mom did this and I said, 'She says it's because it makes me worried.'

'Are you worried?'

'Sometimes.'

Grammie didn't say anything. She didn't tell me I shouldn't be worried like Mom and Dr. Barrett tell me.

I told Grammie I was still worried about Cuddles. Her face said, 'I understand,' and then she said, 'Oh, that's a shame.' She didn't tell me that frogs aren't worth worrying about.

Instead Grammie told me that frogs are like the canaries that miners used to bring into the mine shaft with them. That's because frogs breathe with their lungs but also through their skin. This means they're more sensitive to toxins than other animals are.

I'm starting to think that maybe instead of a general zoologist, I'll specialize and be a herpetologist. They're scientists who study amphibians and reptiles. They have found lots and lots of frogs with missing legs, extra legs, legs that stick out from the body at weird places, legs that are webbed together with extra skin and legs that split into two halfway down. They have also found frogs with missing eyes and a one-eyed frog that has a second eye growing inside his throat. I haven't seen anything like that at the amphibian park near where I live but I once saw a frog missing the legs on one side of his body.

I figure we're going to need a lot of herpetologists since there are about 5,700 different species of amphibians and according to the Red List of Threatened Species 32 percent of them are threatened with extinction.

Actually, I don't really like thinking about this ... but maybe I should have a backup job just in case by the time I'm an adult the only place you can find a frog is in a museum.

In the morning Grammie and I walked on the crunchy snow in the woods. We found the spot where Granddad and I put our time capsule. The summer before Granddad got sick and died, he and I filled up a plastic box with things that would remind us of what we were doing when we dug it up in about ten years. We put in a picture of Granddad and me both wearing big sun hats and birds pecking the seeds off the rims. We sat really still while Mom took the picture. The other things we put in the time capsule were:

1. a lavender bath ball
2. a Canadian loonie with the year's date on it
3. a piece of string as long as I am tall
4. my handprint on some clay we found by the river
5. the ticket stubs that were in my mother's purse from the Harry Potter movie she and I saw that summer
6. apple, cucumber, pea, pumpkin and squash seeds, just in case.

I also put in a letter I wrote to my future self. At first I wasn't sure what to write so I asked my mother. She said how about 'Dear future Phin, are you still sleeping with your mother?' I told her that wasn't funny – especially since back then I slept with her a lot less than I do now. I can't remember exactly what I did write, but it said something like 'Dear future Phin, I am writing this as your eight-year-old self. I hope that by the time you dig this up, species like tigers, apes and polar bears are still walking free someplace on the planet. And I hope you have saved at least one species from going extinct. If you haven't, you'd better work harder. Yours sincerely, back-in-the-past Phin.'

The time capsule is under a big pine tree in the woods. I know exactly which tree it is because it's the one beside a rock as heavy as my mother, which nobody is likely to be able to move without the help of a big machine. My grandmother said we don't have to worry about anyone moving it while she's still here. She's sixty-five and the average life expectancy of a woman is about eighty so I'm super, to-infinity hoping I won't have to dig it up for a lot more years.

Seeing where the time capsule is buried made me think of that picture of me and Granddad frozen in time. I imagined that inside the time capsule, my grandfather is alive. He's sitting reading the newspaper in the garden and drinking his favourite tea. After a while, he tips back in his chair, folds the newspaper over his face and has a nap. I'd rather imagine him in that box frozen in time than in that other box. Every time I think of that other box, I get a really awful feeling in my stomach.

I'm wondering if when future Phin opens the capsule and sees that picture, will he feel sad? Part of me worries that he won't and if that happens, then that means he'll have forgotten Granddad. I think I'd rather he be sad than to forget.

I had an awesome time skating on the river! Mom, Grammie, Uncle John and I got a big sheet and we held on to the edges. The wind caught the sheet and whipped it up into the air like a big sail and it made us go faster and faster down the river. It felt like we were flying. To the gulls way up in the air, we must have looked like a big floating swan.

We skated till we came to a place on the shore where there was a big log where somebody once had a bonfire. We sat down and rested for a while. While Mom, Grammie and Uncle John were talking, I lay flat on my stomach and looked down into the ice. It was as clear as glass and I could see the eel grass frozen on the bottom. I imagined that I was floating above the water. It felt like magic.

If I had a superpower, it would be in a magic potion that I would swallow to make me grow gills for the water. The gills would stay at the sides of my head until I went back on land and then they would disappear. I would have the ability to swim and breathe underwater like a fish and I would be able to understand the language of all the ocean mammals. I would talk to the dolphins and we would figure out how to save them. I would be their human who would go up to the surface and carry out their plans.

Some scientists spend their whole lives studying dolphins – which are mammals like humans and not fish – to see if they're as intelligent as humans. They've found that dolphins can talk to each other and that they even gossip about one another. Each bottlenose dolphin has her own name, which is a certain pattern of whistles and clicks. Sometimes a pair of dolphins will use the name of another dolphin when she isn't around. Dolphins also have meetings where they all stand on their tails in a circle and take turns talking. Nobody knows what they're talking about, but I bet part of it is trying to figure out if humans are as intelligent as dolphins.

It took us a lot longer to skate back to Grammie's house than it took us to skate down the river. That was because the wind wasn't blowing the right way to help us with our sheet sail and so we had to fold it up and put it in Grammie's backpack. I only fell once on the way down the river but I fell three times on the way back. But it didn't hurt very much because Grammie gave me a small, thin pillow to put in between me and my snow pants.

When we got back to the house, my mother went to have a shower and I helped my grandmother make lunch. Then right afterwards, we had to leave to drive back home. Mom and I each gave Grammie a big hug goodbye. Grammie said, 'See you next time, my little frog.' She looked so sad – like how a mother elephant on the Green Channel looked for weeks and weeks after zookeepers took her baby away to put in another zoo.

On the way back home, I saw thirty-one graveyards.

I think my mother was sad when we got home. Visiting Grammie without Granddad there still feels so weird. And I just don't know what to do about that feeling called sad. People keep telling me to remember all the good times and the happy and worthwhile things about my grandfather. What I want to know is where all that good stuff goes when somebody dies. It's not like it's in a bottle someplace.

I asked my grandmother about that and she said that it's in me and my mother and everyone whose life my grandfather affected – little bits of him are everywhere. So I guess that makes us all a bit like bottles.

Bird and I talk about dead people sometimes. Just after my grandfather died – which was almost exactly fifteen months ago – Bird's aunt died. She died in a car accident and Granddad died of cancer. What we both don't know the answer to is once you're in Heaven, do you get stuck wearing the clothes you were buried in for eternity?

I asked my mother about this since she believes in Heaven, and she said she didn't think so because Heaven likely wasn't a material place like earth. She said she thought nobody there would even see a person's clothes if they had any on. People would only see another person's true self, who they were on the inside.

Bird asked his mother the same question and she said they might wear those clothes for eternity but nobody would be worried about that kind of thing in Heaven. But Bird said that his mother and his aunt's husband spent a long time thinking about what his aunt should be dressed in after she died. They finally picked a purple dress because her favourite colour was purple. I sure hope she really, really likes purple if she has to wear that dress for all of infinity.

After Granddad died, my mom reminded me of the saddest example of sad that Jane Goodall said she ever saw. It was when a fifty-year-old matriarch chimp died. Her eight-year-old son sat beside her body, taking her hand in his and whimpering. He wouldn't eat, wouldn't do anything, just like my mom after

Granddad died. I was really super worried then because I knew that after three weeks of not eating, that child chimp died too.

At Granddad's funeral, my mom reminded me of great apes and bears and moose and antelope who won't leave the dead bodies of their family. Her friend Jill couldn't pull her away from Granddad's casket.

This evening, I painted my mom a picture with watercolours. Her favourite garden flower is bee balm, which looks like a crazy alien flower, maybe from Venus. So I painted a picture of her wearing a red bee-balm necklace, like the leis people wear around their necks in Hawaii.

My mom likes my paintings. So far I've given her seven and they're all hanging all along one wall of her study. The one I like the best is of her with her long hair piled on top of her head into the shape of a bird's nest. Inside the hair nest, I painted four little blue robin's eggs. I liked her hair better when it was long like how she looked when I painted that one. Now it's short and in my painting she looks like a crazy bee-balm flower herself. But I likely won't tell her that.

After the painting was dry, I wrapped it in tissue paper and brought it up to my mom, who was working at her desk. She looked up at me and said, 'What's this?' in an excited and surprised voice.

'Just something I made for you,' I said.

'Thanks so much, honey. What's the occasion?'

'I don't know. I just wanted to make something for you,' I told her.

After she unwrapped the painting and saw what it was, she smiled super big.

'This is absolutely gorgeous, Phin, thank you!' she said. Then she pulled me toward her and gave me a big hug and a kiss.

I helped Mom decide where to hang the new painting. As she hammered the nail into the wall, she turned sideways and for a split second, just before she turned back to face me again, I saw a glimpse of Granddad on her face.

This made me think that maybe Grammie's right – maybe there are little bits of him everywhere. I just wish they'd all come back together, just like in a movie I once saw where a bunch of leaves swirled up off the ground and formed into the shape of a dead person. That would be a little freaky at first, but a grandfather shaped out of leaves would be better than no grandfather at all.

Bird and I figure that as soon as we get a hold of Cuddles, we can call the Frog and Tadpole Rescue Group in Australia, and they can help us figure out a way to get him back there. We decided we don't have any choice except to take him. We have a plan for that. We even named our plan. Bird suggested Mission Impossible but I didn't like the Impossible part. So I suggested Amphibian Eco Restore, which Bird said sounded too geeky. So we ended up combining part of his name and part of mine, which made it Mission Amphibian. Mission Amphibian will take place in different steps. These are the steps:

1. The rescue will take place during Wonderful Wednesday art class while everybody is painting and gluing. We decided on this day because the fumes from all those paints and glues will make people more confused than they normally are.
2. I will poke lots of holes in my lunch bag that morning while my mother is in the shower.
3. At 2:50, just before art class ends, Bird will create a diversion by knocking over the jar of water with all the paintbrushes stuck in it.
4. While Mrs. Wardman is helping Bird clean that up (and likely being mad at Bird who says that won't bother him because he's used to it), I will take Cuddles from the aquarium and walk quickly to my

cubby. I'll put him in my lunch bag, where he will be all right until I get him home.

5. I'll put Bird's fake frog in Cuddles' place. The fake frog is brown and Cuddles is green but we figure nobody will notice because of all the fumes.

6. By the time I do this, the bell to go home will have rung.

7. Bird will steal Cuddles' jar of food and put it in his pocket. We want to make sure we have the right food for him because when a frog eats something that's not good for him, he might throw his stomach up so that it's dangling out of his mouth and then wipe it off with his right front leg. That's not something Bird and I want to see.

8. Bird will come home with me, and he and I will pretend to my mother that we want to play in my bedroom.

9. We will put Cuddles in a big box where he'll be okay until we know what to do.

10. We will sneak the cordless phone out of Mom's bedroom and call the Frog and Tadpole Rescue Group in Australia for instructions as to how to get Cuddles to them. We won't call them beforehand because if my mother sees that strange number on the telephone bill, our plan will be foiled.

I am really excited about our plan and nervous at the same time. To calm myself down, I wrote some in my Reull book. The Gorach leaders have a problem. Some of the Bothersome Gorachs are saying that the other creatures of the planet have souls too and maybe Gorachs shouldn't put them in cages and kick and poke and tease them. They've shown pictures of animals looking like they're in a lot of pain as they're dying, and bright lights floating up into the air after they've died. Some of the ordinary Gorachs are also starting to believe that the other animals really do have souls. So the Gorach leaders have told the Gorach scientists who work for them to prove that this isn't true.

To do this, these scientists invented a machine that when you step on it, it measures your total weight. Then it measures the separate parts of the body like the bones, skin, organs and blood. Then the machine adds all those body parts together and subtracts that amount from the total amount of the body. Whatever is left over is the weight of the soul.

The scientists' first guinea pig for the machine was a Plubber. A Plubber is something like the elephant here on earth except it has three trunks – one for eating and drinking, one for protection and one for hugging other Plubbers. Because it has three trunks, it can do all these things at the same time, which makes it very efficient.

The Plubber that was the Gorachs' guinea pig was called Kloop. He had lived in a cage exactly his size – not a millimetre bigger or smaller – for seventy years. Every day hundreds of Gorach children visited Kloop's cage to poke and laugh at him. These days he uses his trunks mostly just to cover his face.

The Gorach scientist used an electric cane to get Kloop onto the soul-weighing machine. The machine churned and churned and finally said Kloop's total weight was 513 kilograms and the weight of his body parts was 512.955 kilograms. This meant that his soul weighed .005 kilograms. 'See!' said the Gorach scientists. 'Just a puny soul, so small it doesn't even count.'

The Gorach scientists then weighed the souls of the Digging Robin, the Electric Cat and many other Reull animals. Each creature's soul weighed less than .006 kilograms, which made the Gorach scientists and leaders very happy.

'But,' said the Bothersome Gorachs, 'you haven't weighed any Gorach souls with this new machine – so how do we know that those souls are heavier?'

This question was never answered because the Gorach scientists just laughed and said it was a silly question asked by very silly Bothersome Gorachs.

After this story I drew a picture of the Gorach scientists weighing the souls of the other animals of Reull.

It's now 10:25 p.m., and I can't sleep. But if I stay in my own bed without getting up to tell my mother that I'm worried, or without getting up in the middle of the night and going into my mother's bed, I will get a loonie. That's what I picked off the list that Dr. Barrett gave my mother. The list had lots of things on it:

Money
Playing checkers
Playing with friends
Swimming
Working with clay
Piano lessons
Singing
Getting a hug or a kiss
Reading
Getting new clothes
Setting the table
Making the bed
Doing the dishes

The reason I remember the first three is because they are things I like. Before my dad and mom got separated, my dad and I used to play checkers a lot, although our favourite game was chess. I remember the fourth one because I'm taking swimming lessons so that I don't drown. I really wish I had a swim bladder like a rockfish. A swim bladder is an organ full of gas that helps the fish swim. The problem is when rockfish are brought to the surface too quickly, the swim bladder can overexpand and burst. This makes the swim bladder push the fish's stomach out its mouth and the intestine out its butt.

I remember the last three things on Dr. Barrett's list because I think it's really weird that some kids would like to set the table or do the dishes for a reward. I thought those ones were just jokes. If my mother said I could do the dishes if I slept in my own bed, I would never sleep in my own bed again – not even when I'm twenty or thirty and have stunted social development like Uncle John has. I don't know why I remember the ones in the middle.

I chose money as my reward, even though what I'm really hoping is that they'll let me watch the Green Channel again if I can sleep on my own – but for now, I'll take the money.

So far, I've been able to stay in my own bed only once in the last five nights. That was last night. That was because yesterday I didn't go to bed until 11 p.m., which is two hours past my bedtime. My mother was being given an award at a meeting for journalists and I got to go as her date. When I finally got to bed, I started to worry about Cuddles and how there are only a few days to go before we rescue him and how I am so worried that something will go wrong. But I must have been really tired because then I fell asleep.

I like it when my mother lets me go out with her as her date. A few other times she had real dates with men. I know this because I heard her talk about it to her friend Jill. I've never met any of those men but I know I wouldn't like them. I was afraid she might have another date with Brent, who is the worst of all. But she must have listened to me when I told her that he upset my homeostatis.

I figure the times that she puts on makeup are when she has a date. Human females are weird like that. All throughout the animal kingdom it's usually the male who tries to attract the female and not the other way around. Male gorillas prance and hoot and beat their chests, male lizards do push-ups, male hippos pee and do a propeller twist to spread it all around and white-fronted parrot males regurgitate food into the mouths of females they like. In most of the animal kingdom, it's up to the male to show the female that he's the strongest and the healthiest and that mating with him would make for healthy children.

I'm pretty sure my mom could get a man without trying a bit. But since she already has a healthy child – me – there's no need for her to look for a mate. There's still my father, after all.

I say that because last Christmas my dad took me to the market to get my mom a present and when we were looking at scarves, he suggested a bluish green one because it would go well with her lovely eyes. Those were his words – he said 'her lovely eyes.' I think he still loves her, and that's half the way to a couple. My mom doesn't say those sorts of things about my dad, but maybe she's just hiding it. Or maybe her love is way down deep in a part of her mind that she isn't even aware of yet.

Since I stayed in my bed all night last night, my mother was really happy this morning and a loonie was waiting next to my breakfast. She said, 'Phin, you did it, I knew you could.' I was happy that she was so happy and decided I would try to stay in my own bed tonight too.

I tried but I just couldn't do it, though. I got up out of bed and told my mother that I couldn't sleep because I was worried about Cuddles. Then all of a sudden, just like that, she was back to her new normal – mad at me. She said, 'For the love of God, Phin, stop! Just stop!'

'But, Mom, Cuddles – ' I said.

'Phineas! Cut it out! YOU'RE DRIVING ME FREAKING CRAZY!' She screamed so loud that Fiddledee ran out of the kitchen and hid under the living room table.

I was going to give her a hint as to what Bird and I had planned but when she said that, I felt the anger pressure move up my throat and words that I knew I shouldn't say came out my mouth like water out of a firehose. I won't repeat them, but some of them had to do with reproduction. I went back to my bedroom and now I'm just going to lie here all night thinking and worrying.

My mother might be able to control what I do, but she can't control my thoughts. Come to think of it, she can't even control all of what I do. Mission Amphibian is only three days away.

Today I saw Dr. Barrett yet again. Just like the other times, the first thing he said after we sat down was, 'Is there anything you'd like to talk about today?' This time I was ready for him.

Before I went to see him, I made up a list of things I wanted to talk about. I figured that having a list would prevent him from getting around to the things I really didn't want to talk about. I pulled out my list. The things I wrote down were:

1. Why don't we get water-logged when we're in water, just like a piece of bread?
2. Would you rather be bad and have everyone think that you're good, or be good and have everyone think that you're bad?
3. Why do I sneeze when I look at the bright sky but my mother doesn't?

I didn't put anything about animals on my list because I didn't want him to be reminded to talk to me about the things I didn't want to talk about.

I asked Dr. Barrett the first question and he said, 'Hmm. I have no idea about that one, Phin. Sorry.'

So then I asked him the second one, and he said he'd rather be good and have everyone think that he's bad. I think he's doing a better job at being bad and having everyone think he's good. At least he's got my mother fooled.

Dr. Barrett changed the subject before I got to the third question. He said, 'Phin, how about we talk about how you've been feeling the last few days? Feeling any better?'

'No,' I said. 'Even though I haven't been able to watch the Green Channel, I'm pretty sure the whole earth situation hasn't gotten any better.'

Dr. Barrett said, 'Phin, you and I can't do much about a lot of what happens in the world – we can't change the world, but what we can change is our reactions to everything so that we feel calmer and healthier.'

That didn't make any sense. Humans made the mess, so it only makes sense that we can unmake the mess – it's not like undoing the laws of physics or something.

I sighed a long sigh, in through my nose and out through my mouth, just like Dr. Barrett taught me. Then I said, 'I'm just so tired of everyone lying to me.'

'Who lies to you, Phin?' said Dr. Barrett, a little surprised.

I didn't say anything.

'Can we talk about that, Phin?' said Dr. Barrett.

I shook my head no. I didn't want to say more until I thought more about it.

'Okay,' said Dr. Barrett, 'but I would like you to write down examples of what you mean by that for next week. Will you do that for me?'

I nodded my head, but I would like to give Dr. Barrett some homework to do too. My homework for him would be to make a list of why he thinks I shouldn't worry. I think he's one of those people who doesn't want to know what he doesn't know.

Before I left, Dr. Barrett taught me some more relaxation exercises. I think that if that man were any more relaxed he'd be dead.

I started a Lie List last night, and at school today, I added two things to it. The first one came in language arts class when Mrs. Wardman read us a story about Terry Fox. He was a teenager who ran across Canada to raise money for cancer research. He had cancer and only one leg, but he still ran because he believed he could make a difference.

After the story, a police officer came into our class to tell us about Cops for Cancer, which means some of the police officers in the city are going to have their heads shaved to raise money for cancer. Then the police officer and Mrs. Wardman talked about how one person can change the world and that it's important to believe that.

At the end when we all got to ask a question if we wanted, Gordon asked if some of the police officers would be fired once their hair was shaved because wouldn't that make them shorter? The police officer said that wouldn't happen because police don't have to be a certain height anymore.

I had a question, but I didn't ask it. I wanted to know why it was called Cops *for* Cancer. Shouldn't it be called Cops *Against*

Cancer? I didn't ask my question because the police officer had to leave just before it was my turn.

After the cop left, I got out my list and added number four. This is what my list looks like so far:

1. Santa Claus, the Tooth Fairy, the Easter Bunny, etc. etc.

I put *etc. etc.* because there are lots of other creatures that are just made up but that little kids are told are real. I think that's just plain mean. One morning when I was six, I woke up with a scratch on my face and thought the Tooth Fairy must have done it to me when she was reaching under my pillow for my tooth. I wasn't sure if it was an accident or something she did on purpose. That gave me the creeps big time. This makes me not so sure there's a God. I can't trust the information I'm getting.

2. There's no such thing as a ghost.

Not true. I've been visited by four and I've only been alive for nine years. One was a ghost cat who used to jump on the end of my bed at night. I could feel his footsteps right up to my head and then he'd jump back down and disappear.

3. It's going to be okay.
4. One person can't change the world.

I added that to my Lie List because Dr. Barrett said we can't change the world. But Mrs. Wardman and the cop said that one person can change the world.

I think it's more likely that Dr. Barrett is wrong because I figure everyone changes the world every day. For example, if Gordon kills the spider that has its web in the corner of the window, then that spider won't be able to eat all the fruit flies that hang around the rotting banana in Kaitlyn's desk and that would mean more fruit flies in this world. This would mean Gordon changed the world all by himself. It also means that everything happens for a reason.

This got me to wondering about the weight of the earth. If all the spiders on earth went extinct, they wouldn't be able to eat insects. This would be a huge problem because the weight of insects eaten by spiders each year is more than the weight of all the people on the earth. Would this mean that the earth would weigh more and more each year?

I thought about this for a while, but then I realized that it wouldn't. That's because when spiders eat insects, they get heavier for a little while until they poop out what their bodies don't need. This keeps all the weight in balance. And besides, those insects have to come from something organic and there's only so much organic stuff on the earth. I figure even though it changes form all the time, the weight of it likely stays about the same.

But then I got thinking about how meteors fall onto the earth from outer space. That weight is added to the earth's weight every year. And also, people are removing helium from underground and putting it in balloons that burst. This allows the helium to float out of the earth's atmosphere. Do these two things mean the earth is getting heavier and heavier? If it is, will this knock it off its orbit around the sun someday? But then I figured this won't likely happen for millions of years. And besides, I have more important things to worry about.

After language arts class, we had French class, and that's when I caught lie number five. Mrs. Reid came back to school after being sick for a month. She told us that she had been in hospital with a blood clot in the vein of her left leg. She said that she was put on medicine to make the clot dissolve but that she had to be very careful over the next few months because if it went to her heart or brain, she could be in big trouble. Then she told us that if she all of a sudden stopped talking or fell on the floor, one of us should run to the front office and tell somebody right away. Kaitlyn volunteered to be the one who ran to the office. She's short and can run fast. I figure that's because her brain is closer to her legs. Then Mrs. Reid said, 'But don't worry, I'm fine.'

I added that to my list. How could Mrs. Reid have clots in her veins that might make her fall on the floor and die and still be fine?

Today at lunchtime, Bird and I managed to get to the swings before anyone else. That's because we sort of cheated. Since Bird lives just behind the school and through the woods, I had a note from my mother that I could go home to eat lunch with Bird because I told her Bird's mother had invited me. She believed me because I'm getting to be a good liar.

The reason I'm getting to be a good liar is because now I don't see the point of not lying. Everybody else does it, and the evidence is my List of Lies. I figure that if you're the only person who doesn't lie in a world full of liars, then you're at a definite disadvantage.

When I started thinking about it, I wasn't surprised that humans lie because animals do too. Mostly it's one species lying to another so that they don't get eaten. For example, a plover will pretend to have a broken wing if a predator comes too close to her nest. The predator chases her as she runs, and then when he's away from the nest, she flies back to her babies.

Sometimes lying goes on between members of the same species too. When a chimp finds some food and he knows another chimp is watching, he'll sometimes pretend not to see the food and walk right on by it. And one time a primatologist saw an old alpha male limping badly after a fight with the new alpha male, but as soon as he got out of his sight, he stopped limping. Because he looked weak and submissive, that likely saved him from being beat up again.

Humans are the species most likely to lie, though. I figure that's because they're the ones doing most of the talking.

The thing is, Bird's mother didn't know we were supposed to go to her house for lunch because Bird doesn't need a note from his mother to go home. So what we actually did was go into the woods between the school and Bird's house and eat the things we had stuffed in our pockets. I ate a bag of Teddy Grahams and a granola bar and Bird ate a bag of peanuts (which we're not allowed to *eat* at school but nobody said anything about having them in your pocket) and a cheese string. We ate as fast as we could, which wasn't easy because we were laughing so hard about the trick we had played on everyone. I told Bird not to laugh with peanuts in his mouth because I figured a peanut is about the right size for a windpipe and I wasn't strong enough to hang him upside down, like what my mother did to me when I choked on a raisin.

After we ate, we ran back to the school playground and jumped on the two best swings before anyone else was even outside. As we swung, I asked Bird if he thought it was possible that climate change could heat the earth up to the point that we all boiled. He said he couldn't imagine that so he figured it wasn't possible. Then I asked him if he could imagine sneezing non-stop for days and he said no, he couldn't imagine that either. Then I told him that a fourteen-year-old girl started sneezing one day and didn't stop for nine months and that a man started hiccupping one day and didn't stop for thirty years. He said that would likely hurt. I figured it would too – just like boiling to death.

When the other kids got out to the playground, they were surprised to see that Bird and I were already there, but nobody asked us how we did it. By that time, we had gotten tired of swinging and were by the big apple tree. I asked Bird if he was worried about the melting of the polar ice cap and the permafrost. He said he wasn't. I told him I was worried and asked him why he wasn't.

'Because I never really thought about it.'

'Now's a good time to start.'

'Okay, I'll try to be worried about it too.'

I could tell that Bird wasn't really worried, but it made me feel better that he said he'd at least try.

Today I played with Fiddledee a lot because I made her a new cat toy. I made it out of an old slipper that Grammie knit me when I was five. It started to unravel so I pulled it around and Fiddledee jumped after it for more than half an hour. I could tell she was really excited because she did things like race around and then lie on the floor and play attack her back paws.

I asked my mom if she thinks Fiddledee has lost any more weight since we took her to see Dr. Karnes. She said she doesn't think so. I picked her up, though, and she seemed lighter to me, but it might just be my imagination. I think it must be weird to be a cat because you get picked up all the time. Can you imagine just walking across the floor and all of a sudden you're scooped up and put down someplace you might not want to be by a creature ten times bigger than you are? That would be weird.

I keep looking in Fiddledee's litter box for red in her poop but so far, so good. My mom thinks that the red we saw before might have been from something she ate. But I'm still a bit worried about her.

After Fiddledee had calmed down from playing with the new cat toy, she climbed up onto my lap and lay down and purred really loud. Fiddledee always seems happy but I wonder if she ever gets depressed, like my mom did after my parents got separated and after Granddad died.

I bet Fiddledee's brain had the happiness chemical when she was on my lap purring. Animals have the exact same emotion chemicals in their brains as humans. I patted Fiddledee as I thought about this and she looked up at me and slowly blinked. Along with happiness, I'm sure she had love in her eyes.

I think it's weird that scientists do all sorts of experiments on animals to learn more about humans, but some of them think that the stuff we know about humans doesn't apply to other animals. That's like bumping heads with someone super hard and even though it really hurts, you say you can't believe that the other person's head hurts too.

I think that since humans evolved from other animals, it only makes logical sense that emotions are gifts to humans – gifts from the other animals.

Tomorrow is Wonderful Wednesday. It's the day to put Mission Amphibian into action. Tomorrow Cuddles will be freed by Bird and me!

When I first went to bed tonight, I lay thinking about how I hope nothing goes wrong. I went over the plan sixteen times in my head. I got up out of bed and triple-checked what Bird and I had written down. I got back in bed and went over it six more times in my head. It was driving me crazy – it felt as though I was caught in a thought maze and couldn't get out.

I considered going into my mother's bedroom so that I could just stop thinking and go to sleep. Even though she's making me more worried, at night she makes me feel calmer. But then I thought how she wants me to stay in my own bed and that she and Dr. Barrett say that I am too old now to need to sleep with somebody. But then I thought about how all other young mammals sleep with their mothers. And then I thought about how even human adults get to sleep with somebody, like when they're married. How come kids don't get to sleep with somebody too?

I gave in and went into my mother's room. She was reading a book with her eyes closed. I sneaked quietly into her bed, but not quietly enough. She said, 'For the love of God, Phin, why can't you just stay in your own bed?'

I said, 'Because I'm worried and you make me feel better.'

She didn't say anything.

Then I said, 'Mom, I'll give you a loonie if you let me stay.'

She sighed but then she turned off the light, pulled me toward her and hugged me.

But I still couldn't get to sleep.

Mission Amphibian was slated for very last period. All day long my stomach was jumping around so much I thought it might get loose and fall into whatever's below it – my bowel, I think. I just couldn't get frog off my brain.

I kept looking at Bird at the front of the classroom, and he kept half standing up and turning around to look at me.

Once he got in trouble for that. Mrs. Wardman said, 'Richard, sit still and concentrate, and stop looking all agog!'

Bird said, 'I wasn't looking at the frog, Mrs. Wardman, honest.'

Mrs. Wardman just gave him a funny look. Bird obviously had frog on his brain too.

I also kept sneaking peeks at Cuddles, who was behind me in his aquarium. I made mental comparisons between him and the rubber frog we were going to put in his place. Although they were both about the same size, I was concerned about the rubber frog being brown. I sure hoped none of the kids or Mrs. Wardman would notice it was a fraud frog before Bird and I managed to get out the door.

I was also concerned about my lunch bag. That morning while my mother was in the shower, I poked holes in it with a sharp pair of scissors. They went through the black outside part easy enough but then I had to push hard to get them through the inside silver part. I only had time to make four holes before I heard the bathroom door open. I quickly put my lunch bag into my backpack. I figure that when my mother sees the holes I'll be in trouble. I'll have to think of a reason for them that has nothing to do with a frog.

At recess, Bird and I went through our plan again. Actually, we went through it eleven times. We both had to memorize the steps. Bird was worried about the fake fraud frog too, but he figured nobody will notice. The kids were excited about Cuddles when we first got him, but lately pretty much nobody bothers to look at him except for me and sometimes Bird.

At noon hour, Bird and I pre-enacted what we were going to do. We made a square with some rocks and put a large rock in the centre and pretended that was Cuddles in his aquarium. We filled a pop can that we found in the soccer field with sticks and put it about four feet away from the aquarium and pretended that it was the jar of paintbrushes that Bird is going to knock over to create the diversion. Then Bird gave me the signal – which is sticking his pointer finger in his right ear – that he was about to knock over the can. This meant that I should walk over to Cuddles' pretend aquarium and get ready for the exchange by reaching into my pocket for the fake fraud frog, which was another rock. I waited till Bird pushed over the can, and then I quickly put the fraud frog rock down and scooped up the Cuddles rock.

We didn't pre-enact the next part but I knew it by heart. I'm supposed to go out to the cubbies while Mrs. Wardman is busy with the paintbrushes and put Cuddles into my lunch bag and then sneak back into the classroom. By this time, the bell should ring and Cuddles should be free. As long as we time this to happen exactly at 2:55, the bell and the sounds of all the kids getting ready to go home should drown out the noises that Cuddles may make inside my lunch bag.

The classes after lunch were in super slow motion. The only out-of-the-ordinary thing that sped it up a little bit was Becky getting sick in the classroom sink and all over the floor. The custodian came in and sprinkled some white powder on it and then mopped it up. It had a horrible smell, and Becky looked like she was going to cry, especially after Lyle said, 'Ooooh, I'll never use that sink again. Disgusting.'

Maybe nobody will use that sink again. That wouldn't surprise me because once a fifth-grader threw up in the water fountain by the lobby and now nearly everybody still fights to use the water fountain by the gym – even though the kid who threw up in it is likely in eleventh grade by now. Every new kid who comes to our school is told about the barf that used to be in the lobby water fountain.

I watched the clock tick to 2:00, time for Wonderful Wednesday. Mrs. Wardman said, 'Okay, boys and girls, let's get our smocks on.' Bird and I looked at each other. I couldn't tell that he was nervous, and I hoped nobody could tell that I was. My palms were so sweaty that I doubted I'd even be able to hold on to a paintbrush.

Mrs. Wardman gave us all big pieces of thick paper and told us the theme today was to illustrate a song from music class that we liked. I thought and thought, but I couldn't even think of a song we did in music class, let alone one I liked – my brain felt like it was bouncing and bits of thoughts didn't have a chance to stick in one place long enough to form into whole ones.

After a few minutes, I looked over at what Laura was painting. She had written the words 'You Are My Sunshine' and was painting a sun. On the other side of me Jane was drawing a rabbit with long ears because her song was 'Do Your Ears Hang Low?' It was then that I felt the crazy laugh in my chest.

When I get really, really stressed out, I start to crazy-laugh. For example, when my mother told me that my grandfather was really sick and was going to die, I started crazy-laughing. I don't know why – it wasn't that I found that the least bit funny – it's just something really weird that happens to me. And when I start to crazy-laugh, it's like I'm floating up above myself with a bird's-eye view, watching and thinking, 'Stop it! Stop it!' but I can't. And if someone looks at me like I've gone crazy, that makes me crazy-laugh even harder.

When I looked at Jane's rabbit with its ears on the ground, I could feel the crazy laugh starting in my belly and working its way up my esophagus and into my throat. I puffed my cheeks and tried to swallow it back down, but it was no use. I started to laugh really hard.

Everybody looked at me and Mrs. Wardman said, 'Phin! Why are you laughing?' But I was laughing so hard I couldn't say anything – and I wouldn't have known what to say anyway. Mrs. Wardman said, 'Phin! Stop that right now and get to work.' This made me laugh even harder. I laughed so hard my face was covered in tears and my chest was starting to hurt. A lot of the other kids started laughing too, which made me laugh even harder, even though it really hurt. Even Mrs. Wardman started to laugh.

Then Mrs. Wardman said, 'Phin, okay, that's enough. Now please go out and get a drink to calm yourself down.'

I got up and ran to the water fountain in the lobby – even though I prefer the one next to the gymnasium too – because it was closer. I took a big gulp of water and then laughed again, which made the water run out of my nose. Finally, I stopped laughing. Water up your nose hurts, and it makes your eyes water. I once saw a show where a man who didn't have an eye could stick his finger up his nose and wiggle it through his eye socket.

After a few minutes, I went back to my classroom. Everybody was looking at me, but I had stopped laughing and was acting as normally as I could. The good thing was that all that laughing gave me an idea as to what song to use for my picture: 'Kookaburra'!

The kookaburra call sounds like human laughter. It sings to warn other kookaburras where its territory is. My dad and I once listened to a whole bunch of kookaburras on the internet. It made us laugh too. You just can't listen to kookaburra calls without laughing. This is kind of ironic because the kookaburras don't mean to be funny at all – they're being quite serious.

As I painted a kookaburra on top of a eucalyptus, I kept a close eye on the clock. The minutes ticked by like they were hours. Bird and I kept looking at each other. Then at 2:47, right on schedule, Mrs. Wardman told us it was time to clean up – only three minutes to rescue time.

I was so nervous I could barely breathe. I patted the pocket of my cargo pants to make sure the fake fraud frog was still there – like he might have jumped out or something. He hadn't.

We all took off our smocks and stuck our paintbrushes in the big jar of water. But then something completely unexpected happened! Something Bird and I never thought of in our wildest imaginations: Mrs. Wardman picked up the jar of paintbrushes and put it in the sink! How could Bird knock over the jar to create a diversion if it was in the deep sink? It's not like he could pick up the jar and put it on the counter and then knock it over and still have it look like a complete accident!

I looked at Bird, and he looked at me, and we both just stared at each other. There was only one minute to go until action time, and we had no way of getting everybody to look in one direction! I felt like my chest was going to explode.

Then Bird smiled at me and did something that really surprised me – he stuck his pointer finger in his right ear. That was the signal for me to get ready for the switch! I didn't know what he was going to do, but I knew this meant I had better get into place. I walked over to Cuddles' aquarium, patted my pocket again and got ready to lift the lid.

Then all of a sudden Bird started making sounds like a dog! He went, 'Arrf, arrf, arff,' loud and then louder. Everybody looked in his direction. Before I had a chance to change my mind, I put Cuddles' jar of crickets in my pocket and then opened the lid to the aquarium and reached my hand in to pick him up. I could hear Mrs. Wardman say, 'Richard, what are you doing? Stop that this instant!'

In my mind I kept telling Bird to keep on barking, and he did. That was a good thing since picking up Cuddles was harder than I imagined because my hands were so sweaty. I had Cuddles in my hand twice, but both times he jumped right out.

I glanced up to make sure nobody was watching me. They weren't. They were all looking down under the art table. Mrs. Wardman was standing where Bird was originally standing and saying, 'Richard! Get out from under there. Right now!'

Then Bird started howling like a wolf, and the kids were laughing and laughing and Mrs. Wardman was saying, 'Children! Don't encourage him. Richard, come out from under there this instant and march yourself down to Mr. Legacie's office!' Bird just kept on howling, growling and barking, and the kids kept on laughing.

Finally, I got a hold of Cuddles in one hand and put in the fake fraud frog with the other. Then I shut the lid to the aquarium and closed my hands over Cuddles and made a fast walk for the door. I couldn't believe nobody had caught me! I was almost frog-free!

As I was walking, I could feel Cuddles trying to jump. Thankfully, this was one part Bird and I had thought about beforehand, and I had left my lunch bag on top of my boots with the lid open. I quickly put Cuddles in and zippered the lid.

Then just as I turned around to go back into the classroom, Bird and Mrs. Wardman were walking out. Bird smiled at me, but I didn't smile back in case Mrs. Wardman was watching.

Mrs. Wardman said, 'Phineas! Get back in the classroom; it's not time to go yet.'

She marched Bird down the hall. I knew Bird was on his way to a misbehaviour, but I also knew it wouldn't bother him as much as it would bother me. It would likely just mean he would lose his Game Boy for a week. I would tell him it was worth it to save a life.

When I got back into the classroom, I kept looking around to make sure nobody was looking at Cuddles' aquarium. Thankfully, they were still all laughing and talking about Bird.

When Mrs. Wardman came back, she told us to put our agendas and homework into our backpacks and get our outdoor clothes on. When Bird didn't come back, I started to get worried again. Then, as I was putting on my jacket, Bird came down the hall with a misbehaviour in his hand. He whispered, 'Did you get him?' and I nodded my head.

As we stood in line to leave, my heart was jumping around so much it felt like Cuddles was in my chest. I really, really hoped Mrs. Wardman wouldn't notice that he'd been replaced by a fraud frog before we got out of the school. I knew someone would notice tomorrow morning, but by then Cuddles would be on his way to Australia.

When the bell rang for us to leave, Bird and I felt like running to my house, but we couldn't because of Cuddles and shaken frog syndrome. Bird carried both of our backpacks and I carried my lunch bag. I could feel Cuddles moving around, which was a good sign.

Bird said, 'What are we going to do when they notice Cuddles is missing tomorrow?'

I shrugged. I had been so worried about the first part – the rescuing Cuddles part – that I really hadn't really thought about that part. It just hadn't seemed important at the time. Now it seemed a little more important.

Bird said, 'But aren't you not supposed to bark up the wrong tree until all your ducks are in a row or something like that?'

'How about we don't do anything,' I said. 'Nobody will know it was us.'

'But we'll be the first to be questioned because we acted so weird,' said Bird.

'That doesn't prove anything,' I said. 'And besides, you act weird lots of times, and a frog hasn't gone missing before.'

'But this was the first time you ever acted so weird,' said Bird. 'You looked crazy like my grandfather after he shot at the squirrels through his living room window without even opening the window.'

'Crazy people don't go around stealing frogs. But I heard sometimes they lick them because there's a chemical on frog and toad skin that makes them go crazier – or was that just a myth? I can't remember.'

'But just in case, maybe we should be the ones who scream out, "Cuddles is gone! Cuddles is gone!" tomorrow morning. That way Mrs. Wardman won't think that we did it because who reports their own crime?'

'Remember Jacob and Sean and their fire?' I asked Bird.

And then Bird said, 'Oh. Right.'

Jacob and Sean who are in fifth grade set a fire in the woods last fall and then reported it themselves. When the fire trucks got there, they asked the firefighters for a reward for reporting the fire. That made it seem suspicious, and they got found out. For punishment, they had to go to every class and talk about fire safety. That would be like Lyle having to talk about being nice.

'But it might work if we don't ask for a reward,' said Bird.

'I don't think it would work,' I told him. 'Lots and lots of guilty people report things because they think that it will make them look less guilty. It doesn't work.'

'Well, then maybe we should go back to the school and open the lid of the aquarium so that Mrs. Wardman will just think that he escaped.'

I thought about that for a moment. That made sense. At least then Mrs. Wardman would just be looking for the kid who opened the frog lid and not for one who actually took the frog.

'How about you wait here and hold Cuddles. I'll go back, and when I see Mrs. Wardman leave, I'll sneak into the classroom and open the lid,' I said.

Bird thought about this. I could tell because when he's thinking, he rubs the soft spot just under his nose. That part is called the philtrum, and it's not for snot to flow down like Bird thought before I told him what it's really for. It's to allow humans to move their lips lots of different ways to talk and to show emotions on their faces. Some other primates like lemurs have this spot too.

'I think I should go back because I can run a lot faster than you,' said Bird. 'And besides, I don't want to be responsible for Cuddles. You stay here and hold him.'

I said okay. I wasn't surprised Bird wanted to do it because I think Bird actually likes being scared. He dropped our backpacks and started running back toward the school. When he got to the corner, he turned and looked at me and yelled out, 'If I get caught, you owe me big time! BIG TIME!'

I sat down next to a tree at the edge of the woods and checked on Cuddles. His throat was moving in and out really fast, and I was worried he was going to have a heart attack or something. I wondered if that happened with frogs. I knew it happened all the time with humans. I also knew that as much as I wanted to hold and cuddle Cuddles to make him feel better, there was nothing I could do to calm him down. He's not a social animal and other beings wouldn't be able to make him feel better. If I touched him, it would make him even more anxious. So I just sat there holding the lunch bag and hoping that Bird wouldn't get caught and would make it back fast.

Fourteen minutes and seventeen seconds later, I saw Bird running toward me. When he reached me, he said, 'I did it! I did it! This is really exciting! I think I want to do this professionally when I grow up.'

'I think you'll be good at it,' I said. 'Maybe you can work for Greenpeace someday. They do animal rescues.'

'Yeah!' said Bird. 'And do you know what else I did? I took the fraud frog out of the aquarium.'

Bird hauled the brown fake frog out of his coat pocket to show me. We looked at each other and started laughing.

'Good thinking,' I told him.

We walked to my house really quickly, but just before we got there, I put the lunch bag back in my backpack. I figured Cuddles would be okay until we got him up to my room. I opened the door and yelled, 'Hi Mom, Bird's here, bye Mom,' and my mother yelled back, 'Okay, great, nice talking to you both.'

When we got to my room, I sneaked quietly to my mother's room and took her phone, and then I tiptoed back to my room. We looked at the number we wrote down off the website for the Frog and Tadpole Rescue Group: 0419 249 728. That was a weird number to us. Bird and I argued over whether or not the zero counted. I thought it must mean something or they wouldn't have put it there, but Bird said a zero in front of a bunch of numbers doesn't make the number bigger than it is by itself. That made a little sense, so I took a deep breath and dialled the number Please hang up and try again.' So I did but this time with the zero in front.

A man answered the phone. He had a really weird voice, and when he said 'Frog and Tadpole Rescue Group,' it sounded like he was twisting the words in the wrong places.

I said, 'Hello. I have a White's tree frog that I rescued and want to give to you.'

Bird poked me in the ribs and whispered that maybe we should ask him for a reward for rescuing Cuddles. I made an angry face at him, and he made an angry face back at me but stopped whispering.

'Okay, mate, how about you tell me where you found him, and I'll see what we can do.'

I wasn't sure I should tell him the whole story, but I figured someone who works rescuing frogs wouldn't call the police on us – and besides, he was at the other end of the world. So I told him that I found Cuddles in an aquarium in my classroom in Canada.

'You found him in an aquarium in Canada?' the man asked.

That's when I came clean, and I told him that I didn't exactly *find* Cuddles. The man was really quiet as I explained. When I was done talking, at first there was no sound, and I thought that maybe he had hung up the phone. But then he said, 'I'm sorry, mate, did you say Canada?'

I said, 'Yes.'

The man was quiet for another moment, and then he told me that what Bird and I had done was very brave and showed a great concern for frogs. That made me smile on the inside. I didn't smile on the outside because I didn't want Bird to start poking at me again.

But then the man told me something that made the room start to go dark on the sides but get brighter in the centre. After he said that thing, I didn't hear much else, even though he talked for what seemed like a long time. After he finished, he asked me if I had any questions. I said no and thanks and then hung up the phone. My mouth all of a sudden felt really dry, and I had a hard time swallowing.

I looked at Bird and couldn't say anything at first. I opened my mouth but nothing came out. It was like the speaking part of my brain was numbed. It was like I was floating up above where we were and was looking down at my room and me and Bird and Cuddles in the lunch bag.

Bird started saying, 'What? What? What?' louder and louder. The only thing that unfroze my brain was when I suddenly had the thought that my mother might come upstairs to see what we were doing if he didn't shut up.

I told Bird that the man said that once a frog was taken from its natural habitat, it could never be put back because it might have picked up a virus or a bacteria that it could spread to other frogs in the wild. He told me that the frogs rescued from bags of groceries and suitcases and things are given to frog foster parents who keep care of them in captivity.

'He said he can't take Cuddles. He said he has to live in an aquarium now because he might have a disease that wild frogs would get if he were brought back to Australia,' I told Bird.

Bird stared at me with his mouth open. Then he said, 'No way! You mean we did all this for nothing? I got a misbehaviour and won't be allowed to play my Game Boy for nothing? Why didn't you know that already? You know everything else! You know I count on you to know this stuff because I don't know it! What the crap are we supposed to do now?'

I didn't say anything. I lay down on my bed and looked up at the ceiling. I couldn't believe I hadn't thought of that. How could I have been stupid enough to think Cuddles could be put back into the swamps of Australia? It seemed so obvious now that he couldn't. And if I hadn't thought of how impossible this was, what other things hadn't I thought of?

Maybe my mother and Dr. Barrett were right after all – maybe there was something wrong with me. Why couldn't I just be a normal kid and be happy and not worry about a class frog? Why did I have to worry so much? Why?

I snapped out of it when Bird yelled, 'What the bleep are we going to do now, Phin? Think!'

'Bird, shhhh!' I hissed. 'You're going to make my mom come up here, and that's the last thing we need!'

'Actually, the last thing we need is to have a bleeping frog in a lunch bag!'

'Well,' I said, 'take him back then. We can't send him to Australia, so go put him back in his aquarium.'

'What? Take him back after all this? Are you crazy or something?'

'Do you have any better idea?'

Bird said, 'But why do I have to do it? Why don't you go do it?'

I would have done it but my legs felt all rubbery and my breathing was all weird and I doubted I could make it to the school and back. So I said, 'And tell my mom, "Bye, Mom, I have to go return Cuddles to his aquarium because the man in Australia says I can't send him there"? I can't leave! If I leave, my mother will think something's up!'

'You've got a point,' said Bird.

'Yep,' I said.

I opened the lunch bag and checked again on Cuddles. He was sitting perfectly still. I figured he'd given up too. I closed the lid and handed him to Bird, reminding him to carry him carefully. I also told him to throw out my lunch bag afterwards. I figured it would be better to tell my mother I lost it than to explain all the holes in it.

'All right, but cross your fingers that I don't get caught doing any of this,' Bird said. Then he sneaked down the stairs and past my mother's office and made it out safely.

I lay back down on my bed. My head hurt and I felt all weak. I closed my eyes, and all I could see was Cuddles. I looked up at the pattern of the plaster globs on my ceiling and thought I saw Cuddles' head and neck. I just could hardly believe it – once a frog was taken from nature, it couldn't go back. Once Cuddles became contaminated by humanness, he was trapped by humanness forever.

This made me think of the true story of Minik, who was an Inuit boy who was taken to New York along with his father and some other men. The men died of disease and their bodies were put on display in the Natural History museum, just like rocks. When Minik found out they were in the museum, he was really, super, to-infinity upset. All his life, he felt that he didn't fit in anywhere – not in New York and not in his native land.

This made me think a horrible thought: what if humans have become so contaminated by the evil of humanness that they never see that what they do to animals is wrong? And what if non-human animals have become so contaminated by humanness that they can never be saved? What if the world is becoming just one great big, enormous Museum of Natural History, and there's nothing anyone can do to stop it?

Once I thought that, I felt like my whole body was growing smaller and smaller and smaller but heavier and heavier at the same time. I read somewhere that since atoms are 99.9 percent empty space, if all the space were sucked out of the atoms in your body, you'd shrink to the size of a grain of salt, even though you'd be the same weight. I felt like I was becoming a seventy-pound grain of salt and was sinking, sinking right through my mattress.

This made me think of the fact that scientists say that most atoms were made a few minutes after the birth of the universe and the rest were cooked inside stars that exploded billions of years ago. They say that 1 percent of the hiss we hear on the radio is the echo of the Big Bang.

I made myself think of more facts about atoms and the universe, and then, finally, my body seemed to go back into its regular size and shape and the pounding in my head stopped. By suppertime, I figured I could fool my mother into thinking that nothing was wrong with me. But there is. Something. Very. Wrong.

Ever since Bird and I found out that there's nothing we can do for Cuddles, I've felt really weird. I feel like it looks when DVDs go wonky and people's bodies are all broken up into little square bits that move slowly around the screen.

I've felt so weird that I actually thought about telling my mom about what happened – but then my common sense kicked in. I also considered calling my grandmother to talk to her. She's the only one who really seems to understand about animals. Just as I was dialling her number, though, a part of my brain screamed, 'No! You can't tell ANYONE! Listen to me!' and won over the other part of my brain that thought maybe my grandmother could help. I'm still not 100 percent sure I shouldn't tell Grammie but I'm a little worried that she might tell my mom. Maybe there's a Giant Rule Book of Life that says that people who know things about kids have to tell their moms about it. I know Mrs. Wardman has been following that rule.

Speaking of Mrs. Wardman, these days I'm liking school even less than usual. Every time I look at Cuddles in his aquarium, I feel really sad and angry all at the same time. I think there should be a word for that feeling.

In math class today, though, I was just plain annoyed. Well, that's like saying the Arctic is a little on the chilly side. In fact, I got very, very mad. It all started with a question from the book called *Math Makes Sense*. It said, 'Add 679 and 451 and then estimate to the nearest hundred to check your answer.' It didn't make any logical sense. I raised my hand and Mrs. Wardman came over to my desk.

I said, 'I don't think this makes sense.'

'Phin, just do as it says,' said Mrs. Wardman.

'But how can I check my answer with an estimate after I actually add those numbers up?'

'Phin, we spent a whole unit on estimation. Remember how we discussed that if you round numbers up or down to the nearest hundred and then add them, your answer should be about the same as when you really add them?'

'I remember that,' I said. 'But how can an estimate be more true than the actual answer?'

Mrs. Wardman told me to just give it a try. I didn't say anything. I added the numbers up, and the answer was 1,130. Then I estimated and the answer was 1,200. I raised my hand again. Mrs. Wardman came over but she didn't look very happy.

'Should I change my answer to 1,200?' I asked.

'No, you've done it right,' she said.

'But you said the estimate should be about the same as the real answer, and it's not.'

'Phin, you've done it right – just go on to the next question.'

I was very, very mad. Normally math makes sense, but this math did not. I thought about all the ways other things don't make sense. I made a list in my mind:

1. At noon hour yesterday, Bird said *shit* and got in trouble for it. But the day before that Lyle said *piss* and didn't get in trouble. Why is it okay to say *piss* but not *shit*?

2. Cans of food with No-Name on the label. How can it be no-name if they call it No-Name? Isn't that a name?

3. Dr. Barrett is supposed to be helping me but so far all he's done is make my life worse.

Then I started to think about how maybe the reason things aren't making sense is because something has infected the brains of humans all over North America. Maybe it's something in coffee or in other stuff adults eat and drink. Maybe it's the pollution or maybe it's the chemicals pillows are soaked in so that people's heads don't catch on fire. Maybe whatever has infected their brains is the same thing that infects the brains of people who are addicted to drugs or video machines.

Then I wondered how long humans can live without brains that work like they should. I read in a book that the reason cockroaches can live for a week without their heads is because they have brains in their bodies too. But they die after a week because they can't eat without heads. I figure humans can live a long, long time with brains that only partly work as long as they can eat and move. I figure they'll just keep on doing the things that make them feel good – until they finally completely destroy the planet.

All this made my head hurt. I could feel my heart beating and my face turning red. I could feel my hands shaking and my brain buzzing. So I dug around in my desk and found a black Magic Marker. I sat there for a second looking down at my math book waiting for my common sense to kick in, but it didn't. Then I did something that I knew would likely get me in trouble – but I didn't care because things weren't making any sense anyway. I wrote on the front of my math book with my Magic Marker. I wrote the word *This* in front of *Math Makes Sense* and then I drew an arrow up between the words *Makes* and *Sense* and wrote in the word *No*.

That's when Mrs. Wardman asked me what I was doing. I didn't say anything. She picked up my math book and looked at it and then at me. I still didn't say anything.

Then she said, 'Phineas Walsh! I don't know what on earth is going on with you. Why did you do that?'

I didn't say anything.

Then she told me that I would have to spend my lunch hour in the principal's office and he would write a misbehaviour note for my mother to sign.

Normally that would upset me, but it didn't – right then I just felt calm.

I looked down at the cover of my math book. At least then it made sense.

Today while my mom was reading an article, I boiled some water and made her some jasmine tea. I even cut a little piece of a lemon because she likes that on the side. She was happy and surprised when I brought it to her study in her favourite tea cup with the lady slippers on it. She took a sip of it and said it was the best tea she'd ever tasted.

I've been trying to make my mother happy ever since I wrote on my math book. After Mrs. Wardman told her what I did, shocked was her first reaction. Then she was mad and asked me if I'd completely lost my mind. I told her that I hadn't, but that it might have been off-line or blinked or something. She told me that what I'd done was called vandalism and was completely disrespectful. This reminded me of one time I was super mad and told her I wanted to kill someone. She was really shocked and showed me how threats were part of the Criminal Code of Canada. She went on about the math-book vandalism for so long that I thought she was going to get out the Code again.

My mother asked me what I thought my punishment should be, and I said it should be to make me live with my guilt for the rest of my life. She said that, no, it would be no computer or TV privileges for a week. I said that was fine because I couldn't watch the Green Channel anyway. Then she just sighed and told me that I would have to scrub the marker off the math book. That's when I could tell that my mother's mad had turned to sad.

I can handle it when my mother is mad because that makes me mad too. And being mad makes me feel a bit more powerful, like I can use that energy to do things. But when she's sad, that's different. I don't like to see her sad. The worst sad for my mom was right after my dad left and after Granddad died. After those things happened, she slept almost all the time and wouldn't eat and her hands shook a lot.

When my mom's sad, I feel sad too and that takes my power away and leaves me with only enough energy to want to make her happier. Luckily this time she was sad about something that could be fixed. After all, it was just a dissolvable marker and it wasn't very hard to get it off.

After I brought my mom the tea and saw that it made her a little happier, I started having second and even third thoughts about that. The more I think about it, the more I'm not 100 percent sure I should want my mother to be happy. If she's happy, that likely means she's getting what she wants. And what she wants is for me to be happy about not being able to watch the Green Channel, and for me to be happy that Cuddles is stuck in a cage for the rest of his life, and for me to be happy that animals are disappearing off the face of the earth and the entire planet is dying.

Yes, the more I think of it, the more I realize that I don't want her to be perfectly happy. In fact, I think happiness might be the whole problem – everyone, including my own mother, wants to be happy all the time and nobody wants to be worried, even though they super, to-infinity should be.

I don't like it when my mom is sad, but maybe that's just the way it has to be. So now I'm thinking that she is *not* going to win this one. I am *not* going to be happy.

Today really sucked extra because Mrs. Wardman made my mind hurt. Again.

She gave out a sheet that said to list the gifts the earth gives us. I put down five things: water to drink, clean air to breathe, forests for homes, earth to grow food in and food to eat. Then the sheet said to list the gifts humans give the earth. I thought about it hard, but I couldn't think of anything good. All I could think of was air pollution and lots and lots of garbage.

I looked up the word *gift* in my dictionary just to make sure I was actually supposed to think of good things. The definition for *gift* was: 'something that is given voluntarily and without compensation.' I guess that means that a gift could be good or bad. So then I wrote down pollution and garbage. I thought some more and came up with ocean aches and forest burns and land disease. That made five. I figured that was enough.

Then the sheet said to draw a picture of the greatest gift humans could give the earth. I thought and thought about that one. There are some things humans can do for the earth like stop chopping down all the trees and stop dumping toxic wastes in its oceans and stop sending poisons up into its atmosphere and stop murdering all of its animals, but the instructions said to draw the greatest gift humans could give the earth. So I drew a picture of the earth with legs and arms dancing around a grave that said 'R.I.P. Humans.' I was so busy colouring my picture that I didn't see Mrs. Wardman standing over my shoulder.

'What does that mean, Phin?' she asked.

I told her it was the greatest gift we could give the earth because then the ecosystem including the atmosphere and all the animals and fish and birds could become healthier and healthier instead of diseased and dying like they are now. I told her that the only thing that would die if humans died out were a few parasites. Now that I think about it, maybe I shouldn't have said that last part because that's when her face started to look weird – like my mother's face looked when she told me about the Voluntary Human Extinction Movement.

Mrs. Wardman said, 'Phin, these drawings are going on our class wall in the corridor. These are drawings to celebrate Earth Day and to teach people about living responsibly. I don't think this drawing is appropriate.'

I told her that the sheet said to draw the *greatest* gift we could give the earth and this was the greatest.

Mrs. Wardman said, 'I am not going to argue with you about this, Phin. I think you know as well as I that this is not a picture we can hang in the hallway for Earth Day. Please draw something different.'

I sat back down in my chair. I couldn't think of anything else to draw. I looked at what Kaitlyn had drawn – it was a picture of humans picking up garbage out of ditches. I couldn't figure out how that was a greatest gift because the humans had put the garbage there to begin with. That would be like somebody setting someone else's clothes on fire and then throwing water on that person to put out the flames and then calling the water a gift. It just didn't make any sense.

I looked to see what Gordon was drawing, and it looked like I don't know what, so I asked him what it was and he said it was a person cutting down trees to make houses. This didn't make any sense to me, but Gordon seemed to be happy enough about it.

When Mrs. Wardman came over to check on me, I still hadn't drawn anything else.

Mrs. Wardman said, 'Phin, why haven't you drawn something?'

'Because I couldn't think of anything to draw that isn't a lie,' I said.

Mrs. Wardman didn't say anything for a couple of seconds and then she said, 'Okay, Phin, you can take the picture you did draw home to show your mother but we won't be putting it up in the hall.'

I said, 'Okay.' But I just knew I was in trouble again.

As soon as Mrs. Wardman left, I got out my List of Lies and added another one:

5. For Earth Day Mrs. Wardman puts lies about humans on the wall in the hallway.

When I got home I didn't tell my mother about the Earth Day picture. Instead I put it in my Reull book. Then I wrote some more of my story to try to calm myself down. I wrote about how the Bothersome Gorachs are getting braver and braver. They're asking all sorts of questions that the Gorach scientists and Gorach Leaders don't want to hear. They're asking things like

'How do we know the Reull animals don't feel pain?' They know they're wasting their breath asking these things of the Gorach Leaders and the scientists who work for them, so they're going to ask these questions of the Ordinary Gorachs at the end-of-the-week dance. They think this is a good plan since during the dances, Gorachs are at their smartest. This is because they dance on the flats of their heads and this makes their purple blood rush to their brains. As a result of the extra blood, they can think really, really super well. When you ask a Gorach a math question when he's dancing on his head, he can answer it three hundred times faster than when he's standing on his feet.

When the Gorach Leaders heard about the questions the Bothersome Gorachs were going to ask at the Gorach dances, they were very, very angry. The last thing they needed was a whole bunch of Ordinary Gorachs bothering them about all that nonsense. So they told the scientists that they had to come up with a reason as to why the Ordinary Gorachs shouldn't dance on the flats of their heads any longer.

The scientists didn't take long at all to think of a reason: Upside-Down Explosiosis. That's a condition, they said, that all of a sudden makes a Gorach's head fly clear off its body because of the pressure of all that blood. Then the scientists got a dead Gorach's body and chopped its head off and took a picture of this to prove this could happen. Then they sent this picture to all the newspapers on Reull along with the headline 'End-of-Week Gorach Dances Now Outlawed Due to Upside-Down Explosiosis.'

Grammie called me this evening. She told me she was making donkeys, which are clumps of bread dough fried in butter in a pan. I love donkeys and could smell them in my imagination as we talked. She said next time I'm at her place we'll make them again.

I told Grammie about a video clip my father emailed me last week. It was of a homeless man in California who has a dog, a cat and a rat for companions. They all get along really well and protect each other. The dog lets the cat ride on top of his back and the rat is on top of the cat. The cat even licks the rat to keep him clean. Grammie said that that is a lovely example of interspecies compassion.

Then Grammie changed the subject and asked, 'How's school these days, Phin?'

I knew where that question came from, and I wasn't falling for it. Whenever Grammie knows about things I haven't told her about and I ask who told her that, she says, 'Oh, a little bird.' But I know it's my mom and she's no little bird. Mom likely even told her about the Earth Day picture thing because it only took Mrs. Wardman about fifty-nine minutes to call my mom after I'd left the school. Let's just say I got in trrrrouble.

'Oh, fine,' I told Grammie.

'Really, honey? You're doing okay?'

'Yep,' I lied.

'Well, sweetie, remember if you ever have something you want to talk about, I'm here. Okay?'

'Yep, I know.'

Then Grammie asked me if there was any more trouble with Lyle. I told her just the same sorts of things like knocking over my things and stuff like that and that I figure Lyle will never stop bugging me. She said I should try to stay away from him as much as possible and to stick close to my friends.

I told her that maybe next time I'm being picked on, I could run up to another kid, scream, wrap my arms around his neck and groom him. That seems to work for chimps. Or maybe I could just bare my teeth or flash my hindquarters. That's what rhesus monkeys do when they approach a dominant group member. It signals to the dominant that he's top monkey and so there's no need to fight.

I told Grammie that if Lyle would just leave me the heck alone, I'd be happy to flash my butt at him. My grandmother laughed so hard I thought she was going to choke on her donkey.

That made me feel good – the laughing part, not the choking part. At least Lyle's good for something.

Cuddles is dead. DEAD. Without any warning at all. One day alive, the next day dead.

This morning just after the bell rang I checked on him like I do every day. That's when I noticed that his throat wasn't pulsing and his eyes were perfectly still. I reached into his aquarium to pick him up even though we're not supposed to do that without Mrs. Wardman's permission. He was stiff and still. Dead. Definitely. Dead.

For a few seconds I had some really crazy thoughts. First I thought maybe Cuddles was faking. I have never heard of frogs faking death, but some grass snakes do. When they're threatened, they puff up their bodies and hiss to try to scare the predator away. If a predator attacks, they fart out a bad-smelling liquid from their anal glands. And if that still doesn't work, they roll over on their backs and play dead. They stay on their backs with their mouths open and their tongues hanging out for up to fifteen minutes. Problem was, Cuddles wasn't on his back and his tongue wasn't hanging out.

My second thought was that I might be able to bring him back to life. I've read that wood frogs freeze in the winter and then thaw out in the spring and are perfectly fine. When they're frozen they look like they're dead, but they're not. But that was a crazy thought too since it was really warm in our classroom.

When my brain finally let me believe that Cuddles was dead, I called to Mrs. Wardman. I said, 'Mrs. Wardman, Cuddles is dead!' She walked back to the aquarium and looked at me holding Cuddles. She said, 'Oh, that's very sad. Phin, how about you put him back in the aquarium.' But I didn't.

Everybody looked at me holding Cuddles and Mrs. Wardman said, 'Children, I have some bad news. I'm sorry to say that Cuddles is dead.' Then she said something about death being a natural part of life and that although it's sad, Cuddles had a good life. That's about as far as she got because then I interrupted her.

Still holding Cuddles' dead body, I said, 'Cuddles did *not* have a good life. He was stuck in an aquarium. An aquarium where all he could do was lie on that stinking log and bang into the glass walls! That's like saying a prisoner has a fun life – and Cuddles didn't even do anything to deserve being in a prison!'

Mrs. Wardman said, 'Phin, I know you're upset, but Cuddles was well cared for – '

'No, he wasn't!' I said. And then I started crying. I cried with tears that ran down my face and dripped onto the floor. I looked at Cuddles, and some of the tears I cried dripped on him too. I cried and cried and even though no sound came out, everybody was looking at me. Bird came over to me and just stood next to me and didn't say anything, but he had a sad look on his face too, which made me cry even harder. The only noise there was in the classroom was the sound of Lyle laughing and then Mrs. Wardman telling him to cut it out.

I cried because Cuddles was dead. I cried because I had failed to help him, and if I can't even help save the life of one frog, how am I going to save whole species of animals from extinction?

I cried harder when I noticed I was the only one crying. That made me feel so alone – like I was the last living thing on earth. Like I was screaming for help but nothing could hear me because the whole world was dead just like Cuddles.

Mrs. Wardman picked Cuddles up out of my hands and put him back in the aquarium. Then she put her arm around my shoulders and led me out the door. She walked me down to Mr. Legacie's office and told me it would be all right. She said I could call my mom if I wanted to and she could come get me and take me home until I felt better.

I didn't want to call my mother. I knew what she would say, and I didn't want to hear it. She would tell me the same thing Mrs. Wardman told me, and that would make me feel all alone again. Instead I just sat down on the chair outside Mr. Legacie's office.

Mr. Legacie came out and asked what had happened, and Mrs. Wardman told him that Cuddles had died and that I was upset. He sat down on the chair next to me and told Mrs. Wardman he would stay with me. Mrs. Wardman went back to 4H.

Mr. Legacie got me a cup of water and after a few minutes I stopped crying. He asked me if I wanted to talk about it, and I shook my head no. I was glad he didn't talk to me.

After a few minutes, I told him I'd like to go back to my classroom, and he said okay. When I first walked in, I could tell everybody was looking at me but I didn't look back. I sat down at my desk and cried some more – but only on the inside.

At noon hour, Bird tried to make me feel better. He told me he learned from his brother that a normal piece of paper cannot be folded in half eight times – it's impossible. He got me to try it and he was right – I could only fold it six times. It took my mind off Cuddles for about sixty-five seconds.

Then, because I still looked sad, Bird said that he figured Cuddles was in a better place, meaning Heaven. I nodded my head. I figured that if there's a Heaven, he must be there because he'd already been in Hell.

I once asked my grandmother if she thinks there are souls and she said she's an agnostic. An agnostic is someone who thinks that the existence of God and souls is unknowable. But she says absence of evidence is not evidence of absence, so she's still open to the idea.

My father is an atheist who doesn't believe at all in God or souls, and he's pretty certain about it. He says this is the only life we'll ever have and if it's going to get better, it's up to us to do something to make it happen.

My mother believes in God and souls and she's pretty certain about it too – just as certain as my father is. They can't both be right.

I wish someone could tell me the right answer. But maybe it's like seeing colours. Scientists have found that some women have an extra kind of cell at the back of their eyeballs that makes them able to see more colours than the average person. Maybe that's like religion – some people see the colours and some don't and maybe what we see while we're alive is what there is for us after we die.

I'd like to believe in God and souls because that would make it easier for me when it comes to death. It would be like losing your favourite thing but knowing for sure you'd find it again.

But if there are souls, when did it happen? Did it happen when we were *Homo habilis* or *Homo erectus* or *Homo sapiens*? It seems to me that there wouldn't really be a perfect time to give humans souls. It just doesn't make a lot of sense. It would be like God saying, 'All humans today, no souls – all humans tomorrow, souls.'

I figure that since we're almost genetically the same as chimps and evolved from the same ancestor, then chimps must have them too. And since every animal came from the same ancestor if you go back far enough, then every single animal must have a soul – including frogs like Cuddles. It just makes logical sense.

Thinking of Cuddles' soul made me all of a sudden wonder where his body was. I asked Bird if he knew.

'Well, Mrs. Wardman said that Cuddles shouldn't have died so soon, so she put him in the class fridge in a paper bag. She's going to take him back to the pet store and get a credit so that she can get another class pet next year.'

'What?' I screamed. 'She's going to take him back for an exchange?'

Bird nodded his head.

I was just standing looking at Bird with my mouth open when the bell rang.

When we got inside, I got my outdoor shoes off really quickly and ran into the classroom while all the other kids were still busy at the cubbies. I went over to the fridge and opened the door. I saw a brown paper bag and peeked inside. Sure enough, there was the body of Cuddles. I took him out of the bag and put him in my desk. Off and on all afternoon I reached in and lay my hand on his cold skin because it was still hard for me to believe he was really dead.

When school was over, I tucked Cuddles in my jacket pocket. I didn't care if Mrs. Wardman found out he was missing. Did she really have to flop his dead body around and turn him in for an exchange like he's a pair of shoes or something? Wasn't it bad enough that she abused his life? Did she really have to abuse his death too?

On my way home, I walked to the edge of a swamp near the school playground. I've heard frogs croaking there lots of times before – not White's tree frogs, but frogs all the same. It was the best I could do. I dug a hole with a stick and put Cuddles in. I looked at him for a few minutes and said, 'Goodbye, Cuddles.' Then I covered him up with mud and tears.

Today's Saturday and I don't feel like doing anything. Not a thing. I feel like I have one of those big, heavy capes on that the dentist makes me wear when she X-rays my teeth.

When I was just sitting rubbing Fiddledee and not saying anything, my mother told me that it was normal to feel like I was feeling but that soon I would be better. Then later when I was crying, she told me that as sad as I am, I had to try to look for something positive in all this. I told her that all I could think of is that my face is cleaner.

Maybe another positive is that she's been letting me sleep with her and not even complaining about it. But it's been nine days since Cuddles died, and I am still so sad. All I can think of is Cuddles and how he spent his last few months – in a cage with humans looking in at him and laughing. I know a little how that feels because when I was seven, I spent a week in a cardboard box that our television came in. I climbed in and closed the flaps. It was big enough to hold me but not big enough to let me move around. I did this because I had read about Laika, the dog in Russia who was launched into space in 1957, and I wanted to know how she might have felt. The problem was I was in my backyard listening to the birds and the squirrels and completely still while Laika could hear nothing that sounded like life, was hooked up to all sorts of equipment and shot into space. I also knew that I could leave whenever I wanted and, in fact, I had to come out for a while every hour because my mother made me. But for all Laika knew, she would never get to move around again, and that's exactly what happened.

When I was in the cardboard box, I tried to imagine Laika's conditions as best as I could. Just before getting into the capsule, she was hooked up to a bag to collect her pee, sponged with alcohol and had electrodes placed on her to measure her body signs.

Then someone led her into the capsule and she went with them because that's what dogs do – they go with their humans. They put her in a harness that would allow her to only sit, stand or lie down in the capsule. They put enough gel food in with her to keep her alive for seven days. The food for the seventh day was poisoned so that she would die after they proved that a dog could live in space. Then they closed the door and sealed her up in there all alone.

When Sputnik II was launched, Laika's breathing rate went up to four times its normal rate and her heart rate more than doubled. By the time it reached orbit, Laika's heart stopped beating. She died of being so afraid.

I tried to imagine how scared she was, but I don't think I even came close to feeling that. She died alone, scared and in a place that was completely unknown to her. To make it even worse, she was a dog and dogs are social animals. That means they love being around other dogs and they love their humans too. Being all alone to Laika would have been even worse than being all alone was to Cuddles when he died.

To make it even worse, Laika may even have trusted the humans. She may have done what they wanted because, being a social animal, she wanted to please them.

To make it even worse, the scientists knew that they were sending Laika to her death. They knew it when they closed the door, and still they did it. I bet they even smiled at her or said, 'Good dog, Laika.' But in Russian.

Part of being social means you feel love for other animals. Scientists have found that most rhesus monkeys will suffer of hunger if getting food means that another monkey will be shocked in the next cage.

I would rather live nine years and die on earth with my family around than live one hundred years in a cage in space all alone.

I couldn't save Cuddles. I couldn't even save one frog. Not even one small, little frog.

I saw on the Green Channel how some people in Spain are trying to get the government to declare that other primates, like the great apes, are humans too. Then they'd have the right not to be locked in cages and used in experiments and killed, their hands used as trophies and their tails used as dusters. So far the people haven't been able to do that, but if they're successful I'm thinking I'd like to apply for a species change.

I've had it with humans. I'd rather be a rhesus monkey.

Today all I could think about was death. Everywhere I looked, I noticed dead things – like the dead spider in a web in the corner of the bathroom whose legs were all curled up. The spider looked like the eyelashes of a doll I once had. Grammie and Granddad – someone else who's dead – gave me that doll when I was three.

Thinking of death started me wondering about how long animals live on average. I looked up the life expectancy of different animals on Google. Then I made a list:

Tree frog: 8 years
Cat: 18 years
Dog: 13 years
Horse: 22 years
Deer: 8 years
Elephant: 50 years
Yellow-headed Amazon parrot: 70 years
Galapagos land turtle: over 100 years
Human: 80 years

You can't count on those averages, though. You never know who's going to get ripped off next. You could be walking along thinking you have another fifty-three years and then all of a sudden you're dead – or worse, stuck in a cage somewhere. It could happen just like that, in the blink of an eye, before you even know what hit you.

I started to feel super, to-infinity worried about who would be robbed next. I kept thinking that maybe it would be my grandmother. This made me feel all skinny inside. I made a list of animals I knew personally who got robbed and how many years each got robbed:

Cuddles (if he was one year old when he was caught, that
    would put him at about seven years robbed, -7)
Karen, a kid I knew in kindergarten who died of
    leukemia (-72)
Jakie, Uncle John's dog who got hit by a car when he was
    six (-7)
Aaron, a friend of my mom and dad who used to come
    for dinner, who died of a brain aneurysm while he was
    driving to work (about -40)
My grandfather (-12)

Although Granddad died at the age of sixty-eight, the very last time I saw him, he looked more like 108. He was in hospital and looked like he was shrinking right down to just his bones. That last time I saw him, my mom left the room to go ask a nurse to give him more pain medication. While she was gone, Granddad, who was trying to sit up, made a motion with his hand that meant push a button on the side of his bed to make the front part go up. I pushed it and it kept going up and up and Granddad didn't say stop. He didn't say anything. He had closed his eyes and his mouth was shaped in an O. He didn't move and he didn't say anything at all. I finally stopped pushing the button when it looked like he was folded over too much. When my mom came back in, she looked at Granddad and then ran and pressed the buzzer to call the nurse in. When the nurse came in, my mom told me to go sit in the TV room. Grammie showed up a few minutes later and she was crying. I sat there some more not watching TV and the nurses tried to talk with me but I didn't want to talk. Eventually Uncle John came to get me and take me to Grammie and Granddad's house. Granddad died later that night.

A few days later, I couldn't stop thinking that maybe I pushed the button for too long. Maybe Granddad got folded over too much and that put too much pressure on his organs or something. Or maybe when Granddad made that motion with his hands, it wasn't that he wanted me to push the button – maybe he wanted me to run for help.

At first, I didn't tell my mom what I was thinking because she was too upset. And then later I didn't tell her because I was afraid I might make her think of something she had never thought of before – that me and the cancer were co-murderers. I know deep down that's not true. But sometimes I still think about it. And now I just can't stop thinking that maybe Mission Amphibian was too hard on Cuddles, and that I'm the reason he died. Not only couldn't I save him, I may have helped kill him.

M y mother keeps asking me what's the matter. 'What's the matter? What's the matter, Phin?' she keeps saying over and over. She's been saying that to me for a week now. I guess she was giving me ten days to be sad and when I didn't all of a sudden feel happy again, she was like, 'Time's up. Smile now.' She sounds like a CD with a scratch on it. I keep telling her nothing's the matter. But that's a lie, and she knows it.

I don't feel well. I don't feel like having Bird over after school. I don't feel like going outside. I don't feel like drawing or writing in my Reull book. I don't feel like playing with Fiddledee, but I do like her to sit next to me. I didn't feel like going to swimming lessons, though my mother made me. I don't feel like doing anything.

My mother said she's worried about me. She says I'm just not myself. I said, 'Why does that make you worried? Isn't that what you and Dr. Barrett want?' She didn't say anything back.

Then after a minute she said, 'Phin, that's not true. Dr. Barrett and I want you to be exactly who you are – only less worried.'

'All right then, be happy,' I said, 'because I'm not worried.'

My mother changed the subject and asked if I'd like her to read to me, and I said no. She asked me if I wanted to play chess, and I said no. She asked me if I wanted to use the internet to look up the answers to questions I have, and I told her that the internet didn't have the answers to my questions. Then she asked me if I wanted an ice cream, and I said no. I went to watch TV. That's all I want to do after school because it means I don't have to move or even think. And I don't even care what kind of TV it is. Yesterday I watched *Doodlebops*. It had a bunch of adults dressed up in bright costumes and wigs. They all jumped around and sang weird songs. Once in a while a moose head on a wall talked and some lady jumped out of the wall and sang more weird songs.

Today I watched *Atomic Betty*, which is really super stupid. It's about a girl whose watch rings every once in a while and a spaceship picks her up and she goes off to fight evil things with an alien and a robot.

While *Atomic Betty* was on, one of the commercials was of a father and son on different sides of the world who eat an Oreo cookie together on a webcam. It made me miss my father even more. It also made me really irritated. Why can't we do things like that while he's away? Some kids have all the luck. *My* father doesn't have a webcam. And he doesn't even like Oreo cookies.

After *Atomic Betty* I watched *Pokemon*. That's where the characters capture this wild Pokemon stored in this little tiny Pokeball and battle other people with Pokemons. I wasn't even sure why they were fighting in the first place. It didn't make any logical sense. But I didn't care.

Then I watched a show called *Animals Flanimals*. It was a cartoon of a giraffe who lived in the jungle. A giraffe living in the jungle. That made my mind wake up. The jungle! Giraffes don't live in the jungle – they live in flat, grassy areas. What the bleep would be the point of a long, long neck if you lived in the bleeping jungle where you could only see one-hundred-foot trees right in front of your face no matter how tall you were?

That's when all of a sudden a thought struck me. And it was almost like it really did strike me because when I thought it, my head whipped backwards and hit the back of the couch.

It struck me that watching all this stupid TV was making me into a moron. I couldn't count on the normal channels to give me good information. I had to get back to reading my books and watching shows that told me the truth. I needed to watch the Green Channel – the one channel in the world I'm not allowed to watch.

Then all of a sudden the sadness went away. It was like somebody opened my lid and tipped me upside down and let the sadness all drain out and then they filled me back up, but with something different: anger. I felt really angry. Really, really, really, really, to-infinity ANGRY.

I got up and turned the TV off, and then I went to look for my mother.

My mother painted the study – again. This is the third time as far as I can remember. First it was white, which she said was too boring, so she painted it burgundy. Then she said that colour was too dark and painted it green, which I liked because it looked like a forest and when I lay on the sofa listening to the sounds at Pete's Pond, I could imagine I was actually there. Now she's painting it yellow, but not yellow the colour of lemons – yellow the colour of buttercups. And pee after you take a vitamin.

My mother asked me how I liked the colour and I said, 'Why do you like to torture me like this?'

She said, 'What do you mean by that? And stop being so melodramatic.'

'I liked the colour it was before,' I told her.

'But that colour was too green,' she said.

'How can something be too green?' I asked. 'Is this about getting rid of something that reminds me that I can't watch the Green Channel? Because I'm not going to forget about that.'

My mother didn't say anything for a moment and then she said, 'This is not about you, Phin.'

'And besides, you're making the room smaller,' I said, 'and I thought you're always saying how you need more space.'

'Yellow will make the room look bigger because it's a lightish colour,' she said.

'But you're actually making the room smaller because each layer of paint adds thickness to the wall. That means the walls are getting closer and closer,' I told her.

She looked at me and laughed. 'I never thought about that,' she said. 'You likely have a point. Your brain is so busy – doesn't it ever get tired?'

'No,' I said. 'Doesn't yours ever get bored?'

She looked at me surprised. 'Well, I see you're feeling better. Would you like to help paint?'

'No! Why would I want to help you do something that looks like the inside of a toilet bowl?' I yelled. I knew this would make her angry, but something in me just didn't care anymore.

My mother turned away from the wall and pointed the paint-brush at me so that little globs of vitamin-coloured yellow paint dripped all over the face of George Bush on the newspaper she had down on the floor. 'Phineas, it's good to see you up off the couch and taking an interest – as critical as it is – but I'm warning you that you are only one more rude word away from throwing it all away for the evening: the TV, the computer, your sketchbook, all of it. So think carefully about what you say and go get a snack to improve your mood.'

So I stomped to the kitchen to look for something to eat.

I found a box of granola bars but they were a different kind than my mother usually gets. I looked on the back of the box for

135

the ingredients. They were: rolled oats, rolled whole wheat, brown sugar, palm oil.

'Mom!' I said. 'These granola bars have palm oil in them! Palm-tree oil! Goddamn palm-tree oil!'

My mother put down her paintbrush and looked at me. She looked at me like I had just told her I found poop floating in the milk. Her eyes were really big and her mouth was open a little. She looked like a Japanese snow monkey that's just seen a snake. 'Phineas William MacKeamish Walsh, that's it – you've lost the TV! Now you'd better think very carefully about where all this is going because I'm not in the mood for any more craziness!'

'Then maybe *you* need some food to improve your mood,' I said. 'And this is all going to Indonesia because I'm not going to eat something that is made out of something else that is killing orangutans!' I screamed. 'And what kind of mood do you have to be in anyway to be a person who doesn't kill animals for no good reason?'

My mother yelled back at me. 'Phin, cut it out! Stop fretting about things that happen all the way on the other side of the world, or you're going to drive yourself and everyone else crazy!'

'That doesn't make any sense!' I screamed. 'That's like saying only be nice to your own kid and don't worry that your next-door neighbour is eating his! Or it's like saying don't learn anything at school because you can't possibly learn everything! How about that, Mom? How about I stop going to school because what's the point? I can't learn everything!'

My mother said, 'I can see that everything I say is going to fall on deaf ears so I'm not going to waste my breath discussing this with you any longer, Phin. This is something for you discuss with Dr. Barrett next week.'

'You're the one with the deaf ears, so maybe it's you who needs to see a doctor!' I yelled. 'I'm not going to waste my breath talking with you!'

My mother dropped her paintbrush on the floor and rushed over to me. She grabbed me by the shoulders and shook me. Really hard. If I were a baby she might have done some serious damage to my brain. 'Stop acting like a crazy person!' she screamed.

When she let go of me, I ran into the kitchen and threw the granola bar in the garbage. And then I picked up the whole box of granola bars and threw them into the garbage can. Then I kicked the garbage can.

I was really surprised that my mother didn't chase me into the kitchen when the garbage can hit the wall. But I knew she heard it. Most of the time she only pretends to be deaf.

I stayed in my bedroom until supper. I was so mad even Fiddledee stayed away from me. I bet she could see the mad heat coming off my body.

After a while my mother came into my room and sat on the edge of my bed. She said, 'I'm sorry, Phin, for shaking you like that. That was wrong and I'm sorry.'

I didn't say anything back.

'Do you want to talk about it?'

I shook my head.

She said, 'Okay then, let me know if you change your mind.' Then she got up and left my room, closing the door behind her.

After I calmed down a little, I wrote in my Reull book. I wrote about how the reign of the Gorachs has come to a sudden end. The creatures of Reull felt they had no choice but to call for help. They knew that each and every time a creature died on Reull, this made a creature-sized hole in the universe. There were so many holes now that the other creatures were afraid the whole galaxy might get sucked in.

The first life forms to hear the cries for help of the creatures of Reull were the Wooloofs from Planet Chary. They sent out messages to creatures on the other planets. Every life form learned of what was happening on Reull and they were all very worried. But the Wooloofs of Chary sent mental messages for them not worry – they would fix things.

So the Wooloofs immediately started landing on Reull, a few ships at a time. Only a few Gorachs noticed them, but when they told the others about the tall thin creatures with huge heads and eleven eyes in ships at the tops of the spikit tuffs, mostly everyone laughed at them and told them they were wonky.

The Wooloofs talked with the creatures of Reull and heard all their sad stories, such as how the Gorachs killed Oster babies in front of their parents by throwing them up in the air and catching them on the ends of their spears. They were brought to big gravesites that held the bones of billions of animals – the skulls of Tussleturtles, the backbones of the Ozies, the feet of the Plubbers, the hipbones of Electric Cats.

The Wooloofs cried and cried when they saw all this evidence. They couldn't believe their eleven eyes. The Wooloofs and the creatures of Reull all put their heads together and thoughts moved back and forth between them all. Finally, they had an idea. An idea that just might work.

A t noon hour, I was having a lonely day because Bird was home sick, and I had nobody to talk to. I thought about maybe trying to join in on a game of tag with the Korean kids, but I didn't feel like being It the whole time. Most of those kids are really fast and can climb up on the monkey bars lickety-split. When I do it, I'm not so fast and it's more like lickety-splat. When I'm It, it's like a groundhog chasing a bunch of squirrels. The only thing that makes it kind of worth it is that one of the kids shares his Korean candy with me. Bird doesn't like it, but I kind of like how it makes my eyes water and my cheeks feel like they're flipping inside out.

I decided my best bet was to race to the swings as soon as the bell rang because that's something you can do well all alone. It sure beats wandering around the playground kicking at the dirt. I knew it was a bit risky being on the swings without Bird – there's more safety in the number two because it's easier to watch out for bullies – but I decided to chance it. I should have known better, though. It was just too much risk. The playground is sort of like the savannah. There are all sorts of predators.

I prefer the bullies who at least give you a warning. For example, there's a bully named Walter who usually says, 'Get out of my way, kid,' which is his strike one. If you don't move, he'll say, 'Get out of my way, you little beep-er,' although the *beep* part is something else. If you still don't move, he'll trip you to the ground. I've never gotten to the being-tripped part, but I've seen some kids who have. It's not pretty.

I like Walter the best of the bullies for another reason too. He bullies because he wants something, and that something is usually pretty easy to figure out. It might be a swing or it might be that you're in his way at the water fountain. Bullies like Lyle are different. They just like being mean, and they really like it when their prey is scared or cries. The man who talked to our class about bullying said that bullies don't feel good about themselves and being mean is how they feel more powerful. I don't think that's true. I think some of the bullies feel *too* good about themselves.

The girl bullies are a little different. They don't kick or punch, but they say mean things. Really mean things. They tell other girls that they can't play with them because they're too ugly or they call them names like she-male.

One time I was on the swings without Bird and these two girls came up to me and told me to get off the swing. I told them I got there first. They started calling me nerdo and brainiac and said they got there first and were going to tell the teacher on me. I said, 'Go ahead,' but they didn't. That's called bluffing. They remind me of a Caribbean stomatopod that has just molted but still threatens intruders by waving a claw. The new claw is too soft and weak for a good fight, but the intruder doesn't know that.

I had been swinging for about seven minutes when I saw trouble. Lyle was heading my way. I looked around to see if I could spot where the teachers were. That's what kids like me do on the playground.

I saw one teacher way off by the slides. She was looking in my direction, but I figured she couldn't make out the look on my face. I looked at the fifth-grade kid swinging next to me, but he wasn't paying any attention and didn't look like he'd be much help anyway. The bully experts say to stand up for each other or run to tell a teacher when you see someone being bullied but most of us don't think that's such good advice. If a kid tells on a bully he's the next one with the bruises.

I tried to get a hold of myself. I forced my face into a full-teeth smile because I knew that would calm me down. When I do that, my mother says I remind her of Snoopy from Charlie Brown or like I'm airing my teeth out. I also stopped swinging and rubbed my hands together to warm them up because on the Discovery Channel it says that you can't feel really stressed out and have warm hands at the same time.

By the time I had rubbed my hands together thirteen times, Lyle was standing beside me. He said, 'Hey, froggie boy, get the fuck off the swing.'

I didn't say anything. I tried to stare straight ahead. Then I stopped warming my hands and started swinging again.

'I said, get the fuck off the swing, you little fucker,' said Lyle. 'What are you, deaf? Your little froggie ears not working?'

I kept staring straight ahead and pumped my legs as fast as I could. I could see the kid next to me glancing over to see what was going to happen. In a few seconds, I was quite high and I could see the top of Lyle's baseball cap. He was standing there with his face all ugly and his hands on his hips. If I stuck my foot out, I figured I could actually kick him in the head. I had to concentrate really hard to get that thought out of my mind. I don't like it when I have thoughts like that because I figure that only a few brain cells stand between thinking about something and actually doing it.

My mother told me a story once of how she hated her best friend's little dog. The dog would growl and nip at her heels and once it bit her hand. One day her friend and the little dog were walking ahead of her on a log over a stream when my mother suddenly had the thought of kicking the little dog off the log. She said the next thing she knew, her foot went out and lifted the dog up and off the log and dropped him into the stream. I figure one or two of her brain cells went wonky. Even though I'd never do that to a dog, I'm afraid that brains cells going all wonky might be a genetic condition. I had to think really hard about keeping my foot away from Lyle's head.

Now that I think about it, that may not have been the best idea. I likely should have kicked Lyle in the head – as long I kicked him hard enough to make him go unconscious. I should have done that before he had a chance to do what he did to me. That's because without any warning – other than another 'I said, get the fuck off the swing, you little fucker' – Lyle grabbed on to my swing which stopped me all of a sudden and made me fall backwards off onto the gravel and hit the back of my head on the ground. Then Lyle immediately jumped on the swing and started swinging, which meant that I had to roll out of the way really fast.

I jumped up quickly and walked toward the school. I could hear Lyle behind me saying, 'Where are you going, you little froggie sookie baby? Do you need me to call a whaaambulance? Whaa, whaa, whaa.'

I was really, really mad, and the back of my head hurt. I walked over to the bench.

Lyle said, 'You'd better not be going to tell on me or I'll be having your frog legs, you little fucker.'

I sat down on the bench and rubbed my head. If I was a capuchin monkey, I'd pee on my hands and feet because that's what the ones who have been picked on do to relieve stress. Thankfully I'm not a capuchin because peeing on my hands didn't sound like something that would relieve stress for me. Peeing on Lyle might, though.

I started to imagine all sorts of things that I would like to happen to Lyle – like an arrow going right through his hollow head or being eaten from the inside out by bot-fly larvae.

Then I started thinking again about how the advice of ignoring a bully doesn't work. Why do they tell us that anyway? I really should have kicked him in the head. I watch Dr. Phil with my mother sometimes and once he talked about how people do the things they're rewarded for. I think if you ignore a bully like Lyle and then he ends up beating you up and getting something he wants, then he's being rewarded for it. I should have kicked him in the head.

As I was thinking about how this day sucked, I saw a shadow in front of me. I looked up and saw the fifth-grade kid who was on the next swing when Lyle attacked me. He was standing in front of me. He was quite a big kid – not big fat, but big tall and big muscular. He had a tattoo of a dragon on his arm. I knew it was likely just a cereal-box tattoo, but it still made him look tough.

'I saw what happened back there, kid,' said the big fifth-grader. 'If you pay me five dollars, I'll beat that kid up for you.'

I looked up. I blinked because the sun was in my eyes. The kid was looking at me, waiting for an answer.

'I don't have any money with me,' I said.

'That's okay,' said the big kid. 'I can do it for you tomorrow after lunch. I'll meet you by the swings. Bring the money.'

'But what would you do to him?' I asked.

'Well, for five dollars, I can hit him or kick him five times,' said the big kid. 'Then I could tell him to leave you alone or next time it will be ten.'

'Oh,' I said, because I didn't know what else to say.

The big kid said bye and walked back over to the swings. So now I need five dollars for five bucks.

That night at supper my mother asked me about my day. I didn't tell her about Lyle pushing me off the swing. What's the point? It doesn't help. This is what happens:

1. She gets mad.
2. She goes to the school to talk to Mrs. Wardman and Principal Legacie.

3. They say things to make her feel better.
4. She comes home and tells me things are under control but to stay away from that kid.
5. Things are better for about three days because the teachers are keeping an eye on Lyle.
6. On day four everyone's guard is down and Lyle strikes again.

After supper I went to my swimming lesson at the Y. My swimming instructor's name is Leah, and the lesson that evening was about what to do if you see a person unconscious in or near the water. There are things you have to look for before you go to help. They are: gas, glass, fire, wire, people, pets and poison. All of those things can be dangerous, and you need to rule them out before helping. It seemed strange to some of the other kids that pets was on the list, but not to me. I know that companion animals – especially dogs – protect their humans. It would be easy for a dog to think you were harming his human if he saw you pushing on his chest.

After everybody could name off the things to look out for, we practiced the back float. I'm actually getting good at swimming, and that makes me happy because many of the species I want to save live in the ocean. There are also species in the ocean that I want to figure out a way to talk to.

One of those animals is the dolphin. The dolphin is extremely intelligent. The dolphin is also very social like humans are. I would like to know what the dolphin is thinking about what is happening to the earth. Maybe dolphins have some ideas about what we can do about it.

That's why a headline in the newspaper yesterday caught my attention. It said: 'Bottlenose Dolphin Attacks Swimmer.' It was about how a dolphin in the waters around England butted a swimmer with his nose and wouldn't let him get out of the water. The biologist said that there have been other attacks on humans by bottlenose dolphins too. He said that scientists are trying to figure out if they got it wrong when they said dolphins are gentle.

I have a different idea: I don't think it's that scientists haven't figured out what dolphins are really like – I think it's that dolphins have figured out what humans are really like. That reminded me of the chimps in a zoo in Sweden who stockpiled rocks and poop and threw them at visitors. They fought back, just like those dolphins.

As I was doing the back float, something green out the window where my mother was sitting caught my attention. I stopped floating backwards and started treading water to get a better look. Sure enough, there was something green standing beside her. I couldn't make out what it was so I did the back float to the edge of the pool to get closer. When I got there, I treaded water again and could clearly see something I'd rather have not seen.

I closed my eyes hard and hoped what I saw would disappear. But when I opened them again, it was still there, green as ever. What's with all the green, anyway? Doesn't he have shirts in any other colour? And didn't my mother say he was away in Europe or Asia or someplace? What was that man doing back in Canada? And at the Y? With *my* mother?

I tried to catch my mother's eye. But she wasn't even paying attention to me. Aren't mothers supposed to watch their kids – especially when they're in a big, possibly dangerous body of water when they can hardly even swim? What if the lifeguard suddenly sneezed and it was at that exact moment that I got a cramp in my leg and sank to the bottom of the pool?

Brent was laughing so hard he looked like a bobblehead doll. I once saw a Jesus bobblehead doll and a Jesus action-figure doll in a store. The Jesus action figure had arms that could move up and down and was on wheels so that you could roll him around. The package said he was the coolest action figure since G.I. Joe. My mother thought it was a little disrespectful. I thought G.I. Joe would be way cooler.

Leah blew the whistle for us to get out of the pool. We all got out as quickly as we could because there are only four showers and ten of us in the swimming lesson. Luckily, I was near the ladder and got out second. I showered and dressed as fast as I could because I couldn't stand the thought of Brent talking to my mother for too long.

When I got out to where my mother was, Brent was still there. He and my mother turned to smile at me. Brent said, 'Hey, Phin, how are you doing?' Then, without even waiting for me to answer, he said, 'You're a good swimmer, Phin, are you going to try to earn badges right up to the lifeguard level?'

I just shrugged.

Then my mother nudged me and said, 'What do you think, Phin?'

I just shrugged and then bent down to tie my shoes.

Then my mother changed the subject. She said, 'Brent, you must be feeling pretty good right about now. The critics loved your book   and I'd have to agree with them, by the way.'

'Ah, Liza, you're too kind.'

'She may look nice, but she's not,' I said as I stood back up.

My mother and Brent laughed, which wasn't exactly the reaction I expected. Then my mother said, 'Well, we'll let you get back to your treadmill, Brent. It was nice talking with you.'

'You too, Liza,' said Brent. 'I'll give you a call soon. Maybe see you next week, Phin.'

I just shrugged. My mother poked me in the side but that didn't make me say anything.

When we got into the car, I knew I was in for it, and I was right.

'Phineas William Walsh,' said my mother, 'that was incredibly rude. When someone asks you a question, answer it. When someone is trying to be nice, and you don't have any good reason for not being nice back, then be nice back. How would you feel if someone ignored you like you just ignored Brent?'

'Depends who it is,' I said even though I knew that was the wrong answer. 'And who says I didn't have a good reason?'

'Phineas!' snapped my mother. 'I don't want to see behaviour like that out of you again. Do you understand?'

I didn't say anything.

Then my mother said, 'If you are rude like that again, you'll lose a privilege.'

That's when I got mad and my mad was madder than hers. I said, 'What are you going to take away? You already took away the Green Channel, and that's about the only thing I want to watch on TV. What are you going to take away next? I know – how about half of my brain? Then I'd be happy talking to that man!'

My mother said in a quiet voice, 'Phin, just consider yourself warned. I mean it – being polite to my friends is not an option; it's a requirement.'

I didn't say anything, and we drove the rest of the way listening to the radio. The song 'Are You Happy Now?' was playing, which I guess is a good example of irony.

At home I went right to my bedroom. I found my wallet and counted out five dollars.

I woke up this morning with a bad feeling in my stomach. Part of it was because I didn't sleep very well. I didn't go to my mother's room because I was still mad at her for the whole Brent thing. I stayed in my room, but I couldn't sleep. The last time I looked at the clock, it was 2:13. When I woke up, it was 6:11, which is an hour before I have to get up for school.

I think the biggest reason for the bad feeling in my stomach, though, was that I was worried about paying that big kid to beat up Lyle. So while my mother was still sleeping, I checked the internet to see if there are areas of the body that the big kid shouldn't hit. I didn't want this to turn into a case of kidslaughter.

One page I found on Yahoo! Answers said there are many major points on the human body that can cause pain, damage, unconsciousness and even death. Most of the death and unconsciousness spots were on the head. I made a note to tell the big kid not to hit or kick Lyle in the head. There were also some other danger spots listed on the site. I wrote down the ones that looked the most dangerous:

1. the windpipe or throat at the centre portion of the neck – a strong hit can sometimes kill a person.
2. the jugular vein and carotid artery, which supply blood to the heart and brain.
3. the heart – a strong blow could cause it to skip beats and in some cases can kill a person.
4. the kidneys – damage can cause internal bleeding and death.
5. the floating ribs since these ribs are not connected to the sternum and can break and pierce the liver or spleen resulting in rapid bleeding causing death.

After learning about all of this, I wanted to make sure I knew exactly where the heart, liver and floating ribs are so I could tell the big kid to avoid them. I typed 'where is the heart' into Yahoo! Answers. All it came up with was: *Looking for where is the heart? Find it on www.eBay.com.*

So then I did a search for it in Google, which led me to Wikipedia. That's where I found that one third of the heart is to the right of the middle of the chest and two thirds is to the left. (I also found out that a person can have heart cancer, although it's very rare, and that people get 'holiday heart syndrome' from drinking too much. The thing in Wikipedia that surprised me the most was that humans can have heartworm, although that's usually found in dogs. In humans, though, the worm usually dies quickly.)

Next I found out that the liver is the largest organ of the body (it weighs three to four pounds) and is beneath the rib cage and on the right side. Then I learned that the floating ribs are the last two ribs (the eleventh and twelfth) on both the front and back of the rib cage. They are attached to vertebrae but not to the sternum, which is a long flat bone in the middle of the chest.

All of this seemed a little confusing written down, so I decided to draw a picture of Lyle and label all the parts that the big kid shouldn't hit or kick. I made Lyle's face mean and angry so it wouldn't seem hard to hate him and hit him in the other parts.

At school, I found it really hard to concentrate because I knew what was going to happen at noon hour. Bird was still sick, and I really wished he were there so at least we could be worried together. I kept sneaking peeks at Lyle to see if he had any idea about what was up. But he seemed exactly the same – mean. He got in trouble twice before recess. Once for peeing all over the floor in the bathroom. Mrs. Wardman knew it was him because he was the kid who went to the bathroom just before Justin, who came back and said there was pee all over the floor. Mrs. Wardman told Lyle that was unacceptable, and if it happened again, he wouldn't be able to pee at school – he'd have to wait until he got home. That's when Lyle got in trouble the second time. He said, 'That's impossible! I can't hold my piss that long!' Mrs. Wardman wrote him up a misbehaviour for saying *piss*. This surprised me because he's said it before without getting in trouble.

At lunchtime I could eat only a bite of my cheese sandwich. I ate only a nibble of my dill pickle and a half a nibble of my apple. If my grandmother had been there, she would have said I was eating like a bird. Bird, on the other hand, eats like a horse.

Finally, it was time to go outside. I patted my pants pocket to make sure I still had the five dollars and my drawing of where not to hit Lyle. Then I went out to the cubbies to put on my outdoor clothes. It felt like I was putting on my shoes and jacket really slowly.

At the cubbies, Lyle was being Lyle and pulling Justin's hat off. Justin likely really regretted letting Mrs. Wardman know that Lyle had peed all over the floor. He was jumping around trying to get his hat back and Lyle was laughing – until Mrs. Wardman saw and told him to cut it out, that he was already in more than enough trouble. Lyle gave Justin back his hat but also gave him an evil grin. I knew that Justin was in for it on the playground, and a part of me felt a little better about what was about to happen. If the big kid beat up Lyle for beating up me when Lyle was thinking of beating up Justin, maybe that would protect Justin and me both. It was like killing two Lyles with one stone. But the killing part was what had me worried.

Out on the playground, Justin headed for the monkey bars, and Lyle headed for Justin. I was right behind them. I kept looking, but I didn't see the big kid anywhere. Justin climbed up the monkey bars, and Lyle stood underneath. I stood back and kicked some gravel while I looked around for the big kid. I could see Lyle's mouth moving, but I couldn't tell what he was saying to Justin, who was up at the top of the bars with his feet dangling down. If he wanted to, he could hang down further and kick Lyle in the head, but now that I know about the effects of that, I wouldn't recommend it.

Finally, I spotted the big kid! He must have spotted me at about the same time because he was walking over to me. He had on camouflage pants, a green jacket and a camouflage bandana tied around his head. This would have made him blend in if he were in the jungle or the woods but out on the playground where everyone was wearing primary colours – even the playground equipment was red, green, blue and yellow – he stood out like a sore thumb, whatever that means.

'Hi,' said the big kid, 'do you have the money?'

I nodded my head and dug into my pants pocket. I pulled out the five-dollar bill and my picture of Lyle with the mean look on his face and arrows to the parts of his body for the big kid to avoid. I handed them to him.

'What's this picture for?' he asked.

'Well,' I said, 'there are some places on the human body that if they're hit hard could cause damage, unconsciousness or even death. I think you should try to not hit those places on the drawing.'

The big kid looked at the drawing more closely. 'But it looks like the only places I can hit that kid is on his arms and legs. How am I going to do that? It's not like hitting someone in certain places is easy to do – kids usually jump around when they're being hit, and where you get them depends on which way they move.'

'Well,' I said, 'I don't want this to be kidslaughter. If something bad happens to Lyle, I'll be in just as much trouble as you.'

The big kid looked at me kind of funny. Then he said, 'Look, kid, I can't make any promises that I won't hit him in those places. Do you want me to do this or not?'

I thought about it for a few seconds. I looked over at Lyle, who was saying things to Justin. Justin was still at the top of the monkey bars and had his feet up high like he was scared Lyle was going to pull them. As much as I hated Lyle, I didn't think I could take the risk. So I said, 'No, I guess I don't want it done.'

The big kid just shrugged his shoulders and handed me back the money and the picture. I was kind of relieved and disappointed at the same time, but I didn't have much of a chance to see which feeling was strongest because just then Justin screamed, 'Get away from me, you F-er!' and moved down the monkey bars as fast as he could. When he got to the bottom and was stepping off, Lyle tripped him. Justin fell back and landed on his butt. Justin screamed, 'F– off, you F-ing F-er,' but Lyle just stood over him laughing and laughing. Justin got up and walked away, and Lyle turned and walked over to the slide to find another victim.

The big kid had also been watching what happened and walked over to where Justin was kicking some stones. I watched to see what was going to happen even though I had a pretty good idea. I couldn't hear what was said, but it looked to me like the big kid was offering the same deal to Justin as he did to me. Even though I didn't do it, I hoped Justin would take the big kid's offer.

When I got home from school today, I was still angry with my mother from yesterday. I was also angry that I had a chance to get back at Lyle and I didn't take it.

My mother said hi from her office but I ignored her. I turned on the TV and watched a show about a bunch of kids who had a pet Komodo dragon. I turned the channel when they put a vest on him to keep him warm. A vest on a reptile! Reptiles are ectothermic, which means they don't make their own body heat. So how the heck is a vest supposed to help him?

I wanted to watch something that made sense. I wanted to watch the Green Channel, so I decided to go ask my mother if I could. Who knows – maybe this was the day she would come to her senses. And how would I ever know for sure if I didn't try?

I poked my head into her office. Then I went over and stood beside her as she typed. She didn't look up. I said in a really quiet voice, 'Mom, may I watch the Green Channel?'

I said it really quietly because sometimes she doesn't really listen to me when she's working hard. If I can catch her at one of those times, she says yes to whatever I ask.

My mother's brain made sense of my words and right away because she looked up from her computer with a surprised face. Then she said, 'Phin, I understand how this is frustrating for you, but no, you may not. You know why.'

I said, 'Then, Mom, tell me what I should do! Tell me what I should do with my time! Tell me something I can do with my brain!'

She didn't say anything.

'Mom, talk to me!' I yelled.

She said, 'Phin, I'm not talking to you. I'm not talking to you while you're acting like this. You're yelling like a crazy person and next thing you know, I'll be one too.'

'Maybe if you talked to me I wouldn't act like this!' I said in a loud voice.

My mother pulled me onto her lap. Her voice got quieter. 'Why don't you do your homework?' she said.

'I said I was bored, not that I wanted to be bored,' I yelled. 'And besides, I'm not doing my stupid homework because it doesn't make any sense to write a page about what I'd do if the prime minister came to our school! That wouldn't make the day special for me! I wouldn't even put on clean underwear for it! And what can Mrs. Wardman really do to me anyway? I don't mind staying in for recess. It's better inside than outside with people like Lyle.'

'How about a walk to the store?' said my mother. 'I will go with you after I finish this report.'

'Anything, but not with you! Why would I want to spend time with the very person who is making my life so miserable?' I yelled.

'How about putting a piece of spaghetti up your nose, or in your ear?' She was trying to get me to laugh, but I wasn't going to fall for it.

'No, nothing involving a piece of spaghetti,' I shouted.

'We could paint your fingernails green.'

'No, nothing that involves you,' I shouted louder. 'And stop being annoying!'

'How about we play a game of Worst Case Scenario?'

'No, nothing that involves you!' I shouted again.

'That's like cutting off your nose to spite your face. You want to hurt me, but it ends up hurting you. Are you trying to punish me?'

'Go away.'

'But you're sitting on my lap.'

I jumped off her lap.

'So a game is out of the question, that's what you're telling me?'

'What's another suggestion?'

'It's your turn; I suggested two things.'

'Let me watch the Green Channel?'

'For the love of God, Phin, no! The answer is no, N – O, NO!' she screamed, forgetting she wasn't going to do that.

'You know you make my life miserable!' I shouted. 'I'm leaving! I'm leaving this place! I'm leaving you!'

She yelled, 'Goodbye, then.' This made me even more mad. I stomped to the foyer and put on my shoes and my jacket. Then I left and slammed the door behind me.

I wasn't sure where to go. I looked up the road, then I looked down the road. I decided to go down since that was to the left and I'm left-handed.

I walked and walked and walked and as I did, I felt calmer and calmer and calmer. I decided to walk to my school and sit under the slide. There was nobody there, which was a relief. I walked under and then sat down and scrunched down as far as I could to the end of the slide. I sat there and looked up at the things kids had written on the underside. I read, 'Poop loves you' and 'I have more brians than you.'

I sat and sat and thought and thought until I saw some feet. My mother's. She had on a pair of brown leather shoes with beige flowers on the sides. I remembered when she bought them. She liked them because they looked like happy shoes. Her feet looked happy but when I looked up, her face sure didn't.

Just before supper, my father called from Edinburgh, Scotland. I was nervous when my mother handed me the phone because I thought I might be in for it. But he didn't mention that I ran away even though I know my mother told him all about it. I'm not sure why he didn't bring it up – maybe my mother told him to wait until he sees me in person. Or maybe he doesn't think it's such a big deal like she does. After all, he ran away too.

My father told me that he's getting lots done in Scotland. He said he's there to interview some environmental activists at an international conference. One's name is Vandana Shiva. She and some other women started the tree-hugging movement in the 1970s when they were trying to stop logging in India. Dad said that because of her and the other women, environmentalists are sometimes called tree huggers.

I wondered if there were people who actually hugged trees to stop them from being cut down near where I live. I saw on the Green Channel that the five big toilet-paper makers use trees straight from ancient boreal forests, like the ones in my province. Those companies don't use much recycled paper because people want something extra-soft to wipe their butts with. But that means that bears and wolves and endangered caribou and lots and lots of birds and all sorts of other animals lose their homes.

On TV commercials for one type of toilet paper, they actually have a big, smiling, clumsy cartoon bear all excited about how extra-soft the tissue is. That's like having a human just about to be shot happily showing everyone how nice and shiny the gun is. I think the people who made up that advertisement were trying to make a satire.

I wondered what it must be like for the animals who live in those forests that are being destroyed. What if someone came to your house, chopped it down and hauled it away to wipe his butt? The suffering of the animals losing their homes to toilet paper is way more than the happiness humans get from wiping their butts with soft toilet paper. I can't figure out how that makes any logical sense.

When I hung up the phone, I asked my mother if there are any tree huggers around here. I figured there must be since there are lots of trees. I heard on the radio this morning that some blue-heron nests were destroyed because a big company chopped down the trees they were in – even though the blue heron is a protected species in the province. What kind of company does that, anyway? That company is on TV all the time and has commercials that say, 'Giving nature the right of way, that's my *what if*.' That would be like Lyle saying, 'Being nice to kids, that's my *what if*.' Whatever.

My mother said the term *tree hugger* is not a very nice one, that it's used to describe people who are extreme in their actions, which means they do crazy things to stop companies from cutting down the trees. I asked her if hugging a tree to stop a man from chopping down a heron's nest is a crazy thing. She didn't say anything. Then I asked her if stopping a company from chopping down the very things that make oxygen so that everything can breathe is a crazy thing. And she didn't say anything about that either. She just kept putting forks and plates on the table for supper.

Then I asked her if somebody was going to chop down a tree that was going to be the only tree that would make enough air for her to breathe, would she hug her tree to stop it from happening? She didn't say anything. Then I said I thought every person on earth should be given a tree to protect. I told my mother that I thought it would be good if everyone was put in charge of his or her own tree and told that it's his or her life support. No tree, no life. Then maybe tree hugging wouldn't seem so crazy. Maybe the only reason it seems crazy is because only a few people are doing it, and they're doing it so that lots and lots of people and animals can survive. Maybe the really crazy thing is that the tree huggers actually CARE! I was being sarcastic. I screamed the word *care*. And that made my mother say something – but not the something I wanted her to say.

She said, 'Phin, you are treading on very thin ice right now. So let's eat our supper, okay?'

She said it in a really quiet voice, like she was telling a secret or something. This is something she does with her voice when my voice is louder than normal. That makes me sound even louder than I would sound ordinarily. This makes me angry and makes my voice go even louder because I figure she already thinks I'm crazy so I may as well act really, really crazy. What's the point of acting normal when someone thinks you're crazy? If they think you're crazy, you may as well act crazy. It's way easier.

When I got mad, I didn't remember the tricks Dr. Barrett showed me and even if I had, I wouldn't have used them. I shouted, 'Mom, do you hear me? Am I in space or something where there isn't air to make sound? Can you hear my voice?'

My mother yelled, 'Phin! Cut it out! NOW!' When she screamed the word *now*, spit flew from her mouth. If she were a spitting spider, I would have been trapped in a web of glue and she would have eaten me.

Her yelling made me feel better, though, because that was at least the right kind of voice to use for something so important. I wanted her to be upset because I was upset. She should be upset! So at least I won that much.

After supper when my mother was talking to someone on the phone, I looked up *tree hugger* on Google. There were 5,920,000 hits. I figured there must be a lot of them out there somewhere. I imagined them with their arms locked around their trees, holding on. Holding on good and tight.

Then I got out my Reull stories and drawings. I drew a picture of a big scale. On one side were the lives of thousands of animals (but I only drew five animals that live in the forest) and on the other side I drew a picture of a human sitting on the toilet (but you couldn't tell he didn't have his pants on) with a roll of toilet paper in his hand. In my picture the weight of the animals was a lot less than the weight of the man on the toilet. Definitely a satire.

I've decided I'm not going to learn anything more at school. I decided this for three different reasons. One is that school is giving me the wrong answers. For example, I got a right answer wrong on my last social-studies test. The question was 'Before humans knew of Mount Everest, what was the tallest mountain?' I answered Mount Everest. Mrs. Wardman said that was wrong and that the answer is Mount Kangchenjunga. That's just plain wrong.

The second reason I'm not going to learn anything more at school is because if my brain gets too full of stuff from school, then there won't be enough room left in it for information that is really important to know for my future job. For example, what if I remember that Mount Kangchenjunga is 8,590 metres and that bumps out the name of the most critically endangered species in South China. (That's the Amoy tiger. None of them are known to be living in the wild – just in zoos. That makes them super-in-trouble and on the Red List of Threatened Species.)

I've read that the human brain is only so big and that there is a slight relationship between head size and intelligence. I measured the circumference of my head, and it's twenty inches. I think that's a good size, but I'm worried that my head might get full of the wrong things.

The third reason I'm not going to learn anything more at school, which is kind of related to the second, is that I'm afraid that if I do, I'll be brainwashed into believing the important things aren't important and the unimportant things are. For example, yesterday Mrs. Wardman made us make pyramids out of our spelling words. This is what we had to do:

Capture

Captur

Captu

Capt

Cap

Ca

C

We even had to take some words home and make pyramids out of them. When my mother saw me doing them, she asked me what the purpose was, and I said I didn't know.

She said, 'Didn't Mrs. Wardman explain it to you?'

And I said, 'No.'

And then she said, 'Well, what do you think she'd say if you asked her?'

I said, 'She'd say she doesn't know.' And I wasn't being sarcastic. What if I learn how to do stuff like that and start to believe it's more important than learning how to save the life of an animal or something like that? I could start to lose my perspective or something. That's a thing that's been worrying me lately.

The problem with my plan not to learn anything more at school is that it's not as easy as it sounds. Some things just sink into your brain without you even trying.

Today I had a plan, though. I know that the best way not to learn something is to have your mind busy doing something else. So last night I ate a lot of popcorn and the shells of the seeds got stuck between my teeth. Pushing on them with my tongue and sucking gave me something to do when Mrs. Wardman was talking.

Then, after first recess, I made a circle and drew a line across it thirteen times. This made twenty-six sections. Then in each section I put the letters of the alphabet in order. Now I can figure out everyone's opposite name by finding each letter of their name and then looking to see what letter is exactly opposite to it on the circle. While Mrs. Wardman talked about graphing numbers, I found out that my opposite name is Cuva and that Bird's is Oveq.

Then at lunch hour when Bird and I started calling each other those names, the other kids wanted to know what we were doing, and now they all want to know their opposite names too. That kept me busy for most of the afternoon.

Do you know what the opposite of opposite is? It's the same.

I did something I wasn't supposed to do this evening. It was a thing that was possible to do because my mother was out at a meeting, and I knew she'd be gone until after my bedtime.

Rena came over to be my pretend caregiver. She acted really nice with my mother but as soon as Mom left, she got on the telephone. Sometimes this bothers me because I want to play games like Worst Case Scenario where you have to guess the best thing to do when you fall through the ice or get stuck in a cougar's mouth or how to survive on a desert island. The right answer for that one is to tie tufts of grass to your ankles so that dew will gather on them and you can wring them out for water. But this evening I didn't even care about playing games because it's been so long since I did what I wasn't supposed to do: I watched the Green Channel.

I felt a little bit guilty about that – but just a little bit. I figured my breaking the law was for a bigger cause. How else am I going to learn about what I can do to save animals?

And besides, what's the worst that can happen if my mother finds out? She'll get really upset and maybe yell at me. I think a question like that should be in the game Worst Case Scenario. It could say, 'What should you do when your mother gets super angry and is yelling at you?' I think the answer is to imagine her as a barking elephant seal.

The first show I watched was about how in Michigan nine dogs were found dead and a few of them had been decapitated. One person wrote a sign to the person who did that. It said, 'You will be caught. You will be punished. You will burn in hell by God.'

Then I watched a show about how when people don't buy other people's products because of how they're made, that's called a consumer boycott. The example they used was the tuna-dolphin problem. That's when fishermen noticed that tuna often swim below herds of dolphins and started encircling dolphins in their nets in order to catch the tuna. The net was then pulled together to keep the tuna from diving out, but dolphins got caught too. Millions of dolphins died this way. When people learned about this, they boycotted. Then the three biggest tuna companies started buying tuna only from fishermen who don't use encircling.

Now people on the Green Channel are working on other problems like the killing of millions of ocean animals by other types of fishing, like bottom trawling. Heavy gates and traps are hauled over the ocean floor and destroy everything in their path – just to get a few shrimp. That makes about as much sense as bulldozing an entire forest just to find some mushrooms.

The Green Channel said there are hundreds of things that we buy that come out of the destruction of wildlife. I knew about some of those things, but I didn't know about most of them.

After that show, I wrote down as many as I could remember. Then I went to my mother's computer and typed in the words *boycott* and *product* I got over two million hits. I read through some of the sites that came up, like ethicalconsumer.org and humanefood.ca and idausa.org.

Then I made a list. And it's a very long, long list.

My mother keeps reminding me that I have another appointment with Dr. Barrett in a few days. I was trying to forget about that, and it makes me angry that she reminds me about it every day.

I said, 'Mom, if you were about to have a piece cut out of your brain and you knew it was going to really hurt, would you want me to remind you of it every day?'

'Does it hurt you to see Dr. Barrett?'

'It doesn't hurt my body but it hurts my mind.'

'How?'

'Dr. Barrett says things that don't make any sense and when people do that it makes my mind confused.' I told her that I figure that's how people's minds feel when they take drugs.

'Phin, maybe Dr. Barrett seems confusing at first, but soon you'll understand what he means and he will help you feel better.'

Hearing that just made me mad. I said, 'I don't know how he's going to do that. Is he going to stop the destruction of the earth? Is he going to bring back animals from extinction? Does he think he's God or something?'

'Phin! You're being very melodramatic! Stop! It's not the end of the world!'

Hearing her say that made me even angrier. 'But, Mom, don't you see? It is! And it's not like a video game – there's no Reset button!'

My mother's voice got really quiet again. She said, 'Phin, please calm down.'

Then I screamed in my loudest voice. I screamed so loud that the sound of my voice scared me even though I felt it come from my own throat. I screamed so loud that if there had been a puddle in front of me, my voice would have made the water move and cause a one-foot tsunami. I screamed, 'Stop lying! Stop telling me that everything will be all right! It will not be all right! It won't be all right until people like you and Dr. Barrett and all the other big, fat, humongous, gigantic, enormous liars start telling the truth to yourselves!'

That's when my mother told me in a very, very low voice to go to the bathroom for a time out to think about my behaviour. She's trying not to argue with me. I know this because I overheard her talking to her friend Jill about how she should stay calm and not argue with me because all that does is make me a better arguer. What she doesn't know is that I don't need a person to say something in order to argue. I could still argue with the look on my mother's face and the way she sighed.

I screamed, 'No – you go sit in the bathroom and think! Go think about your own behaviour!' Then I sat down on the floor and wouldn't move even though she told me three more times to go to the bathroom.

My mother's face looked like the face of an angry baboon. She tried to pick me up under my arms but I made my body go straight. I thought of my mother as the unstoppable force and me as the immovable object, but I knew one of us was going to lose, which made the whole idea false.

She decided to pull me, but still I kept my body straight. She got me across the living room but when she tried to haul me through the door to the stairs, I grabbed hold of the plant stand and it got hauled along with me.

My mother forgot what Dr. Barrett said and turned around and yelled at me, 'Phin! Let go of that plant right now – you're going to knock it over!'

I said, 'I'm not going to knock it over! You're the one creating the force, so you're the one who's going to knock it over! I'm just sitting here!'

That's when the plant stand fell over. It made a loud crashing noise that made me stop talking. It made Fiddledee run and squeeze under the couch. It made the plant pot break in two and the peace lily fall out. And it made my mother even angrier. She looked even scarier than a mad baboon. She looked like a girl I saw on TV one day on the horror-movie channel. The girl was sitting in a bed and her face was like a monster's and then the bed started to move up off the floor and the girl's head started to spin around like a bicycle tire. That's when I changed the channel. I wished I could have changed my mother's channel.

My mother didn't even pick up the plant. She must have gotten some more strength from being angry because all of a sudden she picked me up off my feet and carried me up the first eight steps really fast. She banged my arms and legs against the railing and that's when I said, 'Mom, stop! You're hurting my parts!'

Then she said in a very low voice, 'Phin, if you don't stand up and walk up the stairs on your own, all of your parts are going to hurt! In fact, we're both going to hurt a lot when we fall backwards down the stairs.'

I thought about that. We were on the eighth step and I figured if we fell backwards two steps at a time, when we hit the sixth step, I would land on her. Then two more steps would make her land on me and then two more would put me on her and then the last two would put her on me. That would be the most painful landing since the foyer is hardwood but the stairs are carpet. I didn't think it would feel very good, so I decided to walk the rest of the way to the bathroom. But when I got there, I slammed the door really, really hard.

'And I'm NOT going to see that fucker Dr. Barrett again!' I yelled as loud as I could. Then I had a sore throat.

After my mom told me I could come out of the bathroom, I went to my room and stayed there for two hours. I wanted to make my mother feel bad, but she didn't even ask me to come out like she usually does. I could hear her slamming things around in the kitchen.

For a long time I just sat in there thinking with my hands shaking and my parts hurting. Then after a while I decided to try to calm myself down. I got out my Reull book. I thought and thought about what to write. I was having a hard time because I was still angry.

I lay down on my bed and imagined being at Pete's Pond in Africa. I imagined the sounds of the birds and the wind. I imagined the smell of the grasses and of the water. I imagined being hot, and the hotness made the blood run into my hands and my feet, which calmed me down.

Then I sat up and wrote as fast as I could. I wrote about how one day on Reull things started dropping from the sky. All the Gorachs looked up in awe at the thousands of unidentified shining globs floating down, down, down to the ground. All the Gorachs were amazed and excited.

As the floating, glittering objects started to land, every Gorach on the planet rushed to grab one. The Big Ideas Gorachs pushed and shoved and kicked and shot weapons in the air so that they could collect the most objects. They were thinking that these objects were like the other good things on the planet – they could sell them to the ordinary Gorachs and make a fortune.

But the Wooloofs and the creatures of Reull had predicted that that would happen and so the glittery, shiny objects just kept dropping and dropping like millions of raindrops. Soon every Gorach was holding one.

As soon as these objects made contact with the chemicals in the Gorach's skin, the mysterious globs took a DNA sample of the Gorach holding it and immediately transformed into a perfect little replica of that Gorach. When this happened, the Gorach was amazed. All over Reull, you could hear the sounds of *ooooohhh* and *aahhhhhh*. It was like the planet was breathing in *ooooohhh*s and out *aahhhhhh*s.

As the Gorachs stared at the replicas of themselves, the Wooloofs and the other creatures jumped into action. They encircled all the Gorachs who just couldn't tear their eyes away from themselves. The ones who stopped looking at themselves long enough to see what was happening were allowed to run free. In the end, mostly all the Big Ideas Gorachs and the Gorach Leaders and the scientists who worked for them were caged.

Then the glittery, shiny objects all turned to dust. Those who were in cages looked up for the first time. They couldn't believe their eyes. So they closed them. They couldn't believe their tendrils. So they tied them. They couldn't believe their ears. So they plugged them. They couldn't believe their hands as they grasped the cold steel of the cages. So they clenched them. But as much as they wanted it to, that didn't change the fact – the fact that they were captured in cages.

This morning while I was getting ready for school and while my mother was in the shower, the phone rang. It was only 7:33 a.m. Whenever the phone rings that early, my heart does a somersault. The only person who calls that early is my dad.

I ran to the phone and glanced at the call display before picking it up. Dad has a cellphone and it always comes up *Walsh Will*. But as my hand was on its way to the receiver, I noticed that the call display didn't say that. I jerked my hand back. It said a different name. At first I thought I must be seeing wrong. I blinked and looked again, and yep, that's what it said all right: *Gaskell Brent*. BRENT!

Do you know what it feels like to be expecting one of your most favourite people in the world and to get one of your least favourites instead? It's crueller than cruel. It's like biting into what you think is a big, sweet, juicy purple grape and getting a mouthful of bitter, gross black olive. Or like if you think you won a million dollars in a lottery but it turns out that all you won was a lousy box of Glosette raisins. And raisins make you gag.

I let the phone ring three times and then I picked it up and put it back down. I felt a little bit powerful when I did that. I imagined Brent's confused face. I imagined him thinking that my mother didn't want to talk to him. I imagined him deciding, 'Oh well. I'll just call that other woman instead – the one who doesn't already have a husband.'

Then after a few minutes, I heard another phone ring from inside my mom's coat pocket. I pulled it out and pushed the Answer button on and then off again.

I would have rather my mom got a call from Mrs. Wardman. Or from Lyle. Or from Satan, for that matter.

At school today a bullying expert came to talk to us ... again. This time it was a woman.

She picked a good day because just before she arrived, Ryan borrowed a pen from Lyle but it turned out not to be a pen at all.

It was one of those things that looks just like a pen but it's really a shocking device. When Ryan clicked down on it, it shocked him and he screamed and flung it up in the air and it landed on Mitty's head. Mrs. Wardman was super mad. She grabbed the pen, threw it in the garbage and sent Lyle to Mr. Legacie's office.

This meant, though, that the biggest bully missed the anti-bullying presentation. The expert talked about how bullying is wrong and that if we're being bullied, we should:

1. tell an adult
2. stay in a group
3. join clubs or activities where we'll meet other kids
4. if we're being bullied online, don't reply and tell some-one we trust.

She also said that bullies often will pick on kids who are shy, quiet or seem different from other kids. That was the part that made the most sense to me. Scientists have this theory called the 'oddity effect' that says that fish who stand out are more likely to be chased by predators. This explains why fish prefer to school with other fish who are just like them. Obviously I picked the wrong school.

Just as the bullying expert was getting ready to leave, Lyle came back into the classroom. As he was walking to his seat – and right in front of Mrs. Wardman and the expert – he flicked my eraser off my desk. He did that right in front of everyone just after we had a session on bullying and nobody did a thing! Isn't that bullying? And isn't it also an example of irony or something? As I got up to get my eraser lying in the middle of the floor I was super, to-infinity angry.

After the woman left, Mrs. Wardman told us to each draw a 'Bullying-Free' poster. She said we're going to put them up all around our classroom. She told us to include some of what we learned from the bullying expert.

I sat looking at my blank page for a long time. I didn't know what to draw. I looked at Kaitlyn's poster and it was of a girl talk-ing to a teacher. In a speech bubble above her head it said, 'I am being bullied.' I looked at what Gordon was drawing and it was kids playing in a Lego club together.

I thought some more about what I could draw. I didn't want it to be anything that would belong better on my List of Lies than on the classroom wall. Finally, I picked up my pencil and drew a picture of a kid trying to get his hat back from another kid who was holding it way up in the air and laughing. I made the bully look as much as I could like Lyle and the other kid look like me. Then over top of my drawing I wrote 'Free Bullying.'

When I passed it in, Mrs. Wardman didn't say anything. Not a thing. But I know she's going to talk to my mother again. Oh well.

This evening I called my grandmother. I got right to the point. I said, 'By the way, Grammie, do you know why my parents got separated?'

My grandmother didn't say anything at first. Then she cleared her throat and said, 'Sometimes, honey, people just don't get along very well.'

'So?' I said. 'Does that mean they can't live in the same social group? When chimps fight, afterwards they still live together in the same group. It's not like one of the chimps just gets up, packs his bags and wanders off to another country.'

'Well, if your mom and dad lived together, that might mean a lot of arguing and fighting and hurt feelings that may not be the healthiest thing for either your mom or your dad ... or for you, sweetie,' said Grammie.

I didn't say anything, and then Grammie told me some more things about adults who don't get along. Stuff I've heard before.

After a few minutes I changed the topic and Grammie and I talked some about animals. Grammie mentioned that she saw a snowy white owl while she was walking in the woods yesterday. That reminded me of Jean Craighead George, who wrote that her kids used to have a pet screech owl named Yammer who lived in their bookcase, watched TV and even took showers with the kids.

Her son had once made a sign for the bathroom that said, 'Please remove owl after showering.'

After I hung up the phone, I still didn't understand why my parents had to get separated. It just doesn't make any sense. When two chimps just can't stop fighting with each other, often another chimp jumps in between them and beats them apart. Sometimes when two mountain gorillas fight, an infant will put himself in the middle and the two gorillas calm down.

Maybe I should have jumped in between Mom and Dad that first time they fought. But I didn't. And now it may be too late.

Something happened today with Lyle that gave me an idea. The ironic thing is that the idea came out of something Lyle did that was evil - like the kind of evil that made a man and woman put a dead person's finger in a hamburger in order to get money from the restaurant.

It all started when Ronald McDonald was in our school talking to us about healthy living. I was sitting in a chair between Bird and Gordon and just ahead of Lyle. While Ronald was talking about healthy fruits and vegetables, I all of a sudden really had to go to the bathroom.

When I got back to the gym, I sat down in my chair and leaned back because what had happened in the bathroom sure was a relief. But when I leaned back, I felt something tug the back of my chair and all of a sudden I could feel myself falling back, back, back until *wham!* – my back and head hit the gym floor. Everything after that happened so fast I didn't even have time to think about it. It was as though a part of my brain was on automatic and I couldn't have stopped it even if I had wanted to.

I sat up and screamed something at Lyle that I still can't believe I thought of. I screamed, '*Mo chreach!*' and then, 'Fuck off, you shithead fucking fuckface asshole!' Everybody turned to look at me - even Ronald stopped doing jumping jacks. Lyle looked surprised for about an instant, and then he laughed hard.

He laughed and snorted so hard there was snot bubbling in one of his nostrils.

Bird helped me up and then picked up my quarters and a loonie that had fallen out of my pocket. Then Mrs. Wardman came running over and asked if I was okay, and I said yes even though my head really hurt. She looked at Lyle, who was still laughing with snot bubbling out of his nose.

Mrs. Wardman said, 'Did you have something to do with this, Lyle?'

Lyle stopped laughing and shook his head no. But then Gordon said, 'Yes, he did. He pulled on the back of Phin's chair, and Phin fell back.' Lyle looked like he wanted to kill Gordon. His face got kind of red and his eyes looked crazy like one of them might all of a sudden pop out of his head on a spring like in a cartoon. This made me worried because I think Lyle was born without the do-not-kill-people gene, like what some scientists think happened to Ted Bundy and Paul Bernardo.

Mrs. Wardman looked at Lyle and said, 'Is this true, Lyle?'

Lyle said, 'No – it's not true!'

That's when Gordon said, 'Yes it is! I saw him!'

I'm a little worried about Gordon. I'm thinking that maybe he doesn't have a self-preservation instinct. He'd have been much better off being a peacock flounder fish, which turns the colour of its background. Gordon's eyes or brain or something just didn't seem to be working.

Mrs. Wardman believed Gordon over Lyle. She grabbed Lyle by his arm and marched him out of the gym. Lyle gave Gordon a mean look, and then turned and grinned at me. It wasn't a friendly grin – it was more like the grin of an insane kid without the do-not-kill-people gene.

Principal Legacie came over to me and took me to his office. He looked worried, but I told him I was all right. My head was still hurting but he looked so worried that I didn't want him to feel even worse. He told me that he would call my mother to come get me as a precaution.

I saw my mother coming into the school before she saw me. She looked around and then must have had the sense of being stared at because all of a sudden she turned around and looked right at me. She rushed over and hugged me and asked if I was okay. When I told her I was, she got really angry. Her eyebrows pointed down in the centre of her head, and her lips went really thin. Then she used her sandpaper voice, which is always a dead giveaway.

She turned to Principal Legacie and said, 'How did this happen?'

He told her about what happened, but he didn't say who did it. He just said one of the children.

My mom's head whipped over to me and she said, 'Was it Lyle, Phin?'

I nodded.

My mother's head then whipped back to Principal Legacie. 'I want this to stop, and I want it to stop TODAY!'

Even though my mother yelled the word *today*, Principal Legacie talked in a really calm voice and said that a procedure would be followed, and the child's parents notified. Then he said, 'Mrs. Walsh, I am truly sorry this happened to Phin. Please be assured that we'll handle this. Don't worry ... '

The first mistake Mr. Legacie made was calling my mom Mrs. Walsh. Her last name is MacKeamish. But worst of all were the words *don't worry*. When he said those words, it was if they were coming out of his mouth in slow motion. In my mind it sounded like *dooonnnnnnnnnnnn'ttttt wwwooooorrrryyyyyyyy*. I knew he was in for it. And he was.

The thing about my mother is that she has everybody who doesn't know her very well fooled. She has big green eyes – which look even bigger now that her hair is really short – and a big smile, and she laughs a lot. The average person laughs only eighteen times a day, but my mother laughs at least eighty-six times a day. She looks a little like a big, fluffy, smiling, tail-wagging dog. You think you're safe to pat her on the head, but then next thing you know, she's got her jaws around your throat.

My mother said, 'Mr. Legacie, this has been going on for a long time. If something isn't done and soon, I'll do something about it myself.' She said that in her icy sandpaper voice with acid bursts. That's her worst-ever voice.

I looked at Mr. Legacie's face, but he looked calm. I think he's just a good actor, though, because my mother sounded really scary. If Principal Legacie were a horned toad, he could have squirted blood out of his eyes. If he were a sea cucumber, he could have thrown up his guts at my mother to distract her while he made his escape. My mother, on the other hand, looked like a frilled lizard, which hisses and raises its frill to make itself look even bigger.

Then she turned her back on Mr. Legacie, grabbed me by the hand and we left without saying another word.

When we got home, my mother was a little calmer. She sat with me on the couch and we watched *The Nature of Things*. It was all about the destruction of the rainforest. I had seen this program before. It was about how the rainforests act as the world's thermostat because they control temperatures and weather patterns. More than 20 percent of the world's oxygen is produced by the rainforest and it's home to 50 percent of the earth's plants and animals. Half of the earth's total rainforests have been cleared in just twenty years.

I knew my mother was still thinking about Lyle because she didn't even notice that we were watching a show about the destruction of the earth. Just to be sure she wasn't really watching I asked her if she'd rather be a cuckoo bird or a cuckoo bee. She just smiled and put her arm around my shoulders. And the show didn't even mention cuckoos.

Then all of a sudden my mother said, 'I think you should write a victim-impact statement.' I asked her what that was, and she said it's a letter that describes how you feel when someone does something wrong to you. She said they're used in courts so that the person who committed a crime can see how much they hurt other people. Then she said, 'I'm just kidding, Phin. But really, something had better straighten that kid out now before he ends up a murderer or something.' I think she read my mind.

Even though she was kidding, what my mom said got me thinking. So while she was sitting there not really watching the TV, I went to use her office computer. I typed the words *victim impact statement* into Google and came up with 178,000 hits. One of the sites said that in the letter you should write about the emotional, physical and financial impacts of the crime. So I got out my pen and paper and wrote a letter to Lyle. It said:

Dear Lyle,

I am not sure why you don't like me. All I know is that sometimes when you are doing mean things to me, I wish I were a shingleback lizard that has a tail that looks like a head so that you won't attack my brain.

Then today you pulled my chair back in the gym and I fell, and the back of my head hit the floor and it hurt a lot. I figure I'll have a big bump there for a while.

I didn't lose any money because of my injury but because you rattled my brain in my skull, I may have forgotten important things for my future job working with animals. This may someday cause me economic and social hardship.

Yours truly,

Phineas Walsh

p.s. And please leave the other kids like Bird and Gordon alone too.

I looked at what I had written. I read it over again. And then again. On the fourth time through, I thought about what Lyle would think as he read it. I tried to imagine him sitting in his desk and reading each word I had written. I tried to imagine what he'd be thinking and what he'd be feeling and then what he'd do. That's when I saw him laughing so hard the snot thing happened again.

I tore up the letter and threw it in the garbage. It was a stupid idea.

It's a stupid idea because Lyle will never stop being cruel just because he knows it hurts someone. It's the hurting-someone part that he likes. My grandmother says she's never found a person who is purely good or purely evil. But she's never met Lyle.

After I threw out the letter, I walked to the bathroom thinking about victim-impact statements and how I hate Lyle. But when I got nineteen steps away from mom's office, another idea popped right out of the insides of the first idea.

Victim-impact statements won't work with humans like Lyle – but they likely work for normal humans. And normal humans everywhere are harming animals, but mostly without even knowing it. I think most humans would want to help animals if they really knew what was happening.

In fact, helping another species even has a name. It's called interspecies altruism, and lots of animals do it. For example, pods of dolphins have been seen holding other animals up to the surface so they can breathe as they help them to shore. And some people in Africa heard some whimpering and looked around to see an antelope leading a sick wildebeest, with his eyes swollen shut, to a waterhole. One of the coolest examples of interspecies altrusim I saw on the Green Channel was of a mother cat who adopted seven chicks whose own mother had died. Whenever one wandered too far, she'd gently pick him up and bring him back to where her kittens were.

Humans also show interspecies altruism. For example, a few weeks ago on the news I saw a story about how four white-beaked dolphins were trapped in ocean ice for three days and were close to dying. The humans watching onshore just couldn't stand to watch them suffer any longer so a bunch of men, including a teenager, piled into a motorboat to weigh it down and spent five hours making a pathway through the ice for the dolphins. The teenager even got into the water to help one of the dolphins get free and, in all, three escaped. Maybe stories like this mean that humans just need to be able to see how animals are suffering.

And along with seeing, maybe humans need a way to hear too. Maybe they need a translator to help them understand animals' voices. Maybe it's easier for people not to think of all the ways animals are harmed when they can't even understand the language of those they kill.

Some animals can speak to humans, but not most. I once saw a show about a chimp named Lucy who was raised by a human family in the United States who taught her sign language. She lived there for twelve years, but when she got to be too much trouble (because she threw things around the house and pooped in people's laps), they sent her to a chimp institute in Africa. All of a sudden she was with other chimps for the first time in her life. She was really scared of a big male chimp who chased her around. When her human family visited, she signed, 'Please help. Out.'

There have been parrots who have been taught to speak to humans too. One African grey parrot called Alex was taught to speak English. Once when he had to have a medical exam, he cried out to his human companion, 'I love you. I'm sorry. I want to go back!'

I peeked in on my mother, who was sitting in her rocking chair wrapped up in a blanket, drinking her tea and talking on the phone, likely to her friend Jill. She does that when she's upset. In fact, she's been doing a lot of that lately.

I went back into her study to use the computer. I wanted to see if there were any lawyers who might be able to use some victim-impact statements for animals. I typed in *lawyers* and *animals* and *nature* and came up with two million hits. Most of them were for something called environmental law and eco-justice. I clicked on one of the links and couldn't believe my eyes. There are actually lawyers who sue governments and corporations to get them to stop destroying nature!

Next I typed in the words *environmental law* and then the name of my city to see if there were any of those people around where I lived. And there were! They were suing a university, the city and the province for paving over wetlands and building big-box stores right near where I live.

I clicked on a link that went to the proposal for the whole project written by a construction company. On the front of the proposal were pictures of a moose, a beaver and a brook. What the heck? Why would they put wildlife on their cover? That doesn't make logical sense.

Then I read the first page of the proposal and it got even weirder. They want to name their development after the wetlands they're destroying. That's like calling a prison Freedom Hall. If I worked in the government and got that proposal, I'd think someone was playing a trick on me like on the show *Prank Patrol*, and I'd look around for the hidden camera.

And why do they call it development anyway? The wetlands are already perfectly developed. How come it's not called destroyment?

I wrote down the address of the environmental lawyers and put it in my pocket. I'm going to make victim-impact statements for the animals of those wetlands – like the frogs that live there. I'll do that for Cuddles.

I'm feeling sick to my stomach. I've been sneaking to Mom's computer and reading about what happens when natural habitats are destroyed. I wanted to read all about it because I want to get my letters just right before I send them to the lawyers.

What I found was even worse than I imagined. I guess that's because I've never thought about what happens when bulldozers clear land. I don't know why I've never thought about it because it's happening all around me almost all the time. Maybe that's why.

On one site a man who drove a bulldozer wrote about white-tailed deer running onto a nearby road where they were killed by cars. He also described how lots of animals were buried alive and that he had to keep emptying his bucket of rabbits and squirrels who leapt into it as he plowed through their burrows and nests.

This explained why I've been seeing lots of dead animals like raccoons, groundhogs and porcupines on the road next to where big stores are being built. They were likely running for their lives when the machines started chopping down their homes. My mother and I even saw the bodies of a mother skunk and four babies all scattered along the highway. They made it across two lanes but then there was a big cement wall that wouldn't let them go any further.

Why don't people come up with better ways of getting land ready for building – ones that don't cause so much death? People have come up with thousands and thousands of ways to do things that make life better for humans, so why don't they think of ways to be less destructive when it comes to other lives? Why don't animals' lives matter at least enough to do that? Why do people kill just because they can?

Thinking of all those dead animals made a picture in my mind. So I am going to draw pictures for my victim-impact statements too.

Dear humans,

I am an owl. When you came, I was one of the lucky ones because I heard the warning sounds. I flapped my wings really fast to land in a tree that wasn't knocked down by the teeth. I landed in that tree and closed my eyes tight and tried not to listen to the yelps and the screams and the shrieks from below.

When finally there were no noises, I opened my eyes. What I saw gives me bad dreams every night: I saw big open wounds. I saw broken trees and flattened land and the blood of the dead and the almost-dead. And then all of a sudden, something else I've never seen before happened – the floor of the earth gave a deep, sad sigh and thousands of bright, glowing lights, some big, some small, floated up, up into the sky, toward the sun.

Truly,

Owl

I drew a picture of what was left of a forest. The ground was red with blood and floating above it all were thousands of bright lights – the souls of all the murdered animals leaving the earth.

Dear humans,
> I was a frog. Until you.
> Yours sincerely, once upon a time,
> Frog

This is where I drew a picture. I drew a picture of bulldozers plowing through a forest and trees falling over and frogs leaping all about. Some of them were run over and flattened, their eyes bulging and frozen in fear.

Dear humans,
> I am a deer. When it all began, I flicked up my tail and ran with my fawn as fast as I could away from the sounds of the great toothed beasts and the cries of animals being torn and shredded and buried alive. I can't even describe how afraid we were. All we could do is run, run as fast as we could – to anywhere but there.
> But now my fawn is dead. I heard the sound of her body hit something big and fast and hard. I stopped, looked back and walked as close to her body as I could, but a human was running toward her and I had to run away.
> My baby is dead. This is my pain.

This is where I drew a pain mark. A pain mark is lots of different shades of red. When pain is small – like when you're hungry but not so hungry you would eat broccoli – the mark is small like a dot on a page and pinkish red. But when pain is huge, the mark is huge and very dark shades of red. The pain mark I drew for the mother deer was dark, dark shades of red that covered the whole page. It was a humongous amount of pain. And it was the pain of the mind – which is the worst kind.

I did my very best drawing for those three pictures. I got out my watercolour paints – the ones I save for special projects. It took me a long time to get the colours just right, the way they were in my mind's eye and the way I imagined the victims would see them. I made the owl's picture the most colourful because birds can see all the colours humans can see, and maybe more. I made the deer's picture with less colour because deer see less colour than humans. In fact, they see the world a lot like people who are red-green colour-blind. I made the frog's picture kind of blurry to show motion because frogs mostly just see things as they're moving.

Then I folded my pictures along with a letter I wrote to the lawyers explaining why I was sending them and put them in an envelope. Then I took a stamp from my mother's office. Tomorrow I'll put the letter in the mailbox on the way to school.

Today I got an apology note from Lyle. It said, 'Dear Phin, I am very sorry I accidentally got you hurt. Lyle.'

I don't believe a word of it. I know writing me a note was part of what Mr. Legacie was getting Lyle to do as punishment. Whatever.

I showed my mom the note. She agreed that it was too little too late. She said she has a meeting next week with Mr. Legacie about what happened. She made me promise to tell her if anything else happened. Then she popped some popcorn and we snuggled on the couch and watched *Jeopardy!*. It was almost like the olden days – the days before we started fighting all the time. I think this was because we both had the same big important disaster to deal with: Lyle.

I should have known, though, that it was too good to last. After *Jeopardy!* when my mom went to have a shower because she was going out, the phone rang. *Gaskell Brent*. This time I answered.

Brent said hi and asked me how I was, and I said fine. Then he asked me if I was still taking swimming lessons and I got right to the point and told him my mother wasn't in. Then Brent asked me when I expected her and I said maybe not for a few hours. He was quiet for a few seconds and then asked me to give her a message. His message was: 'Tell your mom I may be a little late getting to the exhibit this evening but that I'll call her cell when I arrive.' I didn't say anything, and when he went, 'Phin, are you still there?' I hung up.

When my mother came back downstairs, she asked who called and I said, 'Nobody special.'

'What do you mean nobody special? Who called?'

'Where are you going tonight?' I asked.

'I told you – to an art exhibit at the gallery,' she said.

'With who?' I asked.

'You mean *with whom*,' she said.

'*With what*?' I asked.

'What do you mean, *with what*? With a lot of people, Phin, people from work, Jill and so on.'

'Well, *so on* says he can't make it tonight,' I said.

My mother's eyebrows went up. 'So it was Brent who called?' she asked.

I didn't say anything.

'Phin, I can see you're upset. Do you want to talk about it?'

'You told me you'd tell me if you were seeing that man!' I yelled.

'Phin, I told you I'd tell you if I ever had a serious relationship with him, or anyone else for that matter,' said my mother calmly.

'Well? Do you?' I asked loudly.

My mother paused. Then she said, 'I've been seeing Brent socially. It's not serious, Phin, but like I told you before, I do enjoy his company.'

'What about Dad's company?' I yelled.

'Phin, your dad and I are separated. That means we aren't a couple, right? In a few months we'll be divorced.'

'Divorced?' I screamed. 'What the heck does that mean?'

'Well ... it means we won't be connected to each other in a married way. We'll be free to date or marry, but I'm not saying that will happen any time soon – '

'But what about me?' I screamed. 'You might be free, but I'm not! I don't feel free, I feel trapped. When you and dad got free, you pushed me into a trap and threw away the key!'

178

I didn't want to do it. I tried really hard not to. I even did some math problems in my head, but I couldn't help it – I started crying. 'So there's no chance you're going to get back with Dad? Not even one tiny little chance – like a .01 percent chance?' I asked.

My mom shook her head no and then hauled me onto her lap and started rubbing my back. Even though a part of me knew it already, hearing my mom say that made me super wish I hadn't asked. I didn't really want to know that for absolute sure. I wished I could grab the words back.

'So I guess that means Dad won't ever have you as a reason to stay at home. And I'm just not a good enough reason,' I said.

'Phin, honey, it's not like that, sweetie ... '

After a few moments I said, 'Sometimes I miss my dad so much that it feels like he's dead or something. And then when I think about how he's alive but I hardly ever see him, I get really angry at him ... ' Then my voice got so high it started coming out silent.

My mom didn't say anything. She waited and rubbed my back until I could say some more.

'Some male primates don't stick around to look after their kids but human fathers are supposed to be more like the marmoset, who does. What the heck's wrong with my father?' I said, but because I had so many tears in my throat, that last part came out more like a long groan.

My mom got up and got me a tissue, and I blew my nose.

'Does Dad have a sense of smell?' I asked my mother after a few minutes.

'Yes, I think so,' said my mother. 'Why?'

I told her that the infant's smell is what makes the marmoset father bond with his infant. That smell lowers the father's testosterone levels and makes him less aggressive and more caring. Scientists think that happens with human fathers too.

'I think there's more to it than that,' said my mother.

'Well, it sure would be better if there wasn't,' I told her. 'Do you think there's anything else that might lower Dad's testosterone?'

Mom laughed a little but she looked tired, like all the muscles on her face were taking a break. Then she said, 'I think, Phin, that maybe you need to discuss how you feel with your dad.'

I didn't say anything.

'He's coming home in a few weeks. I think you should have a heart-to-heart with him. Be honest. Don't worry about hurting his feelings, just say what you need to say. Okay?'

I didn't say anything.

'Are you afraid to tell Dad how you feel?' my mom asked.

I nodded my head. 'I only get to see him every few months, so I feel like we should spend the little bit of time we have having fun. A part of me thinks that if I tell him how I feel, then maybe he'll come home even less often.'

'Your dad may not be around much,' said my mom, 'but he loves you no matter what you feel or think or say. You guys have to be honest with one another – no secrets, no pretending.'

Fiddledee came into the living room and jumped up on my lap. I patted her while my mom patted me.

After a few minutes Mom said, 'How about in the meantime you write down how you feel about him being away and us getting a divorce and whatever else you might be thinking or feeling? Sometimes just writing things down makes people feel a lot better.'

My mom decided not to go out to the art show. She called Jill and apologized for cancelling on her and asked her to let Brent know. Then she asked me if I wanted to talk anymore and I said no. We played four games of Go Fish and I beat her three times.

Later, when she went to check her email, I got out my writing box and started a letter to my dad.

After school Mom told me that we had an appointment at 4:30 to see Dr. Barrett. It's funny, but when she told me this, instead of feeling angry, I just felt calm. Maybe that's because I had my List of Lies all ready and was 100 percent prepared for this appointment. Or maybe I was calm because a part of my mind knew what I was going to do even before the conscious part knew it. Or maybe it was because I was almost all angered out. Even thinking of getting angry again just felt too exhausting. It felt like the anger was inside my body chomping away at muscles and making me weak.

Before the appointment, I worked on my Reull story. When I left off last time, the Gorachs were still in their cages. They were outraged. 'Let us out! This is not right!' they screamed. 'We are not animals! We are highly intelligent beings who deserve to be free!'

But the Wooloofs, who were caring for them by giving them food and water, replied, 'But, Gorachs, we are much more intelligent than you. We come from the planet Chary. We have ships that allow us to explore the universe and other universes as well. Can you do that?'

'No,' said the Gorachs.

'We also can communicate with other creatures on other planets through just our thoughts. In fact, that is how we learned of what was happening here on Reull. We heard the pain in the thoughts of the animals here. Can you do that?' they asked.

'No, but we are highly intelligent beings! This is an outrage!' screamed the caged Gorachs.

'Let me ask you this, Gorachs, why have you put other animals in cages and, in fact, done even worse things to species all over the planet?' asked the Wooloofs.

'Why not? Because we are superior to them, of course!' shouted the Gorachs.

'Oh,' replied the Wooloofs, 'we see. Well, by that logic you should be happy to be in our cages because clearly we are much more intelligent than you. Are we not feeding you and giving you water? In fact, are we not giving you what you gave the creatures you had in cages – and in some cases more? You should be very happy that we are caring for you in this way. It only makes sense from your very own logic.'

Then the Wooloofs turned and walked away, even as the Gorachs in cages screamed and cried for them to come back and let them out.

I sat back and read what I wrote and changed a few words around until my mother said it was time to go.

D r. Barrett started off by asking me pretty much the same question – he asked if there was anything bothering me lately.

I said, 'Yes, there's now a plastic garbage heap the size of Texas swirling about and choking off wildlife in the Pacific Ocean. Not to mention the tar sands, which will destroy a boreal forest as big as Florida.' I had heard both of those on the news this morning.

Dr. Barrett didn't say anything for a minute and then he said, 'Well, that's a lot of worry for a kid. Have you been having trouble sleeping lately?'

'I sleep like a dolphin, half of my brain at a time.'

'Well, that can't leave you feeling very rested.'

I just stared at him.

Then he said, 'When you start to worry, do you try some of the exercises I've shown you, like deep breathing and visualizing being in a place that makes you feel calm?'

'I brought my List of Lies,' I said, taking it out of my pocket. I smoothed out the wrinkles and rubbed a bit of jelly off it. I handed my list to Dr. Barrett.

He looked at it for a few minutes. Then he said, 'Phin, do you know why people might tell lies like these?'

I didn't say anything.

'Well, most lies aren't malicious. Do you know what that means, Phin?'

I nodded my head and moved a little bit forward in my chair.

'So then you know that one of the biggest reasons for lying is to make someone feel better?'

I nodded my head and moved even further forward in my chair.

'And the second biggest reason people might say the things that are on your list is that they don't know the truth. So that's not actually a lie, really. Do you see what I'm saying?'

I moved so my butt was half off the chair and so that my legs were dangling closer to the floor.

'So,' I asked Dr. Barrett, 'are you lying to me because you don't know the truth or to make me feel better?' I already had my ideas about that. I was betting that he was lying because he had his own self fooled and that made him – but not me – feel better. What the heck kind of animal lies to himself? What kind of animal tells himself not to worry at the very time he should be most worried? Animals are all about survival and this just doesn't make any survival sense.

'Phin, I am trying to make you feel better, yes, but I'm not lying to you. I'm trying to get you to see the truth. When you're overly worried about things you can't control, that won't help anything...'

This was when I moved even further forward in my chair, slid out and landed on the floor. I walked over to the door. I heard Dr. Barrett say, 'Phin, where are you going? Do you need to go to the bathroom?' but I didn't look at him and I didn't say anything.

I just opened the door and walked out to where my mother was sitting in the waiting room. I said, 'Mom, I'm going out to wait for you in the car.' She looked surprised and opened her mouth to say something, but I didn't hear her because I was running down the hall.

I ran as fast as I could. My imagination made me think of people dressed in uniforms chasing me with tranquilizing dart guns. This is what they do to animals – like bears, and moose and deer – who are in the wrong places. And I was definitely in the wrong place. I ran like there were wings on my feet.

I woke up in the middle of the night and I couldn't stop thinking about what happened today. I couldn't stop thinking about my mom being so quiet. Quietness in my mother is not a good sign. That's when she's most upset. She didn't say much at all about me running out of Dr. Barrett's office. That surprised me, but it also kind of worried me. This could mean that she's thinking really, really hard about what to do next about me. I could meet a fate worse than having to go see Dr. Barrett ... if that's even possible.

Then I thought about the lie Dr. Barrett told. He said that I was overly worried and that I couldn't change things. That just didn't make any logical sense. I bet that Pete Le Roux's worry made him build Pete's Pond in Africa and that David Suzuki's worry makes him get up out of bed every day and do things to protect the environment and that Vandana Shiva's worry makes her hug trees.

When I thought about this, my thoughts started to multiply. It was like I had on the Cat in the Hat's hat except that it was a thinking hat. Thought One, Thought Two and Thought Three jumped right out, grabbed me by the hand and hauled me out of my bed.

I tiptoed to the stairs. I peeked in my mother's bedroom. She was lying on her back snoring. I crept to the stairs and went down really, really, super quietly making sure not to step on the spots that I know make creaking sounds. Halfway down, I stopped to make sure I could still hear my mother snoring.

When I got to the kitchen, I found a big plastic garbage bag under the sink. Then I put the opening of the bag over the back of a kitchen chair.

I started with the fridge. It took me a long time to go through all the things in there. It was worth it, though, because I found a half-eaten can of tuna and a package of scallops. I threw them into the garbage bag. I figured both of those animals were caught with long-line fishing or bottom trawling. I also found a tub of margarine and a few bottles of sauces and salad dressings with palm oil. I threw all those things into the garbage bag too.

I had closed the fridge door when I remembered something else: over 90 percent of Canada's egg-laying hens are kept in battery cages. The hens are crammed into small cages for all of their lives. Many of them have their feathers chafed off and are covered in poop. I opened the fridge and looked at the eggs in there. They didn't say *free-range eggs*, a label that means the hens are allowed to move around in farmyards. So I threw them out.

Then I went on to the freezer. I didn't find much except ice cream and frozen French fries, but there was a package of Eggo waffles with palm oil and a package of pork chops that didn't say anything on the label to make me think they weren't from pigs raised like most of the pigs in the country are raised, where sows are in crates for most of their lives and the crates are so small the sow can't turn around and can take only one step forward and one step back. She eats and sleeps in this tiny little space. Her poop falls through slats in the floors where there's sewage underneath her. I threw out the package of pork chops and then found a package of hamburg and threw it in too because most cows are raised in pretty much the same way.

Then I went to the cupboard where Mom puts all the snacks and crackers and things. I read all the labels and found lots of stuff in there with palm oil: a Coffee Crisp bar, blueberry oatcakes, raspberry spread, All-Bran Snack Bites, Yogos berry fruit snacks, Raisin Bran cereal bars, instant noodle soup and coffee whitener. I threw them all in the garbage bag.

I started to go through the cupboard with the flour and spices and things but wasn't really sure about some of them. Like, what the heck is allspice? So I threw it out just in case.

I was going to go through the other cupboards, but I decided to go to where there are the next most things to throw out first: the bathroom. In the cabinet I found a lip gloss and some shampoo with palm oil in it. I also found toothpaste and shampoo that come from a company that still uses animal testing. In the bathtub, I found a bar of soap that didn't have a label on it, so I threw it out just in case.

I looked at my bag of things. It was almost completely full. I knew that not eating and using all that stuff was actually a waste but I felt better because I had done something. My father would call it the principle of the matter.

As I was about to go back upstairs to bed, I heard my mother coming down the stairs. When she got to the bottom to where I was standing behind the door, she jumped back. She said, 'My God, Phin, you scared me! What are you doing down here in the middle of the night?' But before I could even answer, she walked around the corner to the kitchen and saw the garbage bag. 'Phin! What is this? What have you been doing?'

I opened my mouth to say something but she peeked into the garbage bag and I knew it was game over. She reached her hand in and pulled out the bottle of shampoo, which had egg white dripping off it.

'Phin! What in the name of God is this? What have you done?' She looked at me with her eyes bulging, still holding the shampoo bottle, which was now dripping egg on the floor.

I said, 'Mom, I did something that you're not going to like – I threw out all that stuff because it was made in ways that harm animals. But please don't be mad. Please.'

My mother stared at me. She opened her mouth to say something, then closed it again. She turned away from me and looked out the kitchen window. Then she dropped herself into a chair, put her head in her hands and did something that really shocked me. I'm talking the kind of shock that I hadn't felt since Cuddles died. She started crying. And not quiet sniffling noises but out-loud choking noises like how Jody cried when she was sent home for telling other kids that breath mints could make them jump high. My mom cried like she did in the days after Granddad died. That sort of crying makes my heart beat really fast. It scares me because usually my mom is really happy. Except for when we've been fighting lately, she makes more jokes and laughs more than any other person I know. She's the one who's always cheering other people up and doing crazy things to make them feel better. Seeing my mother cry was like seeing a nurse kick a little kid or a police officer rob a bank. It made me feel like the things I thought I knew for absolute sure weren't for sure at all. It scared me and I wasn't sure what to do.

I went over to her and I touched her shoulder. Her crying got quieter. Then I said, 'I'm sorry, Mom. I'm sorry,' and her crying became just a few sniffles. Truth is, I wasn't sorry for throwing all that stuff out but I was sorry for making my mom so sad. Really, really sorry.

My mom wiped the tears off her face with the edge of her nightgown and then she looked at me. Her eyes were still all teary. She looked awful: sad and tired and confused all at once. To make it even worse, her nose was starting to run.

'I'm sorry, Mom,' I told her again.

She didn't say anything. She got up and walked over to the couch and patted the cushion beside her for me to come sit down. Then she reached in her housecoat pocket and found a tissue and blew her nose really loudly and looked at me with her lip twitching just a little. Then Mom said, 'Okay, Phin. Explain this to me. I'm listening.'

I took a deep breath and I told her all about how I learned on the Green Channel (but I didn't tell her that I'd watched it last week – I'm not that crazy) that people can make a difference for animals and the environment if they are careful about the sorts of products they buy.

I looked at my mom's face, but she still didn't say anything. She just looked straight ahead even as Fiddledee batted at her head. Then after a moment she said, 'Phin, did you buy those things that you threw out?'

'No, you did.'

'That's right. I bought them with money I earned through working really hard. Even though you might not like where they may have come from, who would you say those things belong to?'

'You.' I was figuring out where this was headed.

'Do you think you have a right to destroy something that doesn't belong to you?'

'No ... I guess not. But people destroyed animal homes that didn't belong to them to make those products – '

'Hold on, Phin, just a second now. Do you believe in a tit for a tat – that if one person destroys something that belongs to another person, then it's all right for that other person to destroy something of theirs to teach them a lesson?'

I thought about that for a few seconds. I wasn't 100 percent sure there wasn't a time when that would be the right thing to do. But I figured that maybe most of the time it wasn't. So I said, 'No.'

My mother was quiet for a few minutes and then she said, 'Phin, next time we go for groceries, I'll listen to your point of view. Does that sound fair?'

'Yes, that's fair.' I actually felt a lot better after she said that – even better than I felt after I'd finished throwing all that stuff in the garbage bag.

'Okay then, let's put those things back. It's a waste to throw them out. Don't you agree?'

'Yes – but it was the principle of the matter.'

'Well, you acted on your principles and you made your point. Now let's put them back, okay?'

'Okay, but I'm not using that stuff.'

'Like I said, that's fine, Phin – as long as you don't complain that you don't have the things you want for breakfast or something.'

After we finished putting all that stuff back – except for the eggs, which were all cracked – we went back upstairs. I asked if I could sleep with her and she said yes right away. I hugged my mother and told her I loved her.

I think my mother releases calming pheromones just like other mother animals because when I sleep with her I fall asleep as soon as my head hits the pillow. You can buy those pheromones in a spray pump for puppies to help them with separation anxiety. Maybe if my mother wants me to sleep on my own, she should bottle her pheromones for me and spray them on my pillow.

Today was a training day for teachers, so I got the day off. I thought I was going to have to play quietly at home while Mom worked, but she surprised me. She had an interview with a person who lives near where Grammie lives, so I got dropped off at Grammie's – and just in time too because just after I got there, her raven friend came right to the patio door and waited for her to come out. She calls him Plato and feeds him peanuts out of her hand. I stayed inside and watched because he's not used to me. It was way cool. As he was eating, my grandmother squatted down and the raven cocked his head sideways and they looked each other in the eye, bird to human. When the peanuts were gone, she held her empty hands up. He flapped around the yard as if to say thank you and then flew off.

Ravens are much, much bigger than crows and have flatter heads and bigger beaks. There are also lots of crows at Grammie's and she feeds them too. Sometimes when she comes out of the house, they'll swoop down around her to get her attention.

A few months ago she saw about twenty crows swooping down over the river and cawing. She couldn't see a predator or anything, but then she spotted a dead crow on the beach. The other crows were circling around him. Grammie said they were saying goodbye. She said goodbye too by finding his dead body and burying him after the others had left.

After lunch, Grammie said, 'How about we go to the ocean?' Since I hadn't been there since last fall, I was super excited. It was still way too cold to swim, but we could look for rocks and shells and ocean animals.

Grammie and I were surprised to find that we were the only two on the entire beach. We spent a long time picking up and looking at things like barnacles, sand dollars and sponges. After a while we climbed up onto the rocks and watched the seagulls around the shoreline. I asked Grammie if she noticed that there are fewer birds. She said she had noticed that. 'There used to be a lot more thrushes and sparrows and grosbeaks,' she said.

I told Grammie that I once saw a show on the Green Channel about how some Canadian scientists set up nets in marshes in Ontario to catch and tag and weigh birds every year. They've found that the number of songbirds has dropped 80 percent over the last forty years. Not even the common tern is doing so well.

'They'll have to change that bird's name to the uncommon tern,' joked Grammie.

I smiled – but at her joke, not at the fact the common tern is becoming uncommon. Then Grammie and I sat quietly, looking out at the ocean. She told me once that the Celts believed that the ocean is a place where the barrier between the living and the spirit world is thin. I know she was feeling Granddad.

'I feel like there's death death death everywhere,' I said after a few minutes.

Grammie looked over at me, pushed her long grey hair behind her ears and said, 'Tell me about it, Phin.'

'Granddad, Cuddles, the extinction of whole species,' I said. I was starting to get tears in my eyes so I blinked a few times really hard.

My grandmother put her arm around my shoulders and pulled me toward her and smoothed my hair. That's when I started crying. Grammie held me tight and said, 'Shhh, shhhh, shhhh,' in a really soft voice that didn't mean I should stop crying.

After a few minutes, Grammie looked me in the eyes and said, 'I understand, Phin, why you are worried about the animals and the environment.'

'Are you worried too?'

My grandmother nodded her head and said, 'Yes, sometimes I am. And you know what? I learned from a therapist friend this week that there's now a word for what you and I feel. It's called eco-anxiety – not that we need a word to make it real. But the point is, we're not alone.'

'Is it an inherited brain disorder?' I asked Grammie, joking, but not really.

Grammie laughed. 'No, heck no. I mean about the disorder part. But I sometimes envy all those people who don't worry, don't you?'

I nodded my head really hard and said, 'Bird doesn't worry much – but he's trying.'

Grammie laughed again. 'You know, when I'm really worried I talk with other people who are worried too – and trying to do something about it.'

I thought about that for a minute. 'But what happens if you're a kid and your mom worries that you're a crazy person and takes you to a doctor who tries to change you into some sort of zombie robot kid instead? And what if that makes you fight with your mom so much that you make her cry – really, really hard?'

My grandmother put her hands on my shoulders and said, 'Phin, I know this is all so confusing for you, but I do know some things for certain, and one is that you and Mom will work this out. You and Mom will be just fine. Don't worry about that.'

'But I think I may be giving her post-traumatic stress disorder,' I told Grammie.

Grammie smiled. 'It's easiest to be hard on the people you love the most, eh? Because they're always there and always loving you, no matter what. I once screamed so loud at Granddad that I scared Callie.'

That made me laugh because Callie is Grammie's deaf cat.

'I didn't like it when I lost my temper, but when I did, I knew your Granddad loved me no matter. Because of that, we always told each other the truth – even when it meant a disagreement. I liked to think of our fights as kind of like sandpaper that smooths all the edges. That's the kind of relationship you have with your mom. You and Mom will work it all out,' said Grammie again.

I sat and thought about that. Hearing Grammie say those words did make me feel better. I'd say about 31 percent better.

Then after a few minutes Grammie said, 'Do you know what else I do when I'm a little eco-anxious, Phin?'

I shook my head.

'I rub my worry rock,' she said and pulled a smooth white rock out of her jacket pocket and handed it to me. 'I always have an ocean rock or two in my pocket. It reminds me of peaceful places like this. It connects me to the earth, anchors me. And I find rubbing the rock in a rhythmic way, back and forth, makes me feel a bit calmer. Try it. You can even close your eyes if that helps.'

I held the grey, round rock in the palm of my hand and then rubbed it between my thumb and pointer finger. I closed my eyes and concentrated on its smooth coolness. My grandmother asked if it was making me feel any better and I nodded my head. It was.

'Well, Phin,' said Grammie, 'I think we should find you a special worry rock.' She and I slid off the big rock and we headed down to the ocean floor. It didn't take us long to find lots of small, smooth rocks. We put them together in a little pile. Then after trying each out in my palm, I had it narrowed down to three. I couldn't decide which was the best, so my grandmother suggested I put all three in my pocket.

As we were walking back to the car, Grammie said, 'If you could work to help protect an animal, any animal, which would you choose?'

I thought about it for a few moments and said, 'I think amphibians.'

'Amphibians. Of course! Excellent choice,' said Grammie.

When I got in the car, I noticed my mindache was gone. I think Grammie may be a healer or something. I saw that on a show once. This woman put her hands on a man's sore back and when she took her hands away, he danced around the room like there was nothing wrong with him. I think my mindache was gone because Grammie put her hand on my head.

Today at school there was a new kid in our class even though there's only a month left of the school year. His name is Yoo Seok. He's from South Korea.

Just like when Mrs. Wardman introduced Mitty, I knew that Yoo was in big trouble. It didn't take long – only about two minutes and forty-four seconds – for Lyle to start calling him something other than his real name. He waited until Mrs. Wardman left the class to photocopy some papers and then said, 'Hey, You Suck, you're sitting next to Shitty.'

The good thing is that Yoo can't speak English yet. I could tell he didn't have a clue what Lyle said to him because he just smiled and nodded his head. Mitty's face went really red, though. Too bad for her that she speaks English.

Lyle didn't get in trouble because Mrs. Wardman didn't hear him. Gordon got in trouble, though. Mrs. Wardman was calling out spelling words and making up sentences to go along with them so that we would know exactly what each word was. Three of the words on the list were *to*, *too* and *two*. They've been in every spelling book since first grade. I figure that if there's a kid who doesn't know them by now, he likely knows how to sleep with his eyes wide open, like cows and giraffes.

When Mrs. Wardman got to the word *two*, she said, 'I have two eyes, two ears, two arms, two hands,' and that's when Gordon said, 'Two boobies.' He didn't say it very loudly, but I heard him because I sit right next to him. I don't think he actually meant to say it either. I think it was like when I screamed '*Mo chreach*' and then 'Fuck off, you shithead fucking fuckface asshole' at Lyle. It just kinda popped right out of his mouth like that popped out of mine. After he said it, his face turned really red and he wouldn't look up at Mrs. Wardman, who was standing right next to our desks. The other kids didn't seem to hear him say it, but I could tell that Mrs. Wardman did. Even though she didn't say anything to Gordon, it took her more than a few seconds to think up a sentence for the next word, which was *too*.

The fun thing about today was that after lunch we went on a field trip to O'Dell Park. We do that every spring when it gets nice out. We had to take the bus there and Bird and I got to sit together. Once we were all in the bus, Mrs. Wardman went over the bus rules. They are:

1. Stay in your seat.
2. Talk quietly.
3. Don't eat or drink on the bus.
4. Listen to the bus driver.
5. NEVER put your head or arms out the window.
6. Know where the emergency exits are, but don't play with them.
7. Don't throw things.

When she got to rule five, she told us the same story from the beginning of the year when we went on a field trip to pick apples.

She said that she knows of a person who had his hand out the window of the bus when all of a sudden the bus tipped over and landed and skidded on his hand so that he had to have it amputated. She said that even though it was amputated, it pained for all of his life after that.

I told Bird that I once looked up why that kid's hand still hurt after it was amputated. I found on Ask.com that there's a part of the brain that makes pain for the hand and it doesn't always turn off like it should when the hand's missing. That's why he still feels like he has a paining hand. It's called 'phantom limb.'

Bird said, 'Wow, that would really, really suck,' and I agreed.

'Maybe Lyle has phantom brain,' said Bird. That made me laugh really hard.

When we got to the park, we had an awesome time. We walked the hiking trail, which took us almost an hour. We had to walk slowly because some of the kids aren't very fast walkers but it was still fun. It was even more fun than usual because Lyle had to walk beside Mrs. Wardman at the front of the line and Bird and I were at the back.

We took turns closing our eyes and walking. This meant I had to trust Bird and he had to trust me not to lead him right into a tree or a swamp or off a cliff or something. Once Bird pretended that I was close to a cliff and that he was going to let me go over it, but I trusted him. In harsh environments, you've got to have at least one good friend you can trust.

Usually we go to the farmers' market first thing Saturday morning but today my mother said how about we get our rubber boots on and go to the amphibian park instead? She said there's a spring cleanup and volunteers are going to pick up garbage around the trails. They do the cleanup after the snow melts so that the park is healthier for all the frogs, toads and salamanders that live there. I ran and got my rubber boots on right away.

When we got to the amphibian park, there were about nineteen other people there, including six other kids. A tall woman named Caroline told us all thank you for coming and that our work this morning is very important to the wildlife at the preserve. Then she gave us each a big garbage bag and some garbage pickers that looked like big lobster claws, and broke us into groups assigned to different parts of the trails around the ponds.

My mom and I got assigned to a group with Caroline and a woman who looked to be about my grandmother's age. She was so old that her face looked like an apple ring after it has been in my grandmother's dehydrator. She said her name was Beth. She talked with a British accent, which made me think that everything she was saying was really smart and super important.

When we started off toward one of the ponds, I walked behind Caroline and Beth, and my mom walked behind me. She kept grabbing my pants with her garbage picker and I kept swatting her away. Did I ever mention that my mom is a big teaser? Never give a teaser a tool that's more than a foot long because then they can irritate you even from a distance. My granddad used to do that to me too but with a really long blade of grass, which he'd use to tickle the back of my neck as we walked in the field.

When we got to our pond, we could see where the beavers had built a dam on the other side. Caroline told us that if we came back at dusk, we might actually get to see them hard at work. There were so many animal sounds – like frogs and birds and squirrels – that it was hard to believe we were so near the city. The only sign of humans was the garbage – and there was lots of it: Tim Hortons cups, plastic bags, beer bottles, even an old car tire that Beth, who's really strong for such an old woman, lugged out onto the path so we could roll it back to the road.

As we worked, Caroline explained that there are sixteen species of amphibians found in our province and that the amphibian park is home to most of them, including seven different types of frogs. The one that's of most concern is the grey tree frog. Although it's not on the Red List of Threatened Species, there aren't very many of them left in our province. Caroline told us that grey tree frogs can turn many different colours from white to black to green. The ones that stay grey are the ones that are either dead or in aquariums. That made sense. It also made me think of Cuddles but I didn't have time to feel sad because there was so much work to do.

We worked for over an hour and then it was time to head back. At one point, Caroline took us off the trail into the woods and lifted up a few big stones. Under one was a yellow-spotted salamander. She told us some things I already knew but that I like to hear about, like that salamanders belong to the *Amphibia* family, along with frogs and toads. They eat things like insects, worms, snails and slugs and use their sight and smell to find their food because they can't hear, although they can feel the ground vibrate with their legs and jaw. They can actually regrow a leg if it's bitten off by a predator like a bird.

We looked at the salamander for a few seconds, but we didn't pick him up. Not only would he not like it, but human skin has oil in it that is toxic to the salamander. Caroline then put the stone down next to him but not on top of him because he had moved and doing that would squish him.

Further up the path, Beth pointed out some deep purple trilliums. She said that the nature preserve is also home to different types of rare plants too, including red milkwort and narrow-leaved gerardia. She said years ago women ate milkwort to help produce more milk for their babies.

Then Beth talked about how many, many plants – including those used to make drugs to treat things like cancer and AIDS – are at risk of going extinct because we're destroying the forests and other natural habitats. So basically we're destroying the very things that can be used to heal us.

'My grandfather had a Gaelic expression for that,' I told Beth. 'It was *cac sa nid*, which means *shit in your own nest*.'

My mom said, 'Phin!'

But Beth and Caroline just laughed.

Our team collected four bags of garbage. When we added ours to the other teams', altogether there were twenty-three bags. That's a lot of *cac*.

When I got home from school today, my mother came out of her study with an envelope in her hand. She said, 'Phineas William Walsh, have you committed some crime we need to talk about?'

At first I didn't know what the heck she was talking about. Then she handed me the letter and I saw the address of the environmental lawyers on the front. I tore open the envelope as fast as I could. This is what I read:

> Dear Phin,
>
> My name is Julius Crandle and I am one of the lawyers working to help save the woodlot. I got the victim impact letters and pictures you mailed to us, and I am amazed and impressed by the quality of both what you wrote and the accompanying artwork.
>
> I think that your words and pictures speak very well for wildlife. I would like to run your work in the local and provincial newspapers as a way of making people aware of the consequences of developing the natural areas we are trying to protect.
>
> We would like to discuss this further with you and your parents and ask you to please give us a call at the number above.
>
> Yours most sincerely,
>
> Julius

I could hardly believe what I read and had to read it again to make sure I saw all the words properly. My mother was standing in front of me waiting for me to explain. I was a little nervous to look up at her face because I wasn't sure she'd be happy or mad.

'Well, Phin, what is the letter about?' she asked.

'Do you really want to know?' I asked.

'Yes, of course.'

'Really, really? Even if it's not good news?'

'Yes, Phin!'

So I told her about how I'd written victim-impact statements for the animals of the wetlands and sent them to an environmental lawyer.

Her mouth hung a little bit open and she didn't say anything right away, so I said, 'Actually, Mom, you gave me the idea when you said I should write a victim-impact statement to Lyle.'

'Oh, don't credit me with this, Phin!'

I didn't say anything.

'So, what ... ? Is the law firm writing to thank you for your letters?' asked my mom.

I handed her the letter and watched her face as she read it. At that moment I wished I was a chameleon whose eyes tell his brain what colour to turn – or at least had on a shirt the same colour as the wall.

After a minute, she looked up at me. Then finally she said, 'What do you think about what they're asking, Phin?'

'Awesome?' I said but kind of asked.

My mother looked at me like she had just noticed something different about my face. Then she looked down to the letter and back at me again.

She said, 'Okay, Phin, if this is really something you think is important and want to do, then it's all right with me.'

When she said that, you could have knocked me over with a feather. Really. Truly. With a teeny weeny little black-capped chick-adee feather!

I jumped up ran to the phone to call the number on the letter to tell Julius Crandle he could use my pictures in the newspaper!

When Bird and I were walking home from school today, it started to rain. Bird started to walk really fast, saying, 'Hurry up, Phin, we have to get out of the poison.'

'What the heck are you talking about?' I asked, looking up at the sky.

Bird said he heard on the news last night that chemicals that make female hormones have been found in the rain and snow.

'What do you think would happen if we got too many female hormones?' asked Bird.

'Well, I think we'd likely have higher-pitched voices and maybe grow breasts,' I told him.

'What do you mean?' yelled Bird. 'Really? You think it could make us grow boobs?'

'Yep, among other things,' I said. What I didn't tell him is that scientists have also found that human boys' penises are getting shorter because of chemicals in plastics.

'Arghhhh!' howled Bird.

We decided we won't catch the raindrops on our tongues anymore like we used to.

When we got to Bird's house, I asked him if he's worried about what's happening to the environment now.

He said, 'Yep. I don't want boobs. My mom says a good bra is really expensive and I'd rather spend my money on video games.'

I figure that if the people like Bird, who doesn't get worried very often at all, are now starting to become worried, then that's a good thing - even if it's only because of boobs.

When I got home from school today, Mom had a big smile on her face and a newspaper in her hand.

When my mom and I met Julius at his office last week, he said that likely my pictures would be on half a page, but they were on an entire page! Julius Crandle put all three animal victim impact pictures and statements in the paper at the same time, and they took up a whole page. The entire page!

I was really excited and talked super fast and Mom laughed at how excited I was and helped me scan the page to email it to my grandmother and my dad. I also emailed it to Bird, who must have been sitting at the computer because he wrote me back right away. He wrote, 'Thats wicked!!!!!! your famus and we could be even more famus if we tell everyone about how we tried to rescue cuddles!!!'

I wrote back that I didn't think it was a good idea, but I don't know how long I can keep him quiet about that.

The next day, Mrs. Wardman brought my pictures into school to show everyone. Then she posted them up on our Morning News board. That was kind of funny to me because of how my Earth Day picture didn't even make it onto the Earth Day wall. But I was feeling too good to let it ruin my day.

I was feeling so good that outside at recess when Lyle started bugging me, I wasn't even bothered, at least not at first. I reached in my pocket and rubbed my worry rock and tried to ignore him.

But then Lyle said, 'Your pictures sucked, froggie boy. You're nothing but a little fucker,' and then he shook his middle finger in my face.

Maybe it was because I was feeling so good that I said what I said. I said, 'I sure hope *you* never become a fucker.' A reproducer is the last thing I want Lyle to be. Then I stared back at him and tried not to blink. Bird tugged on my arm so I stepped back a bit.

And then Lyle said, 'What are you talking about, you fuckface froggie fucker?' and stepped toward me with his face all scrunched up like he was trying to turn it inside out.

Bird stepped between me and Lyle and said, 'Get lost, Lyle, or I'm going to use this on you,' and pulled out a little spray can that said *pepper* on it.

'What's that, little Birdie boy, you think you can scare me with a little can of fruit spray?' said Lyle.

Bird took the cap off the bottle and held it up so Lyle could see it better. He said, 'If I press down on this, Lyle, you'll get a face full of pepper that'll make you want to tear your eyes out.'

Lyle said, 'Yeah, right,' and stepped so close to Bird that later he told me he could smell Lyle's breath and it reeked like rotting meat, likely from the kids he's eaten.

Bird held the can up level with Lyle's face and put his finger on the nozzle.

Lyle said, 'You don't scare me, little birdie boy,' but his mouth twitched a little.

Bird pressed down a little more on the nozzle. 'Try me, Lyle, just try me,' he said.

Lyle growled, 'Where's your Try Me button, you little brown fucker?'

Bird said, 'I mean it, Lyle. This will burn your eyes out.' He moved the bottle even closer to Lyle's face.

Lyle paused for a second and then he backed up and said, 'I'll get you later, you little scumbag shithole,' and then he spat on the ground and walked off, likely looking for someone safer to bother.

I couldn't believe what Bird had just done. 'Holy crap, Bird, thanks!' I said.

Bird just shrugged, but his eyes were bugging out and I could tell that he couldn't believe what he had just done either.

'Where did you get that stuff, anyway?' I asked.

'From my grandmother. I told her what Lyle did to you. I sure hope he doesn't tell Mrs. Wardman about it because I sure don't need another misbehaviour. And what the bleep's wrong with you, anyway, Mr. "I sure hope you never become a fucker"? Are you trying to get the crap beat out of you?'

'Let's just hurry up and get rid of the evidence in case Lyle's on his way to Mrs. Wardman.'

Bird and I decided to bury the pepper spray in the gravel next to the apple tree. I stood in front of him to hide what he was doing while he dug the hole and put it in and covered it up. We agreed that if Lyle looked like he was going to hurt one of us, the other would run for the pepper spray and use it if he had to.

I don't think I'd have a problem doing that these days either. Things are changing now that I'm almost ten. So long, Mr. Nice Guy.

Today I mailed a letter to my dad. I wrote a little bit each day for over two weeks. It's four pages long. I followed my mom's advice and told him how it feels to hardly ever see him. I tried to say it in a nice way but in an honest way at the same time.

To write one part of my letter, I watched the evening news for a week. I did this so that I could find out about some of the horrible human-rights things that are happening right here in Canada. I'm thinking that if Dad knew about them, then maybe he would be interested in doing stories closer to home. I made a top-three list:

1. The murdering of Native women in the west of the country, which the police don't seem to do much about.
2. The fact that the Canadian government still allows asbestos to be sold to people in other countries – even though they know it kills. Isn't that just as bad as the melamine in foods from China that gets lots and lots of news stories?
3. Oil and gas companies being bullies with people who want them to stop ruining their land and making them sick.

Near the end of my letter I told Dad that Mom sometimes sees another man and that I can't help thinking about how that's not right. Every time I see her with him, I get angry. I told him that Mom says that she and he will never be back together. I asked him if he feels that way too. I just want his honest opinion. Then I drew him a few pictures of the creatures on Reull and explained what has been happening there.

I felt relieved to drop the letter in the mailbox, care of the news company he works for. My dad is coming home in a few weeks and I know my mom is going to make me talk with him about all that. She calls it 'the big talk.' So I figure it's better that he knows some of it in advance so that he's prepared. I hate it when I'm not prepared for bad news.

Also, since my mother doesn't make much sense when she tries to explain it to me, I'm hoping that maybe my dad can tell me exactly how it is that a person can love someone one day and then not love them the next? I don't think any animals in the world do that. Maybe if humans were in a social group together and they all had to work really hard to get enough food to eat and keep them all alive, they would stay together. Maybe then they'd be like the other animals who really do mate for life, like the shingleback lizard, the Canadian goose and the grey wolf.

But maybe I've got it all wrong. Maybe humans aren't animals who mate for life. Maybe they're more like the mate-for-a-season animals.

I know what my mom thinks about her and Dad, but I also need to know what Dad thinks. If his and Mom's season is up, I need to know that for absolute sure.

This morning just as Mom and I were about to go to swimming lessons, the phone rang. It was Caroline calling to ask us to please come help with a toad rescue taking place in the wetlands – the very same wetlands that now has a big road right through it, the one where Julius's law firm is trying to stop further development. She said that hundreds and hundreds of toads are trying to get across the road to their mating grounds on the other side but are being squished by cars.

My mom said going was up to me but that I'd miss my swimming lesson. I got my rubber boots on right away. Then I remembered that when I told Bird about cleaning up the amphibian park, he said that he would have liked to help too and why didn't I call him? So I asked my mom if we could pick Bird up on our way.

When Mom, Bird and I were almost to where other cars were stopped along the road, I couldn't believe my eyes. I was sure I was having a daymare. At first it looked like hundreds of small rocks on the road. But when we got closer, I could see that some of them were hopping and some of them were just twitching about a little. When Mom stopped the car and we got out, I saw the horrible, terrible, awful truth: hundreds of toads lying dead on the road. Toads lying with their bodies flattened and their eyes bulging out. Toads with their insides squeezed out of splits in their skin. For about half a kilometre all you could see was dead bodies and hundreds of other moving, jumping, hopping, frantic bodies.

Bird and Mom and I stood and looked at the scene of life, half-life, death and dying. It reminded me of the victim-impact letter I wrote for the frog. For another few moments, nobody said a word – which was really unusual for Bird who always, always has something to say. As I counted up the dead bodies just in the metre in front of me, I got a skinny feeling all inside my chest and I felt like I couldn't breathe. My mom came over to stand beside me and rubbed my back.

Then Bird said, 'If I toad you once, I toad you a thousand times – you can't build a road right over top of a migration path.'

I laughed without meaning to and that forced the air back into my lungs.

'Well, Phin,' said Bird, 'let's go save some toads.'

We went over to where Caroline was passing out buckets and shoeboxes to about thirty people all gathered around her. I saw Beth and she gave me a wave. I also recognized some of the other people who were at the amphibian park last week.

Caroline was telling everyone to try to grab the toads as gently as possible and to please, please watch out for traffic. Luckily, from where we were we could see cars coming from about a kilometre away.

Bird and Mom and I got to work. Because there were just so many of them, it was easy to catch the toads, but you really needed both hands, which made it hard to hold on to a bucket at the same time. So we worked out a strategy. My mom held the bucket and Bird and I filled it up. Each time we had a bucket almost full, Mom ran it across the road and dumped the toads safely out.

The really horrible thing was watching the toads we couldn't save get run over. That's because every so often, we had to let cars pass through and they would squish everything in their way. It was super, to-infinity hard to stay still and not run out and try to save the toads that were still moving. Most people mouthed *sorry* as they were driving through and I think they really were. But some people just pretended like nothing bad was happening and one man even rolled down his window and shouted, 'Get a life, you bunch of nutballs!' Bird gave him the finger as he drove away, but Mom told him he shouldn't do that.

Caroline came over to stand with Bird and Mom and me as we let cars through. 'Sorry about that, boys. I hope that didn't upset you. Some people are pretty rude.'

'Heck no,' said Bird. 'Kids like Lyle call us a lot worse than that at school, don't they, Phin?'

I nodded my head and my mother fake-smiled.

'Yeah, unfortunately *nutballs* is pretty mild compared to the goings-on on the playground,' my mom told Caroline.

'Okay,' said Bird, with his head hanging sideways, his eyes rolled back in his head and his tongue hanging out, 'let's all of us nutballs get those toads off the road!'

So we all got back to work. As we rescued dozens and dozens of toads, we noticed more and more people showing up to help. They came in ones and twos and in whole families! There must have been almost a hundred of us nutball humans there by the end of the morning. When I saw how we were all working together to save the toads, I got a toad in my throat.

That guy should have shouted, 'Give a life!' because that's what we did. Lots and lots and lots of them.

Fiddledee got Bird good. That's what my grandfather would say if he were alive. He'd say, 'She got ya good, didn't she, Bird?' Or he might have said, 'Well, Bird, now that's a fine how-do-ya-do.'

Fiddledee didn't mean it, she just got too excited. Bird was running around the living room with a piece of yarn and she was chasing him. Then when he all of a sudden stopped running and plunked down on the couch, she jumped up on him after the yarn that was dangling out of his hand. That's when she scratched his wrist and it started to bleed a little.

Bird yelled, 'Ow! Ow! OW!' and danced around the room holding his arm. Once he even said the F word, but under his breath.

I asked him to let me look at it and it looked pretty nasty. It even dripped some of his DNA on the floor. After he'd wiped it off with a cloth, I told him I had a way of making it feel better and he said okay and held out his arm. I went and got a washable marker and when he saw it, he got a little suspicious and jerked his arm back.

I said, 'Bird, just trust me. I know what I'm doing.'

And he said, 'All right, Phin, but if you hurt me more, you owe me big time. *Big* time.'

I said, 'Okay,' and circled the cat scratch.

Bird said, 'What the crap are you doing, Phin?' and I told him those were the boundaries for the pain that would knock against the lines and in a few minutes wear itself out and be gone. That's what my grandmother did for me once when I fell and scraped my knee and it worked. Bird rolled his eyes at me, but guess what? It worked. In a few minutes, Bird said the pain was completely gone.

I told Bird that it's a good thing he feels pain because if he didn't he'd keep doing stuff that damaged his tissues and bones and stuff. Some animals including humans have a weird condition where they don't feel pain and they end up in pretty bad shape, sometimes dead.

I wish I could draw pain boundaries for other animals too – like the bull I once saw on a show who was being castrated with a big rubber band. He was lying on his side and moaning. But when someone walked over to the fence, he jumped up and behaved like he wasn't in pain. Then when the person left, he lay back down on the ground and moaned and moaned. When I saw that, it was like someone grabbed me on the inside. But that's a different kind of pain.

If I imagine the pain mark on earth right now at this moment, it's humongous and deep red and ugly and is spread out over the entire earth. If I zoom in in my imagination, like you can on Google Earth, I see the pain mark in my very own city and it's also red raw.

But now I'm thinking that maybe one way to draw pain boundaries is to do work for animals – like what my mom and Bird and I have been doing in the amphibian park and in the wetlands. I'm super, to-infinity happy about this because I thought I'd have to wait until I was an adult before I could start my work saving animals.

So now in my mind I'm imagining the edges of the pain mark in my city as a little less red – even a bit pinkish.

After lunch hour, Lyle came in with a swollen lip and blood on his cheek.

Mrs. Wardman said, 'Lyle, for the love of Pete, what happened to you?'

Lyle just shrugged.

'Did someone hit you?'

Lyle just shrugged again.

'Lyle, please go down to Mr. Legacie's office and explain to him what happened,' said Mrs. Wardman.

'I have nothing to say,' said Lyle.

'Please just go,' said Mrs. Wardman.

Lyle got up out of his seat and left. The funny thing is that he did it without arguing or sneering or laughing or anything. It was not at all like Lyle. Since I had told Bird about the big kid's offer a few weeks ago, Bird turned around in his seat and looked back at me. I raised my eyebrows and shrugged. This was way weird.

After Lyle had left, Mrs. Wardman said, 'Anybody know anything about this?'

Nobody said a thing.

'Okay,' said Mrs. Wardman, 'get out your language arts Duo-Tangs and write a descriptive paragraph using as many adjectives as you can, like we discussed yesterday.'

I got out my Duo-Tang. I thought about what I could write. Last time we did this I wrote a whole paragraph on how it feels for a person to scrape his fingernails across a big, dry, chalky blackboard. The time before I wrote about how it feels for a person to listen to that. I used tons of adjectives like: dry, scratchy, high-pitched, excru-ciating, annoying. I had a list of other annoying topics for language arts, like how it feels to have lice crawling on your scalp and laying nits and the symptoms of pinworm. Today, though, I felt like giving Mrs. Wardman a break, so I wrote about the toad rescue instead.

About halfway through class, Lyle came back in. He sat down in his seat and got out his Duo-Tang, even without Mrs. Wardman telling him five times.

I wonder what the heck happened to him. I wondered if some-one finally paid the big kid to beat him up. Or maybe some other kid did it all on his own. Maybe there's a kid out there on the savannah who is challenging Lyle for the alpha-male position. In some groups of primates, weaker members form alliances. This is how two or three medium-strong monkeys can fight any big alpha male – two heads and two sets of teeth are better than one. When a smaller primate wants to form an alliance, he spends lots of time grooming another primate, removing parasites from his hair.

Bird and I need to find another kid or two to groom.

When I got home after school, I saw a strange car in our drive-way. It was one of those little tiny cars that only two people can fit in. I didn't know anyone who had one of those cars. I ran up to the door and my mom was standing there with a strange look on her face. At first I thought, oh no, maybe the new not-tested-on-animals moisturizer I persuaded her to get yesterday has burned her skin. But then she smiled really big and said, 'Phin, we have a visitor.'

I looked in the living room and there was Julius. He stood up and shouted, 'Great news, Phin, the province has ordered construc-tion to stop!'

Julius was smiling so big it looked like his teeth might pop out.

I screamed, 'Awesome!' I could hardly believe it!

Julius told us that my pictures were a big hit. After they were in the paper, a whole lot of people wrote to the Minister of the

Environment, who took another look at the case. He made the decision that the construction was in 'an ecologically significant area' and it should be stopped immediately.

And then Julius said, 'I have something for you,' and hauled out a whole whack of letters from his briefcase. They were all addressed to me and the postmarks were from all over the province. I ripped open the first one as fast as I could. Julius asked me to read it out loud so we could all hear. This is what it said:

Dear Phineas,

I saw your pictures and letters in the paper and just wanted to tell you what a wonderful idea your victim impact statements are. Your work has prompted our organization to open a nation-wide call for statements for animals written by children like yourself. These submissions will be posted on our website and in our newsletters. Your voice added to those of the many around the world advocating on the behalf of animals will result in more compassion for and the ethical treatment of animals. Keep up the wonderful work!

Yours sincerely,
Morag McCann
Director of Wildlife Rescue Fund

I counted them and there were eighteen more letters from people who saw my pictures in the paper. My hands were still shaking and my eyes felt all jittery and my mother kept grabbing my hands with hers and holding them still and laughing because she was happy I was so happy.

Most of the letters were from ordinary people in our province and city. They all wrote to tell me that they liked my pictures and victim-impact statements. A few people said that I had really made them think about something they'd never thought of before. One girl sent me an invitation to speak to her Kindness Club!

My brain was buzzing so much that I didn't even hear what my mom and Julius were saying. I just kept flipping through the letters. When my mom went to make some coffee, Julius said, 'You know, Phin, I don't think the Minister of the Environment would have had another look at the wetlands if it hadn't been for your victim-impact statements. They really touched a chord in people.'

I just looked at him with what was likely a really dumb smile on my face because I couldn't think of what to say. I just couldn't even believe it.

While Mom and Julius drank their coffee, I read through the letters again and again. Before Julius left, he reached out to shake my hand and then grabbed me and gave me a hug.

Then my mother said, 'This calls for a celebration.' She put on her Celtic fiddle music and grabbed me by the arms and swung me around. We made the floor shake so much that Fiddledee got the heck out of there and headed for the basement.

At one point my mom stubbed her toe on the big, fat dictionary that holds the dining room door open. She hopped around with her foot up in the air, saying, 'Ow, ow, ow!'

When I said, 'Hey, Mom, who says words don't hurt?' she grabbed and tickled me until I laughed so hard my elbows hurt.

Before bed, my mom made me some warm honey milk and then she read to me. We started a book called *101 Useless Things You Need to Know and Some You Don't*. I wasn't listening very well, though, because about 64 percent of my mind was still thinking about what had happened during the day. I thought about how along with famous people like David Suzuki and Pete Le Roux, there are lots of ordinary people concerned about animals and the environment too. My mom and I have even met some of those people, like Julius and Beth and Caroline and all those others who helped with the toad rescue. Maybe some of those ordinary people are even in my own neighbourhood, and maybe I walk by them every day on my way to school and don't even know it – it's not like they look or sound or smell any different than other humans, so how would I ever know?

Then I started imagining that these people are living in little pockets here and there and everywhere. And just like those who wrote letters to me, they're out there signalling to others too. 'I am here! I am here!' they're signalling. This helps them find one another so that they can join together and grow their numbers minute by minute, day by day – hundreds, then thousands, then tens of thousands, then millions.

Thinking this reminded me of locusts. When there aren't many of them, they're solitary insects and live in little pockets all over the land. But when their population grows to a certain point, all of a sudden the pockets join together and form a gigantic, humongous moving swarm. This makes it impossible for their predators to keep up with them. It makes them an unstoppable force. I imagined all the pockets of people moving together like a cloud of locusts, chewing and swallowing up all the pain and suffering and death all over the earth.

As I imagined all of this, I leaned against my mom and listened to her voice through her chest. My thoughts made me feel like how I imagine a deer feels when he's standing in the middle of his herd – calm and alert all at the same time, surrounded by family.

Today I talked to my father on the phone. He was excited to hear my news and told me he was looking forward to seeing all the letters. He said I used my talents in a creative way for a great cause and that he was very proud of me. He also said that maybe some of the other environmental groups, such as Greenpeace and PETA, would be interested in what I've done. When I told Mom that, I could tell she wasn't as excited about that idea, but she didn't say anything.

My dad told me that he will be home in exactly eleven days and asked me to make a list of things I'd like to do with him.

This is my list:

1. go to the ocean
2. visit Grammie, who says she has a gift for me to celebrate my important work

3. go to the science museum
4. go to a movie and maybe take Bird with us
5. have what Mom calls the 'big talk'
6. get some constructive criticism on my stories from him

Since I want my dad to read the entire Reull story and give me his honest, professional opinion, I got it out and wrote the last chapter.

I wrote about how the caged Gorachs have been screaming and crying and pleading for days. But the Wooloofs have been letting them believe that they will stay in cages forever and ever.

Actually, though, they wouldn't do this because they know that all parts of life are needed to make the whole of life complete – even the parts that are thought to be bad because they know that sometimes bad is good and good is bad.

It took the Wooloofs and the other creatures of the universe one full revolution of Reull around its star and a lot of thought fights and even thought wars before a decision was finally made as to what would be done with the Gorachs.

And this was the decision: the Gorachs in the cages would each be given his own tree to take care of and be taken care of by. If a Gorach can live for a full Reull year with just this one spikit tree, which gives him food and a home but nothing else – no Jingle-worm bracelets, no Oster nostril nozzles, nothing extra – then he will be released from the spikit tree and allowed to roam Reull. But if he can't live … well, then he can't live. His soul will be returned to the life spirits of the universe.

And so that was the way it was, and the life spirits of the universe breathed a sigh of relief that was felt by all the creatures of the universe as a joyous thought. This made every creature – and especially the ones on Reull – very happy because something had been done about the Gorachs. And everyone knows that it's what you *do* with the thought that counts.

The (but hopefully not for the Gorachs) End.

Acknowledgements

After the idea for this novel was formed, it was as William Faulkner described: 'It begins with a character, usually, and once he stands up on his feet and begins to move, all I can do is trot along behind him with a paper and pencil trying to keep up long enough to put down what he says and does.' Phineas William Walsh ran through every aspect of my life for several years, and if it weren't for those who kept me trotting along, he would still be arguing and insisting – but from the inside of my head.

I am deeply grateful to my agents, Carolyn Swayze and Kris Rothstein, for their much-needed encouragement and support and for championing this manuscript.

Immense gratitude to my editor, Alana Wilcox, for her enthusiasm, insight, keen eye and thoughtful edit. Also, a big thank you to Evan Munday, Christina Palassio and the incredible crew at Coach House Books.

Heartfelt thanks go out to the Gunn family: my parents, David and Carolyn, my sisters Heather Gunn (who read the first scenes of this manuscript just before giving birth to twins), Susan Henderson and Teri Anne Stairs.

And then we come to the core: my sons. What can I say? While I was writing and researching this book, they shared their facts, brilliant insights and astute observations. They inspired, challenged and made me laugh so hard my neck spasmed. Better pains in the neck there never were.

Finally, deep gratitude to Chris McCormick, who constantly assuaged my insecurities, read scene after scene, draft after draft and listened to me prattle on about Phin for several years. If it weren't for his advice, support and encouragement I most certainly would have stopped trotting along long ago.

While writing this novel, I consulted numerous books (such as *Natural Conflict Reconciliation* edited by Filippo Aureli and Frans De Waal) and research articles (such as those by Dr. Sam Gosling) and listened to many of Bob McDonald's fascinating interviews with animal researchers on CBC Radio's *Quirks & Quarks*. Phin's story of the Ozies was inspired by an April Fool's joke that aired on this program April 1, 2006.

Unlike Cuddles, the frog on the cover is not a White's tree frog, but a South American red-eyed frog. Although not yet endangered, its habitat is disappearing at an alarming rate.

About the Author

Along with writing, Carla Gunn works as an occupational consultant and teaches psychology. Her writing has been published in the *Globe and Mail*, the *National Post* and heard on CBC radio. She lives in Fredericton, N.B. This is her first novel.

Typeset in Legacy and Legacy Sans
Printed and bound at the Coach House on bpNichol Lane, 2009

Edited and designed by Alana Wilcox
Author photo by Graydon Gruchy

Coach House Books
401 Huron Street on bpNichol Lane
Toronto on M5S 2G5

416 979 2217
800 367 6360

mail@chbooks.com
www.chbooks.com